To Dr. Dave
I hope you
enjoy th
much as I
writing Absu

Sue Catrambone

# Absolution

## *A PARENT'S HEART HELD HOSTAGE*

*An Italian Saga Brought To Life*
*Volume Five*

## by

# Elizabeth Quintino

authorHOUSE

*1663 LIBERTY DRIVE, SUITE 200*
*BLOOMINGTON, INDIANA 47403*
*(800) 839-8640*
*www.authorhouse.com*

First published by AuthorHouse 03/29/04

ISBN: 1-4184-0627-9 (e)
ISBN: 1-4184-0626-0 (sc)
ISBN: 1-4184-0625-2 (dj)

Printed in the United States of America
Bloomington, Indiana

This book is printed on acid-free paper.

Edited By:
Denise Logan
Angela Martello

Cover Concept & Design
Frank A. Seder

To my parents,
who through their example
taught me to give of myself
unselfishly to others.


To my family and friends
who never allowed me to give up
in spite of all the road blocks
in my way.


To those numerous children
whose growth is being suffocated
by the abuse they experience
daily in their lives.


To those who willingly walk
through a dark journey,
helping these children defeat their
'Demons.'

# Table of Contents

# Forward

Life has many roads that we must travel. Often times they are dark and dangerous. Signs along the way cause us to detour, leaving us frustrated and restless. It is our inner strength and determination that enable us to continue endlessly.

Inner strength and determination were what the Italian immigrant's took to America. It allowed them to sustain their heritage down even the roughest roads. It's to these people that we, as Italian-Americans, owe a debt of honor. If it weren't for their insistence that tradition be upheld, we would have suffered a great loss.

As their ships neared New York Harbor, the immigrants happily caught a glimpse of the first sign of freedom. They emerged in awe of the Lady with the Torch of Freedom in her hand, the Statue of Liberty. Families would huddle together seeking her comfort. Cheers would break out, accompanied by tears of joy at the vision of her beauty. Their long journey was finally over.

Every member of the family carried merely a small suitcase that contained all of their worldly possessions. After passing through customs, they would seek out the family and friends awaiting their arrival. Some, unfortunately, had no one to greet them but faced the challenge none-the-less. A great deal of the Italian immigrants settled in New York City. There was yet another segment that journeyed further to Philadelphia, Pennsylvania.

South Philadelphia, in particular, became their haven. It reminded them of their homeland. Upon settling, they would immediately seek employment. Many had expertise in carpentry, construction, plumbing and tailoring. Others were laborers who chose to work the farms in New Jersey. Whatever path they took, they would overcome the obstacles in their way.

This story is about the Italian immigrants who became the backbone of our Italian Community after World War I. They would tell stories of the devastation of war and their struggle migrating to a new land with unfamiliar surroundings and language. Their children would be raised in a culture rich with Italian heritage, a heritage deep rooted, even until today.

The Italian immigrants formed a circle of love and support wherever they settled. That circle would grow every day as new immigrants moved into their neighborhoods. With every birth and marriage, the circle grew larger. Every joy they shared added more love to the circle. Each death or crisis faced together gave strength and tolerance to the circle.

In South Philadelphia, where I grew up, the Italian Market, corner grocery stores, drug stores, and candy stores all made life a little easier for these people who struggled to fit into a society not their own. Without formal education in the English language, they were able to communicate in what became known in South Philadelphia as 'Broken English'. I prefer to call it the 'Language of Love'.

My inspiration for this book comes from the Italian immigrants closest to my heart. Leaving their families behind, they crossed the ocean in a crowded ship while their heart ached for their homeland. When they came to this country, they had only a suitcase and a burning desire to start life in a new country. They encountered a great deal of hardship along the way, but never wavered in their love for God and their fellow man. If it weren't for these people, I wouldn't have the Italian heritage embedded into my mind and heart. I dedicate this book to my grandparents, Maria and Antonio Enrico.

# Chapter 1

## Trip Down Memory Lane

Throughout early childhood, Paulo Altro watched his father struggle to provide for his family. His father died in an industrial accident when Paulo was only eight years old. Equipment at the printing company he worked for was in disrepair and conditions were hazardous. Rather than invest in new printing presses, the company continued to use equipment that was more than forty years old.

The particular printing press Paulo's father operated was braced against the wall for stability. He would often complain to his supervisor that the screws used to hold it in place were becoming loose. The complaint would be sent to maintenance and placed on a list. The list was so long, however, that they never got around to making the necessary repairs. As fate would have it, one day, the huge printing press detached from the wall and crushed Paulo's father to death. Suddenly, Paulo's mother was faced with the responsibility of being the sole provider for three sons.

The company paid her a lump sum for the accident. It was just enough to pay off their bills and loans, with the exception of the mortgage. Paulo's mother had to find work in order to make ends meet. Not having the advantage of a complete education, she went to work in a nightclub. She would leave her three sons at ten o'clock every evening and waitress for six hours. Paulo could remember the late nights his mother would sit at the table counting change to buy food. Watching her struggle, he promised himself that his wife and children would never have to experience such hardship.

Paulo eventually became a self-made millionaire who, at times, seemed 'Old World'. European men pride themselves on being the breadwinners and protectors of their wives and children. They also demand respect. These qualities in Paulo were mixed with a deep concern for his fellow man and extraordinary love for his children.

Finding it hard to sleep one evening, Paulo Altro got out of bed and walked over to his bedroom window. Opening the window, he felt a crisp breeze blowing across his face. Looking out, he observed the incredible progress being made on the homes under construction on his estate.

Paulo recalled how he and his second wife Anna were so overwhelmed with joy after their daughter, Assunta, gave birth to their first grandchild. Paulo and Anna had invited Assunta and her husband Franco to move in temporarily after the baby was born. Two weeks later, their daughter-in-law, Donna, gave birth to twins. Paulo and Anna invited Donna and their son Gino to spend some time at the estate as well. This made it possible for Anna to be of assistance to the girls anytime of the day or night. During their stay, it became quite evident that their children found peace and serenity there. Paulo and Anna, feeling the same, offered them the use of their grounds to build homes for their families.

Looking back even further, Paulo remembered the day he and his beloved deceased wife, Martha, saw the house for the first time. There were eight bedrooms in the main wing that he hoped to fill with a large family. Now, with his children and grandchildren remaining with him until their homes were completed, his dream finally became a reality.

Still feeling restless, Paulo decided to go downstairs rather than risk waking Anna, his second wife. Once inside the library, after dimming the lights, Paulo gazed upon the family portraits lining the wall. Looking toward the fireplace, the photo albums, in their place of honor, caught his eye. He picked up the first three and brought them over to the conference table. Unbeknownst to Paulo, his butler, Thomas, had come in behind him and was watching him curiously.

Thomas and his wife Marisa have worked for Paulo for over thirty years. They far surpassed the status of ordinary employees. Their loyalty and devotion have earned them a special place in the family.

"Mr. Altro, is anything wrong?"

Paulo jumped at the sound of his voice. "Thomas, you startled me!"

"I thought I heard a noise in the family room and came in to investigate."

"I'm sorry to have disturbed you. I couldn't sleep. Since you're here, would you care to join me for a trip down memory lane?"

Thomas walked around the table and sat down next to Paulo. "Delighted, sir!"

The first album opened with a picture of Martha, Paulo's first wife. She was Paulo's childhood sweetheart. As children, they played together on the street where they lived. There were no toys, computers, or televisions at the time so they had only their imaginations to keep them occupied. As they got older, they explored the neighborhood together. Even in the dark of night, they could be found wandering the streets of South Philadelphia. Martha felt totally at ease with Paulo by her side.

She wasn't a remarkable person with respect to wealth or intelligence, but Martha possessed a winning personality accompanied by natural beauty. Her dynamic character was one of her biggest assets. As the wife of Paul Altro, the self-made millionaire, she impressed many people

2

and commanded admiration. Martha, however, preferred spending time at home being a wife to Paulo, and surrogate mother to Michael, the boy they adopted at the age of eight years old.

"This picture was taken the day Martha and I married."

"Mrs. Altro was a beautiful woman physically and spiritually. She had a way of making Marisa and I feel right at home."

Paulo smiled as he turned the page. There, before him, was a picture of Michael's tenth birthday gift, a blue trailblazer bike.

Thomas laughed as he remembered the day. "Michael was ecstatic when you arrived with his gift. The blue bow was almost as big as the bike."

"I remember the day he took his first bike ride into town. Martha paced back and forth on the porch, praying silently. I put my arms around her, assuring her of his safety, but she never stopped worrying. She could never conquer the fear of losing Michael. Without realizing it, she became over protective and doted on him constantly."

Thomas thought back on his own childhood. "I believe worrying comes with the territory of being a mother."

Paulo nodded in agreement then turned the page. The next picture was of Paulo and Michael playing chess.

"Mr. Altro, how well I can remember watching Michael struggle to make the right move."

Paulo nostalgically recalled the good times they had when they were just a budding family. "Martha insisted I leave my work at the office at the end of the day. She believed that evenings and weekends were to be spent with the family. Looking back, I realize how wise she was. The time I spent with Martha and Michael saved my sanity. Running a business can be like sailing in stormy weather, or as peaceful as the summer breeze. I was the captain of my ship, driving it out to sea. Martha was the navigator, constantly steering me toward peaceful waters."

Turning the pages of the album, Paulo thoughtfully fingered the pictures. "This is a picture of my brother John, Martha, Michael, and myself, taken on the day we opened the doors to Altro Electronics. John and I were close growing up. We had another brother who was killed in an automobile accident at the age of sixteen. Marc was five years older than myself, and seven years older than my brother John. One evening, the State Troopers tried to stop Marc for speeding. He was driving a stolen car and had no license. He thought he could beat them out by taking off. In the end, he lost his life.

"My mother withdrew into her own world after Marc's death. She was just going through the motions of life. His death brought John and myself

3

closer.  When our mother would go out to work, we talked about how, after making it in the business world, our mother could retire, stay home, and enjoy life. Unfortunately, this never came to be.  She died of a broken heart one year after we buried Marc."  Paulo stopped momentarily to wipe a tear from his eye.  "We moved in with our aunt and uncle.  They did the best they could to make us happy.  However, they couldn't fill the void of our mother's death."

Paulo looked with pride at the rest of the pictures of the opening day of Altro Electronics.   "When we talked about purchasing the electronics factory, we realized we didn't have enough money to do so.  I suggested we go to the bank and try to take out a business loan.  I knew it was a long shot since I was only twenty.  Nevertheless, I had this gut feeling we could make the company successful and save jobs.  Martha was instrumental in securing the financial loan needed to start Altro Electronics.  The bank president agreed to take a chance on a young kid, wet behind the ears, because of Martha's friendship with his wife.

"Martha struggled with me during the formative years of Altro Electronics.  She gave me the perseverance to go on in spite of my doubts.  Martha never lost faith in God and His ability to see us through the turbulent waters that we sailed.  When facing financial problems, Martha would give me the courage to go on.  She told me that God would provide the finances I needed.  I must admit the payroll was always met.

"Michael was only four years old when we opened Altro Electronics.  It had been a long morning, too long for Michael.  When we were getting ready to cut the ribbon, Michael fell asleep in my arms."

On the next page, Paulo found the first pictures of the house.  "These pictures were taken the day Martha and I moved in.  When Michael saw the size of the house, he became frightened.  He jumped into my arms and held on for dear life."

Paulo moved on to the next picture.  "This is a picture of Michael playing out back before we had the garden.  How he loved playing in the dirt!  When Martha would give him a bath at the end of the day, she would often remark that Michael was meant to be a ditch digger."

Paulo continued turning the pages while Thomas looked on with interest.

"This picture was taken of Michael on his first day at school. It was only kindergarten, but it felt like we were sending him off to college.  When he walked into the school building, it took ten minutes to calm Martha."

Paulo closed the first album and opened the second one.  Thomas proceeded to explain the scene.  "I remember the day these pictures were taken.  This was the day you and Mrs. Altro adopted Michael.  That was

4

the first formal dinner Marisa and I prepared here at the house. We were only in your employment for a few weeks when you informed us of a sit-down dinner for thirty people. Marisa and I were a nervous wreck until it was over."

"I remember that particular dinner very well myself. Martha and I received nothing but compliments for weeks afterward. Thomas, did I ever tell you how Martha and I came to adopt Michael?"

"No, sir. I often wondered, but thought it was none of my business."

"Martha and I, with the help of Deacon Pollato, decided to move to a new location. We chose New Jersey because it wasn't far from Philadelphia. We had a great deal of friends and acquaintances we made over the years that we promised to stay in contact with."

"Deacon Pollato knew a lovely couple, John and Mary Tambrino, who lived in Cherry Hill, New Jersey. They were raising their grandson, who was left in their care temporarily after the death of his mother. However, it became a permanent situation. They were both in their early sixties, and having a difficult time keeping up with their grandson. The same as any other toddler, he was energetic and curious.

"Deacon Pollato contacted the Tambrinos on our behalf. They became instrumental in helping us find housing on their street. When we moved in, Mary helped Martha organize the house. Mary could sense Martha's loneliness as they unpacked and it gave her an idea. She couldn't wait until John came home to discuss it with him.

"After dinner that evening, Mary sat down telling John of her observations. They decided to host a small get-together in our honor. Out of everyone we met, only one stood out, a small boy by the name of Michael. We later found out Michael was John and Mary's grandson. He captured our hearts from the start. From that evening forward, we spent all our free time with Michael and his grandparents. The more we saw of Michael, the more we wanted to be with him.

"Living on the same street as Michael made it easy for us. Michael spent the day running back and forth between his grandparent's and our home, and eventually started spending weekends and holidays with us. We lived there until Michael was four years old."

"Did Michael have a hard time adjusting once you moved away from him?"

"That was never a problem because soon thereafter, we agreed to share custody of Michael. We had him with us as much as possible.

"It all started when Michael's grandfather invited Martha and me to dinner. He told me he had an important matter to discuss. We walked on eggshells until the evening of the dinner. We feared Michael's grandparents

5

felt we were spending too much time with him."

"Were you right in your assumption?" Thomas inquired.

"No, just the opposite. Michael's grandparents wanted to thank us for the love and attention we showered upon Michael. Before leaving, they asked Martha and myself to consent to becoming Michael's surrogate parents. This was a dream come true for us. Michael would be the son we could never have.

"Deacon Pollato, who later went on to become Cardinal Pollato, stayed in close contact over the years. He had a sense of humor and could make light of any situation. I remember one particular story that I often tease Michael about."

Thomas expressed surprise. "Cardinal Pollato has always reminded me of a stern man, never smiling."

"Not true. Shortly after we settled in the house, Martha and I invited Deacon Pollato, Michael, and his grandparents over for lunch. Finishing lunch, Michael asked to be excused. He walked toward the family room. A few minutes later, I couldn't believe my eyes. Michael put on Deacon Pollato's shirt, collar, and jacket. He was very proud of himself, but I wasn't pleased.

"'Michael, why are you wearing Deacon Pollato's things?' I asked.

"'I think they look good on me.'

"The only one who smiled was Deacon Pollato. 'I think you look handsome, Michael. Someday you may wear the same clothing I wear, and take over my job. Would you like that?' Michael thought for a few minutes and then responded. 'I think so.'

"The evening Michael announced his intentions of entering the seminary, I wasn't surprised. Martha had some concerns. She wasn't sure he would be able to give up all the worldly things he had become accustomed to, being raised by us. I felt differently. Watching him that evening, I felt energy in the room that I couldn't describe."

Paulo looked into Thomas' eyes. "Today, when I speak with Pope David, I find it hard to imagine that the young Deacon Pollato is now the leader of the Roman Catholic Church."

"I knew you were friends with Pope David, but, I didn't know how far back your friendship went."

Paulo smiled. "My friendship with Pope David has spanned many years. Not only was he instrumental in our adoption of Michael, he was ultimately responsible for my only meeting with Michael's biological father."

"I thought Michael's parents were both deceased, sir."

"Michael's mother passed on after Michael's birth. His father was so distraught that he left Cherry Hill seeking new employment. The vocation that drew Michael's father like a magnet meant he would have to leave Michael behind. That's how he wound up with his grandparents.

"Deacon Pollato had set up a weekend fishing trip with Michael's grandfather, a close friend of his, Tanose Frenzio, and myself. I felt completely at home with Tanose. I found him to have a pleasant personality.

"I talked about Michael the entire time we fished on Saturday. At one point, I apologized for bragging about Michael. Tanose looked at me with understanding and asked, 'What father doesn't enjoy bragging about his son?' I felt relieved and continued to talk about Michael.

"That evening, after dinner, we relaxed around the fireplace. Tanose listened while Michael's grandfather and I exchanged more stories about Michael. I waited for Tanose to excuse himself out of boredom. Instead, he encouraged us to continue.

"On Sunday morning when we went to church, I was surprised to see Tanose celebrating the Mass. I thought it was odd that Michael's grandfather didn't mention Tanose was a priest, and then decided it wasn't important. I liked Tanose for himself, not because he was a priest.

"While waiting for Tanose to join us after the Mass, Michael's grandfather informed me that Tanose was Michael's father. I couldn't believe what I was hearing. Finally, it dawned on me, Tanose didn't enter the seminary until after his wife died. Very little was said on the way back to the cabin. I needed time to get my thoughts together. Later that morning, Tanose and I went out back to do some more fishing. Michael's grandfather excused himself. He decided to give us time to talk alone.

"This time, while speaking about Michael, I could see the love in Tanose's eyes. When we finished and I started to gather up my gear, Tanose stopped me. He admitted being Michael's father, and then he asked me if I would consider adopting Michael. Tanose feared the authorities would take Michael away from his aging in-laws. Realizing the devastating effect this would have on all of us, I agreed to adopt Michael. Tanose and I talked into the early morning hours. We discussed goals for Michael's future.

"After that weekend, I had a deep respect for Tanose. If I ever had a doubt in my mind that Michael's father loved him, it was gone."

Following the fishing pictures, were page after page of Michael's involvement with sports. "I can still remember Michael waking at the crack of dawn every morning to go down to the stables with me. That was my way of spending private time with him."

Paulo's facial expression showed pride as he reached for the next album.

"This is the last album of Michael. These pictures were taken during

Michael's years at the seminary. When Michael came home for the Christmas Holidays, he brought Timothy with him as a houseguest. Martha and I were enchanted with Timothy from the moment we were introduced. During the break, Timothy received notification that he was being suspended for poor grades. Timothy admitted his wrongdoing but had no idea how to go about getting reinstated. I could tell Timothy was sincere, so I made a call to his father informing him of the situation. Timothy's father couldn't care less about his studies. He never wanted Timothy to enter the seminary. I found out much later that his father was against it because he, too, wanted to enter the seminary when he was a boy, but his father wouldn't allow it. He regretted not fighting his father the way Timothy did him. I felt it was up to me to help so I phoned the Dean of the seminary to see what could be done. Timothy was placed on Academic Probation for the next semester.

"That day, Timothy and I had a heart-to-heart talk concerning his studies. I told him that I would help him in any way I could if he wanted and that I would monitor his progress. By his senior year, Timothy excelled in all classes. Had it not been for my intervention, who knows what Timothy would be doing today.

"Michael and Timothy were both excellent students. I was very proud of them when they completed their studies. Michael graduated first and Timothy graduated second in their class of two hundred fifty young men. Before their ordination, they put in a request as to where they would like to begin their ministry. Even though they were close friends, they had very different destinations in mind.

"Michael decided that he wanted to be sent to a foreign mission. The idea of helping people to live in a better environment for themselves and their families captivated him. He wanted to work hand-in-hand with the poor, bringing them many of the things we take for granted. Most importantly, he would bring the gospel of Jesus Christ to their civilization.

"The area Michael was sent to lacked sturdy housing, medical assistance, food, education, and much more. Before leaving they were living in homes constructed of brick and cement. He was also instrumental in building the first hospital and school before leaving the mission.

"Timothy's calling was to help the sick. While studying at the seminary, Timothy became friendly with a young man named John Rao. John confided in Timothy that he had AIDS in the final stages. In the final hours of John's fight for life, Timothy never left his side. During this short period of time, Timothy met many of John's friends; most were HIV-positive, the same as John. They reminded Timothy of the early Christians waiting to be executed by the lions. Instead, they were waiting for this vicious disease to devour them. He walked that long hard journey with each one individually, from HIV to AIDS, and finally to death."

Paulo closed the album, then went back to the fireplace and lifted the other five books off the shelf. Thomas followed to be of assistance. "Thomas, are you sure you would rather not go to bed?"

Thomas smiled. "No sir, I'm enjoying this."

Paulo proceeded without hesitation. "This album starts out when Anna and I were married. When Martha died, I thought my life ended. Hearing Anna's voice brought me back to life. Did I ever tell you how I met Anna?"

"No, sir, but I do remember the first time Mrs. Altro visited the house. You had that look in your eyes. The look that had been missing after your wife's death."

"One of my engineers left the company without notice. I had to hire someone quickly to replace him. My policy was to promote within the company whenever possible. In the past, I always followed this policy, with the exception of my engineers. After giving it serious thought, I decided to offer the position to someone within the company.

"Salvatore Greco, supervisor at Altro Electronics, suggested I offer Gino Bruno the position. Even though Gino didn't have an engineering degree, Salvatore felt he was qualified. It meant Gino would have to go to college and get his degree. Since I knew Gino didn't have the money to go to college, I offered to pay his tuition as long as he maintained a B average.

"Gino jumped at the opportunity. When he told his mother, she found it hard to believe. Gino phoned me at home, asking me to explain to his mother about the position I was offering. When I spoke with Anna on the phone, I instantly fell in love. The rest is history."

"I'll never forget how beautiful Mrs. Altro looked on your wedding day!"

"That she did, Thomas!" Paulo brushed his fingers over the picture as if he were touching Anna. The album finished off with their honeymoon in the Swiss Alps. Looking at the pictures brought back all the wonderful memories they shared.

Paulo picked up the next album. The first page was an engagement portrait of his daughter Assunta with her fiancée.

"They are a handsome couple, Mr. Altro."

"Gino and Franco were the best of friends growing up. When Franco moved to Cherry Hill from Vineland, he stayed with Gino sharing the expenses of the apartment. Once Gino moved here, Franco had a hard time managing the expenses alone. Anna always treated Franco like a son, so it was no surprise when she asked if he could move in with us. We had plenty of room so there was no problem." Paulo picked up his head.

"Early on, Franco and I got along well but right before the engagement my attitude toward Franco changed." Paulo faced Thomas. "Remember how furious I became when I found that pornographic film in the house?"

"I'll never forget that day," Thomas responded.

"What made it worse was that Franco tried shifting the blame from himself to Assunta. It didn't take me long to realize that Franco was cunning, devious, and shrewd." Paulo paused momentarily. "Assunta and I connected right away after being introduced. I could see she needed a father figure, and I fit the part perfectly. During one particular conversation we had, Assunta confided in me that her father was abusive during her childhood. She never went into details but the look in her eye told it all." Paulo's expression showed his heartache. "After Assunta's engagement to Franco, I had a feeling that he was abusive to her, but I couldn't prove it. Unofficially, I took over the role of father and kept a close watch. Looking at Franco today, I find it unbelievable the man he used to be. I had given up on Franco back then, but Anna never did. She saw through the facade, hoping his true character would emerge. Anna was right in her logic. I, on the other hand, totally misjudged Franco's capabilities.

"I'm the first one to admit when I make a mistake or misjudge someone, and that's exactly what I did when it came to Franco. When I think of the turnaround Franco made, it amazes me. He left here an abusive, arrogant, sarcastic, and immature boy, and returned home a mature, young man ready to take on the responsibility of husband and father. It took a total stranger to bring Franco around and I thank God he did.

"Today, Franco is one of the top businessmen in the area. He's known in the business community as fair, understanding, and ready to lend a hand when the opportunity arises."

"You taught him well, sir."

"The day that Franco changed his name to Franco Paulo Altro-Cordova was one of the proudest days in my life. The boy I had totally given up on was paying me the honor of adding my surname to his." Paulo could feel himself becoming emotional.

Paulo flipped through the pages of the album once again, pointing everyone out to Thomas. The wedding pictures followed the engagement pictures. The next album started out with Donna and Gino's engagement portrait.

"Mr. Altro, they too make a lovely couple."

Paulo smiled with approval. "Anna and Donna's mother became friends while Gino and Donna were in grade school. They had a great deal in common. They both lost their husbands at a very young age.

"Sadly, when Donna was in junior high, her mother died suddenly; but not before teaching her the art of being a seamstress. Anna opened her heart and home to Donna. She moved in until she finished junior high. After graduation, Donna went on to be one of the top bridal gown designers in the area.

"When I asked Anna to marry me, she decided to have her wedding dress custom made. Since Anna always admired Donna's work, she hired her to design and make her wedding dress.

"The morning of the wedding, Donna made an appearance in the library. She had come in to pick up her flowers since Anna chose her to be her witness. In spite of the many fittings Anna had for her wedding gown, Gino hadn't seen Donna since she graduated junior high. When he finally laid eyes on her, he was instantly captivated. Donna and Gino walked out at the end of the ceremony arm in arm. They started keeping company from that day forward."

Closing the book, he laid it aside and reached for the next album. "This album represents my heart." Paulo went on to reveal page after page of his grandchildren. It wasn't difficult for Thomas to see that the children brought new vitality back into their grandfather's life. When he finished looking through the pictures, he closed the album and placed it alongside the others. Picking up the final album, he handed it to Thomas.

"Now, it's your turn to show me the pictures."

Thomas opened the album and found pictures of when he and his wife attended his family reunion. "Mr. Altro, you knew all along," he remarked astutely.

"Thomas, you, of all people, know by now that very little slips by me undetected. I found the VCR tape after returning from vacation. That night I had a special presentation in the library for the family. I wish you could have seen the look on everyone's face. They were just as shocked as you when they realized I found out. Anna and I were very proud of what the children did for you and Marisa. I must admit, if I were here, I would have done the same thing."

"Mr. Altro, I can't begin to tell you the happiness that reunion brought Marisa and myself. My family all did well for themselves, with the exception of me personally. When the reunion would come up each year, I would make an excuse for not attending. When Assunta and the family started planning a way to have our dream become a reality, we couldn't resist. For one weekend, we weren't the butler and maid for the Altro family, we were people of distinction. Your children gave us the opportunity to experience 'Camelot' in our lifetime. For this, I'll always be grateful."

Paulo smiled placing his hand on Thomas' shoulder. "I want you to remember one important thing from this day forward. You were never my butler and Marisa never my maid. You were always thought of as family." Sitting back, Paulo made himself comfortable. "Tell me about your family."

Thomas pointed out his relatives one at a time. When he finished, he closed the book and placed it on top of the others. Paulo realized it was already six o'clock. Thomas and Paulo had spent many pleasurable hours looking through pictures in the family albums.

"I'll return these albums where they belong, sir."

Paulo thanked him then gazed at the pictures on the wall, admiring his family.

Thomas saw the pride in Paulo's eyes. "Mr. Altro, you have a great deal to be proud of."

"I realize that. I also realize that what we think is a punishment from God, can be a blessing in disguise. God may not have blessed me with children of my own, but he saw fit to send children of other parents, who needed my guidance and love to fulfill their destiny in life. My inability to father children enabled me to be there for these children. I may not be their biological father but, none-the-less, I'm their father. I couldn't love them any more if my blood ran through their veins. My children and grandchildren are my heart and I'll always carry them with me even when I depart this earth."

"Mr. Altro, if you will excuse me, I want to take my shower now. I have to wake Marisa soon."

"Thomas, do you believe we have been here for four hours?"

"I believe we have, sir, and I wish to thank you. You and I rarely have time to spend together."

Paulo smiled. "We should get together more often. Maybe you and I can go fishing down at the cabin soon."

"I would enjoy that very much, sir." Thomas turned to walk away and then faced Paulo once again. "Mr. Altro, thank you for considering Marisa and me part of your family. The day you hired us was a blessing from above. Up to that point, we couldn't find suitable employment. In your home we are treated with respect instead of as servants."

"In our home, you are both treated with respect for the work you do every day and you're loved by the family because of the people you are and the love you share with us. Without you, my family wouldn't be complete."

On that note, Thomas left Paulo in the solace of his thoughts. Paulo strolled slowly by the individual portraits once more. These images represented the fulfillment of all Paulo's dreams and expectations. Life couldn't get any better than this, he thought, suddenly feeling exhausted.

Before heading to bed, he checked all the locks again just to be on the safe side. Lately, he paid special attention to securing the house at night. Now that he had everything he ever wanted, a large family, wealth and happiness, he wasn't about to let it slip away. On his way upstairs, his mind quickly wandered to happy thoughts of his upcoming vacation. Somehow, before then, he'd have to catch up on his sleep.

# Chapter 2

## Paulo's Enemy Makes His Move

The weekend after the Fourth of July holiday, Paulo and Anna left for a long-awaited vacation with their grandchildren and their daughter's in-laws, Antonio and Maria Cordova. Preparations had been in the works for some time now, including a shopping spree at J. C. Penney for their grandchildren's necessities. It was the perfect way for all of them to spend time with their grandchildren, and besides, they enjoyed the Cordova's company. Ever since the union of their children, they had become very close. A good time was sure to be had by everyone.

Michael took advantage of his parents' absence to call an urgent meeting with his brothers and sisters. On the agenda was what to do for Paulo's fifty-fifth birthday, which was just around the corner.

"Papa's birthday is August 13th. He will be fifty-five years old. Perhaps we can all get together and do something special. I'm open for suggestions."

"Why not throw Papa a big party," Assunta suggested. "We can have it at Giuseppe's. I bet Papa would enjoy that. Better yet, we could have it a week ahead of time and make it a surprise party."

Michael checked his calendar. "It's already the second week in July. That would only give us three weeks. If we were to pull this off, we would need to do a great deal of preparing in a short period of time."

"Please, Michael!" Assunta batted her big blue eyes at him. "I know we can do it! Papa deserves it for all he does for us!"

Michael looked around the room and asked if anyone had another suggestion. No one did so he moved on to discussing the details.

Assunta placed paper and pencils around the conference table as she always did before a meeting. Family meetings were a common occurrence at the Altro residence but this one was different, there was a driving force missing among them that they all felt. This was Paulo's conference table, yet he wasn't there directing the meeting. Michael realized it would be like this permanently someday and the thought sent chills up his spine.

Assunta noticed Michael daydreaming and tugged at his sleeve. "Are you going to start or not?"

Her remark brought him back to earth. Normally, Assunta would object to Michael conducting meetings but this time she seemed not to mind. Maybe, she was finally accepting his authority.

"Wonders never cease to amaze me," he said under his breath before taking his seat.

He immediately put together a list of what had to be accomplished. "If we are to pull this thing off, it will require a great deal of planning. Gino, I want you to make a list of Papa's closest associates. Since you're at the company, you should have that information on hand. Then we'll need a second list of Papa's friends. We can probably use the guest list from your wedding."

Having Gino's full cooperation, Michael moved on to the next item on his list. "Donna, you can be in charge of the invitations."

Donna wrote a reminder note and put it in her pocket. "Tomorrow, I'll take a ride down to Esposito's and ask if I can borrow one of their books."

The next item on Michael's list was the menu. "Franco, you take care of the menu. Stop by to see Giuseppe and work it out with him."

Franco nodded and Michael continued."Timothy and I will concelebrate Mass at Holy Spirit before the dinner. Did I forget anything?"

Franco raised his hand to suggest they have the Brusco children sing at the Mass. The Bruscos were well-known in the church community and everyone loved their performances so Michael happily agreed.

Assunta listened patiently as Michael assigned jobs to everyone but she was starting to get upset now. After all, the surprise party was her idea and he hadn't given her anything to do. She suddenly looked very disappointed and Michael noticed. He decided it was in everyone's best interest to tell Assunta what her job was before she exploded.

"Assunta, I saved the best job for you. How would you like to work on the decorations for the . . ."

Assunta didn't give Michael a chance to finish. "That's exactly what I wanted to do in the first place," she said excitedly. " Thank you for letting me do this. You won't be disappointed. I already have a lot of ideas!"

As there was nothing left on his list, Michael adjourned the meeting. He didn't pay much attention to everyone as they left but he did notice that Assunta was humming as she walked out the door.

Michael turned to Franco. "Franco, you know Assunta better than I do. Is her humming a good sign or a bad sign?"

"Neither one. I think it's an expensive sign," he said and they both laughed at the thought. The two of them continued talking in the library when Assunta came rushing back in.

"Michael, since I'm decorating the restaurant, can I decorate the church?"

"I didn't give much thought to decorating the church. I intended to have a bouquet in front of Our Lady of Fatima and one in front of the Sacred

Heart."

"I promise I won't do anything until I check with you. You'll have the final word."

Michael paused for a moment. "Put your ideas in writing so we can sit down and go over them. But I must warn you, I won't permit balloons in church."

Assunta jumped for joy. "Thank you. I'm going to start on it right away. Once again, she rushed out of the room and Franco soon followed. He was curious to see what she was up to.

Satisfied that his work was finished, Michael decided to turn in for the night. He checked to make sure everything was secure before going upstairs. Normally, Paulo would do this but, in his absence, it became Michael's job. Following in his father's footsteps, he also couldn't go to bed without first saying goodnight to everyone. He started with Gino and Donna then moved on to Franco and Assunta. They were still awake when he knocked.

"Come in," Franco called out.

Michael announced as he peeked in the door, "I just came to say goodnight."

"Michael, come in. It seems your sister doesn't remember what you said about balloons in church. Can you refresh her memory?"

"No balloons in church!"

"My girlfriend had balloons at her parents' fortieth wedding anniversary. Their grandchildren gave them each a balloon as a sign of peace." Assunta gathered her thoughts before speaking. "I mean you no disrespect, but can you tell me why not?"

"No balloons in church because I say so! Is that a good enough reason?" Seeing Assunta becoming upset, Michael toned down his attitude. "Assunta, you're my sister and I love you dearly, but the answer is no. Are we clear on that?"

Assunta nodded her head. "If we can't have them in church, can we at least have them in front of church. As Papa is coming out, we can release them into the air." Assunta waited for an answer.

Michael looked at Franco. "What do you think?"

Franco nodded his approval. "Sounds okay to me."

Assunta was thrilled and couldn't wait to get started. She thanked Michael again before heading for the shower.

They all went to bed that night thinking about the party. The family had to work quickly because in a few days, Paulo and Anna's vacation would be over and they would be returning home.

On the day of their arrival, Thomas was called to pick up the Altros at the airport.  Thomas knew how much Assunta and Donna missed their parents and children so he invited them to take a ride.  They made it just in time to see them coming off the plane.  Their appearance at the plane's exit was comical.  Assunta and Donna couldn't help laughing.  Anna, Maria, and Antonio each held one of their grandchildren, while Paulo carried three diaper bags; one on his right shoulder, one on his left shoulder, and one between his hands.  They talked and laughed about it the whole way home.

As soon as they arrived at the house, the girls put the children down for a nap while Paulo and Anna settled everyone in.  Something suddenly reminded Thomas of the envelope that was delivered that morning for Paulo. He retrieved it and brought it to Paulo right away.

"While you were away, some man was trying desperately to reach you. This morning, this envelope was hand-delivered to be given to you upon your return."

"Thank you, Thomas.  This may have something to do with the merger."

Paulo opened the envelope with great enthusiasm, anxious to see its contents.  He had been hoping for good news of the impending merger he had so diligently been working on but instead, he held before him an atrocity. Antonio noticed the shocked look on Paulo's face and became concerned.   In his customarily straightforward style, he asked to know what was wrong.

"Antonio, please come with me."  Paulo signaled Antonio to follow him into the library then locked the door and pulled the curtains.  He handed Antonio the brief hand-written note.  Antonio read it with disbelief.

*"You don't know me, but I know you well, and I know you love your family.  It would be a shame if I had to hurt them.  Do as I say or there will be hell to pay.*

*"Deliver three million dollars in small-unmarked bills to PO Box 666.*

*"P.S.  Don't contact the police!"*

"Do you think they are serious?"  Antonio asked.

Paulo's silence explained it all.  Paulo picked up the phone and made a call to Stone Security.

"Mr. Stone, it's important that I see you right away.  Another threat has been made on my family.  I believe this one is serious.  I received several calls while I was on vacation. Early this morning someone hand-delivered an envelope.  I can be down there within the hour.  I don't mean to come off abruptly, but I'm frightened for my children's safety."  Paulo hung up the phone contemplating his next move.

"Antonio, take a ride with me."  They headed straight to Paulo's car.  On arrival at Stone Security, Paulo handed Robert Stone the envelope.

Robert Stone read the letter carefully. "Unfortunately, this looks like it could be the real thing. We began surveillance on your family a month ago. I have daily documentation on each of your children. If you give me a few minutes, I'll get the reports."

Antonio snapped at Paulo. "You knew since June and never told me?"

"The only person I told was Michael because I was going on vacation. I wanted him to be aware everyone was under surveillance." Paulo hadn't counted on upsetting Antonio.

"Why was I not informed?" Antonio was obviously furious.

Robert answered in a serious tone of voice, "I requested no one become aware of the threat because the more people that know, the more chance of a slip up. As long as Mr. Altro was aware of what was being done, no one else mattered."

"You don't understand, Mr. Stone! Franco is my son!" Antonio stood up facing Robert Stone.

Paulo tried to calm Antonio down. "I started to tell you a number of times. Unfortunately, one of our wives would walk in. Antonio, please accept my apology." Antonio realized that Paulo's actions were justified.

"How can I be angry? All that you had in mind was protecting your family, which includes Franco. I want you to know I appreciate you doing this for my son."

"The most important thing right now is my family's well being. Do you hear me, Mr. Stone? I will hold you personally responsible if anything happens!" Paulo's tone was threatening.

"Leave me the envelope. Perhaps I can lift some fingerprints. I'm also going to double the guards around your home."

"My children's lives are at risk. I meant what I said about holding you personally responsible! God help you if anything happens to any one of them!"

Robert Stone suddenly became pale as a ghost. "Starting today, you will see men patrolling the premises. They will be wearing green work suits in various shades. I intend to plant them at each of the construction sites, doing the gardening, working on wires, and odd jobs on the property. If you see anyone else on your property, you're to phone me immediately."

Paulo nodded. "If someone was threatening your children, how would you react? "

"I would react the same as you. Give us a few days. I promise we will have some information for you."

Paulo and Antonio left reassured and headed for home. On the way, they discussed if the others should be told and both agreed that they are better off not knowing. Paulo would give Robert Stone some time to figure this out before having to worry his family.

At the house, Anna was going out of her mind with fear and anger. Paulo was late for lunch and hadn't left word with anyone as to his whereabouts. This was unusual behavior that Anna couldn't tolerate especially after her dream the other night. As soon as he stepped foot into the house, she let him have it. "Paulo Altro, where have you been? I have been searching high and low for you! If you couldn't tell me where you were going, you should have left me a note, or would that have been too much trouble for you!"

The longer Anna talked, the angrier Paulo got. He wasn't accustomed to being yelled at by his wife.

"Anna, something came up that I had to take care of before lunch. I'm sorry you worried. I'll leave a note next time. Let's eat, I'm starved."

"Just like that! You have some nerve! You can eat by yourself! I have suddenly lost my appetite!"

Paulo had heard enough. He asked Antonio and Maria to excuse them for a few minutes so they could speak privately but Anna objected voicefully.

"Maria and Antonio are family, whatever you have to say can be said in front of them!" Anna banged the table. "There's no need for either of them to leave!"

Paulo did all in his power to hold his temper. "Antonio, I want to speak privately with Anna. Will you please excuse us?"

Antonio held Maria's hand and walked toward the kitchen door without saying a word. Once outside, Antonio questioned Maria.

"What's that all about? I have never seen Anna act that way."

"Anna was frightened that something happened to Paulo. She had this dream a few nights back, with visions of blood all around Paulo's office. All she could remember was the sound of ambulances, and seeing bodies on stretchers. She couldn't distinguish any faces. Anna began to sob uncontrollably while telling me the story; fearful her dream would turn into reality. Anna was getting ready to send Thomas down to the company when Paulo pulled in the driveway."

"I think the best thing right now is for Anna to tell Paulo what has her so upset."

Antonio and Maria continued to walk toward the garden. In the meantime Paulo and Anna were still going at it in the house.

"Anna, what's wrong with you? You have never acted this way especially in front of company." Paulo expressed his bewilderment.

"Perhaps that's the problem! If I had told you off a long time ago you would have to follow the same rules that everyone else follows! You had no right leaving without letting me know when to expect you back! You would want me to do the same for you!"

"Anna, that's enough! On a scale of one to ten you're close to twenty. I want to speak with you in the library, now!"

"I would rather speak right here!"

"Now, before I do something out here that you'll definitely regret!" Paulo's eyes expressed his frustration. They walked into the library and took a seat.

"Calm down and talk to me."

Anna stomped her foot and looked the other way.

"Why are you acting this way?"

"If the children and I have to follow certain rules, then I expect you to abide by them as well! I want to know where you're going at all times!"

After Anna stormed her way to the bathroom, Paulo scanned his property through the patio doors. It wasn't bad enough he had a ransom note delivered to his home, now he had his wife acting like a lunatic.

When Anna came out of the bathroom, he ushered her to the sofa. Anna tried to pull away, but did as Paulo requested.

Paulo sat quietly trying to find the right words to say. "Since we married, this is the first time you have spoken to me disrespectfully. It's so far out of character for you. Will you tell me the reason you're so upset?"

"Nothing has upset me, I simply overreacted."

"I really don't have time to play games. I guarantee before going to sleep, you will give me the answers I'm looking for."

Anna and Paulo went outside to find Maria and Antonio sitting talking with Franco. Franco stood up when he saw Paulo and Anna. "I forgot some paperwork this morning."

Paulo sat down.

"We were just about to have lunch. Since it's such a nice day we're going to eat out here on the patio. Why don't you join us?"

Franco looked at his watch and laughed.

"Lunch at the Altro home at two o'clock? That's one for the books! Lunch is served at noon and noon only!"

Paulo gave Franco a stern look and Franco knew he had said the wrong thing.

"I'm sorry I can't stay. I already had lunch. After lunch when Quintino and I started going over the paperwork on the building we are trying to purchase, I realized I left the estimates home for the renovations. I came home to pick them up."

Franco turned toward Maria and Antonio. "Mama, when will you and Papa be returning home?"

"This evening, right after dinner."

"I'm glad. That will give me a chance to spend some time with both of you."

Franco walked over to Maria and Anna giving them both a kiss. Then he turned to Paulo.

"Papa, may I have a word with you. Something came up at the bakery I would like to discuss."

Paulo stood up. "If you will excuse me, this shouldn't take more than a few minutes." Paulo and Franco walked into the library through the patio doors.

"What's the problem?"

"Nothing, I just wanted to speak with you privately. I didn't know if you were aware that Mama seems upset over something. I can see it in her eyes."

"When we came home today I found a message requiring me to go to town to see an acquaintance of mine. Your Papa took a ride with me. I should have looked at my watch before leaving. When we returned, it was one o'clock and Mama was furious. She lashed out at me for being late for lunch without waiting to hear my explanation. She sounded like Assunta and I reacted the same way I do when Assunta mouths off to me."

Paulo looked at his watch, "I better join Mama or she might send out the National Guard."

Franco laughed leaving the library when he remembered something.

"One evening last week when I came down for a glass of milk, I found Mama crying. I asked her if anything was wrong; she told me she had a bad dream that upset her. Maybe, the way she spoke with you, had to do with that dream."

"Did she tell you what it was about?"

"All she told me was the dream frightened her. I wonder whether her behavior this afternoon and the dream are connected somehow."

"I don't know, but I intend to find out."

Paulo walked Franco to his car and then returned to his lunch. The rest of the day was quite pleasant. After dinner, Paulo and Antonio walked around the grounds.

"Did you find out why Anna was so upset before lunch?" asked Antonio.

"No, and frankly I'm concerned."

"Maria told me why Anna was upset. It has to do with a dream she had recently. In the dream she saw your office splattered with blood. Anna

22

could hear the sound of ambulances, and see bodies on stretchers. When you were gone, she took for granted you went down to your company and her dream would become a reality. That's why she spoke with you the way she did. It was out of fear."

"That's the dream Franco was referring to this afternoon. Franco found Anna crying in the kitchen one evening after everyone had retired. Anna explained to Franco that she had woke up out of a bad dream and came down for a glass of milk. She never told him any of the details. I can't understand why she didn't tell me when I asked her. It's not like her to speak with me that way. Now I understand."

While Paulo and Antonio were walking the grounds, Anna and Maria were inside the house making sure Maria left nothing behind.

"Anna, I want to thank you for everything. Antonio and I loved spending time with Antonio. He's a beautiful child. Assunta is doing a fine job raising him."

"Franco is an excellent father as well. They teach him right from wrong and provide all the love he needs. I wish the twins were being raised the same, but. . .," Anna put her head down momentarily, and then changed the subject.

"Maria, I have pictures from our vacation in Rome. Let's take a look before you leave."

When Antonio and Paulo walked into the dining room, they found the table full of pictures. Paulo explained where each picture was taken since Anna wasn't familiar with Rome. Finally, it was time for Antonio and Maria to start for home. Everyone walked them out to the driveway. The love between Franco and his mother was obvious. With his father, it was a different story. Franco hugged and kissed his mother good-bye but only shook hands with his father. It wasn't noticeable to anyone with the exception of Paulo. The reason he picked up on it was that he came from the same type of relationship with his own father.

Once they were out of sight everyone returned inside. They sat around the fireplace to unwind and drink coffee. After a few minutes, Paulo decided to take a walk in the garden.

"Anna, let's take a walk in the garden. We haven't done so since before we left for the shore."

Paulo escorted Anna out. They walked slowly, holding hands. When Paulo suggested they sit, Anna pulled her hand from him quite abruptly.

"Anna stop acting childish!"

"Paulo, I'm sorry. I guess I'm angry for the way you spoke with me this afternoon. Your tone of voice was embarrassing and humiliating."

"Do you think for one moment I wasn't embarrassed or humiliated by the way you acted in front of the Cordovas? I could have embarrassed you in front of the Cordovas, but instead, spoke with you privately."

"I'm sorry for the way I spoke to you. Can you forgive a foolish old lady?"

"Anna, you are not an old lady, nor are you foolish. There's something you're keeping from me that has you upset."

"I don't know what you're talking about."

"I can't help you unless you level with me."

Anna looked away realizing he didn't believe what she was saying.

"There's something bothering you. Tell me what it is, perhaps I can put your mind at ease."

Anna kept staring at the ground as he spoke. Paulo wasn't getting anywhere with Anna so he decided to give it a rest. "I think we should turn in early. It has been a very trying day. I hope you will reconsider by the time we go to bed."

The reluctance was quite noticeable in Anna's eyes. If she could have avoided going to bed until Paulo was asleep she would have done so. Anna didn't want another confrontation. Paulo held out his hand and helped Anna up. Together they walked back into the house. Everyone was still in the family room.

"Mama and I are turning in early this evening. I'll stop by later to see each of you before going to bed." Paulo and Anna walked upstairs in silence. When they entered their room, Anna went directly to the window.

"Anna, I'm going in to take my shower. Give serious thought to telling me what's bothering you when I'm through."

Anna realized he wouldn't stop until she told him about the dream, yet she didn't want to frighten him. When Paulo came out of the shower, he found Anna in the exact spot where he left her.

"The shower is all yours. When you're finished with your shower, we'll talk some more."

Paulo sat on the loveseat wondering how he could get Anna to open up. Once she did he could put her mind at ease. Anna came out of the shower and started rearranging the clothing in her drawers. It was a stalling tactic she hoped would work. Paulo watched her for a few moments gathering his thoughts.

"Close the drawer and come sit next to me."

Anna continued doing what she was doing. "I won't take much longer."

"Anna, now!" Paulo spoke in a harsh tone.

Anna closed the drawer and sat next to Paulo.

"This will be the fourth and last time I ask! What was bothering you so much that made you act the way you did when I returned from town?"

Anna looked away from Paulo. "I don't know what you're talking about."

"Stop being so stubborn!" Paulo kept up the pressure. "I'm through playing games with you!"

Anna couldn't take it anymore. "Okay, I'll explain why I was upset with you."

"A few days ago I had a nightmare. I found myself looking at your office at the company. There was blood all over the office. I could hear the sirens, of the ambulances, as they were arriving and departing. When you disappeared this afternoon and I couldn't find you, I thought the worst."

As Anna was relaying her dream, Paulo could see Anna becoming physically shaken and emotionally upset. He had never seen his wife sobbing so frantically. The only thing that stopped him from doing so was that he knew she had to get it out of her system. Paulo lifted Anna's chin until their eyes met. He took his handkerchief out and wiped the tears from Anna's face. Then he held Anna in his arms.

"Anna, when I asked you why you were upset, why didn't you tell me the truth? If you had told me the reason, I would have understood why you acted the way you did. What you had was only a dream and nothing else."

Anna curled up on the loveseat, lying in Paulo's arms.

"I know at times I cause you pain. It is never intentional. If anything happens to you, I'll kill myself."

This revelation stunned Paulo.

"I better never hear those words out of your mouth again! If anything happens to me you're to go on with your life. I'll always be by your side."

They kissed passionately.

"I'll be back as soon as I say good night to the children. Wait for me."

Paulo returned in less than ten minutes; this night belonged to his wife. Anna lay in Paulo's arms while he ran his fingers through her hair. For the first few minutes or so not a word was spoken. Paulo gently turned her face toward his. As he gazed in her eyes, he spoke softly to her.

"When I awake, I thank God for making me see the light of day and for bringing you into my life. Before going to sleep, I say a prayer of thanks for sharing my day with you. When I attend daily Mass, I pray for the guidance to make the right decisions, especially when it comes to you. You give me the courage to continue even when I fail. A moment ago, you said you cause me great pain. Not so, Anna, my pain stopped the day I married you. I'm sorry about this afternoon. It is never pleasant when I have to deal with my family privately, especially you. I was wrong for not letting you know I was going into town, but it came up so fast that I wasn't thinking clearly. Tomorrow is Saturday, after breakfast we're going to have a family meeting. I intend to tell the children, that from now on, they are to let you know when they are leaving and when they are expected back. If anyone will be late for any meal, they should phone ahead. I'll enforce this rule quite stringently with our children as well as myself."

Anna curled up next to Paulo feeling the warmth of his body. Paulo couldn't help but wonder if perhaps the dream was a warning. Then he wiped the thought out of his mind. It was only coincidental. Some day in the future he would share the note with Anna, but now wasn't the time.

On Saturday mornings Paulo's whole family, including his grandchildren, ate breakfast together. Everyone was at the breakfast table at nine sharp. Paulo sat at the head of the table with his granddaughter Anna sitting on his lap, his grandson Antonio to his left, and his grandson Paulo to his right. After holding Anna for a while he would pass Anna to her Mom Mom and pick up Antonio. He would do the same with Paulo. Paulo would continue to take turns with each child until breakfast was over. Paulo or Anna never actually ate breakfast. Occasionally, they sipped a cup of coffee. The entire time, the children ate from their grandparents' plates. Paulo and Anna wanted their grandchildren to experience the closeness of having breakfast with their family, especially with their grandparents. When breakfast was finished Paulo would have Anna on his lap again. She had a slight edge over the boys, but no one cared since Paulo doted over all his grandchildren.

After breakfast, Paulo asked Thomas and Marisa to take the children into the family room for a short time. He wanted to have a family meeting. Paulo and Anna kissed all of their grandchildren on their way out. Michael and Franco removed the high chairs from the table.

"Starting today, I'm going to strictly enforce a few of the rules I laid down from when Mama and I married. Over the years I have been lax in following through with them," Paulo declared. "I expect everyone to be present for breakfast at seven sharp. Assunta, Donna and I will join Mama for lunch. If any of you boys find time to come home and eat lunch with us, you're more than welcome. Dinner will be served at six sharp every evening. Phone ahead if there's any reason you won't be on time.

"Michael, Timothy, let Mama know ahead of time the nights you're coming for dinner. Phone Mama if you make arrangements to eat elsewhere. I expect both of you for dinner on Friday evening. Last but not least, phone Mama once a day since she likes to hear your voices." Everyone laughed. "Also, today I'm having textured glass doors installed with an intercom at all the entrances leading into the house," Paulo continued. "Before letting anyone in, put the light on, look through the glass, and inquire who's at the door. The first person that doesn't follow my directions will answer to me privately. Assunta, I hope you understand what I'm saying. You love to run to the door and open it to anyone. As of today you better think twice before doing so. Soon you'll see men changing the patio doors as well. They are installing shatterproof textured glass. The other day I read where a tree fell on a playroom enclosed with glass and shattered the glass to pieces. Luckily there were no children playing there at the time. When you leave our home, you're to let Mama know when you're leaving and when you intend to return. If, for any reason, you're delayed, I expect you to phone Mama and let her know. Donna, I have noticed that you like jogging on the freeway. There have been too many accidents on that road involving joggers. I would prefer you jog on our property."

"I have noticed a lot of traffic on the freeway lately myself and was considering changing locations," Donna responded.

Assunta looked at Donna sarcastically and mumbled something under her breath. Franco heard what Assunta said and gave her a sign of warning, all of which Paulo caught sight of.

"Assunta, when we're through with this meeting, I would like you and Franco to remain," Paulo said.

Assunta banged the table with her fist and made a face. Paulo looked in her direction. Words weren't necessary.

"Anyone who doesn't follow the rules that I have just stated will answer to me."

"Why are you treating us like children?" Assunta blurted out.

"I'm not treating anyone like a child. I'm only reminding you what I have always expected. If anyone objects to what I said a few minutes ago, I would like to hear from you."

No one said a word.

"Everyone is excused. Franco, you and Assunta can wait in the library."

Franco helped Assunta out of her chair.

"Let's not keep Papa waiting."

Anna started to get up when Paulo signaled her to remain seated.

"Not this time," he said.

Anna knew Assunta was capable of getting in trouble with her mouth as easily as she could walk with her feet.

Franco and Assunta took a seat as Paulo checked his phone messages. "Watch the way you speak with Papa. Don't upset him!" Franco whispered in Assunta's ear.

Paulo put down the phone and stared at Assunta. Before he had a chance to question her, she decided to volunteer the information.

"I know why you called me into the library."

"You never know when to keep your mouth shut!" Franco interrupted Assunta. This time it was Paulo's turn to interrupt Franco.

"Franco, I want to hear what Assunta has to say."

Assunta sat up straight looking at Paulo.

"I interrupted you while you were speaking with Donna! When you suggested Donna jog somewhere else, she agreed just to make points with you! Donna likes to come off as 'little miss goody two shoes' and she's doing a damn good job!"

"Assunta, watch your language!" Franco interrupted.

Paulo kept looking at Assunta with a stern look on his face.

"Franco, please let Assunta continue."

"I meet with you almost every day. You never meet with Donna. Donna is the 'good little girl' and I'm the 'bad little girl'."

Paulo leaned back in his chair momentarily and then spoke again.

"Donna and you are not little girls. You're both adults! There's one difference between you and Donna. Donna acts like an adult while you, at times, act like a child! I get no pleasure out of meeting with you privately. As for Donna, I'm going to tell you a story you're never to repeat to anyone. If Mama finds out, I'll know who told her!"

Paulo began to tell his story.

"One evening, Donna wanted Gino to drive her into town. Gino had a hard day and refused. They argued upstairs until Gino fell asleep. Donna left with the keys to the car. She drove straight to the freeway. She never imagined she would get stopped for speeding. She was going eighty miles an hour, and when the sheriff pulled her over, she tried to explain her way out of the situation. She blamed Gino for not fixing the speedometer and misplacing her license. Then she told the sheriff her name hoping the Altro name would get her off the hook. But the sheriff didn't buy her story. While she waited in the patrol car, he called to verify her identity. Mama turned in early, leaving me time to work on paperwork when the phone rang. It was Sheriff DeVito. He had stopped a young lady on the freeway driving Gino's car. She said she was my daughter-in-law. 'I'm sure my daughter-in-law is home', I told him, but when I went up to check, I noticed the bedroom door ajar. It seemed as though two people were in bed. On closer look, I realized I was incorrect. Donna had stuffed a blanket in her place. When I returned to the library I had Sheriff DeVito describe the girl to me. I knew it was Donna. I went upstairs and told Mama I had to go to the company; something was wrong with the alarm there. Sheriff DeVito sent an officer to pick me up since I wanted to drive Gino's car home. I asked Sheriff DeVito not to use sirens or lights. Within ten minutes, I was on my way to meet Donna. When we pulled up, Sheriff DeVito was standing outside his car. He asked me to identify the girl.

"As soon as I opened the door, the car's interior light activated, illuminating Donna's frightened expression. I was furious and she knew it. She tried to explain, but I wouldn't let her speak until we got home. Sheriff DeVito released Donna to my custody.

"When we arrived home, Donna waited in the library while I had a cup of coffee. I needed to calm down. I entered the library and sat down behind the desk. Both of us were speechless at this point until I conjured up the right words to say. I decided to tell her the story about my brother Marc.

"When Marc was sixteen years old, he decided to borrow a car and go joy-riding. Marc was driving at eighty miles an hour without a license! When the State Troopers started chasing him, he panicked and never made it out alive. My mother blamed herself until the day she died. There's nothing worse than watching a parent bury a child. I pray to God that I'm never put in that position! I told Donna I wouldn't tolerate such irresponsible behavior on the part of any of my children. What happened to my brother could have happened to her that evening.

"That night Donna vowed never to drive any car until she first got her license. That's why Donna is always in agreement to what I say. Donna isn't trying to act like 'little miss goody two shoes'. She vowed never to meet with me privately in the future. Now what do you have to say?"

Assunta remained dumbfounded. "I had no idea. You never said a word about this before now."

"When I meet with you, do you think I go out and tell everyone what took place? If you do, you're dead wrong!"

"I'm sorry for the way I acted in the dining room."

"This time you'll get away with a lecture. Go before I change my mind!" Assunta and Franco joined the others for coffee and cake.

The following week, everyone did exactly as Paulo requested. Anna was beginning to relax realizing now her dream was just that, only a dream. Paulo was even beginning to feel as if the ransom note was a hoax. Robert Stone and his men had the entire Altro family under surveillance for the week without any indication of trouble.

Dinner Friday evening was exceptionally pleasant. The whole family was there, and everyone in good spirit. Paulo took the opportunity to announce his plans for the following day.

"Tomorrow, Mama and I are taking the children down to the summer camp. We'll be home for dinner."

"I'd like to take a ride," Timothy interrupted. "I promised the boys I'd stop in and see them."

Paulo smiled. "Try to be ready for eight o'clock. I want to get an early start."

The following morning, Paulo left immediately after breakfast. With Paulo and Anna away from home, everyone had a chance to work on the plans for the party and finish the invitations. If they sent them out now it would give the guests a week to respond. Franco's mother would record the responses. They would use her list for seating arrangements.

The invitation was in the shape of a dove. On one side there was a note written by Franco. On the other side Donna listed all the information regarding the Mass and dinner. In haste, Donna forgot to include the date. Assunta wrote the date in the lower right hand corner with red ink. Before Paulo and Anna returned, all the invitations were in the mail.

Paulo and Anna arrived home to find everyone in the family room. Dinner had been kept warm. No one intended to question Paulo as to why they were late, no one except Assunta.

"Papa, why are you and Mama late for dinner? Dinner at the Altro home is at six o'clock sharp! You and Mama are one hour late. It's a rule of the Altro family that you call home when delayed."

Everyone thought Assunta had dug her own grave and waited for her body to drop.

Paulo gazed at his daughter and decided to tease her a little.

"Assunta, come here."

Assunta had only intended it to be a joke, but feared Paulo didn't take it that way.

"The rules of the house apply to everyone. In the future, I'll be more responsible. I give you credit for saying what everyone else was thinking."

A smile broke through on Assunta's face. It was an enjoyable evening with everyone talking and laughing about how Assunta reprimanded her parents. That night, as Paulo and Anna lay in bed, they both laughed.

"I often felt that Assunta never paid any attention to me when I spoke, I was wrong. Her actions and the way she spoke when we arrived late reminded me of what I'd have done. Now that I've finally taught Assunta to listen to what I'm saying, the next step is to get her to follow through."

`Anna laughed.

"No matter what her Papa does, Assunta's love grows stronger by the day."

Paulo smiled running his fingers through Anna's hair.

"As does her Papa's love for her and her Mama," he added.

It had been a long day for both of them. Before long they both fell asleep.

The week went by quickly.

There was a certain peace that returned to the Altro home. Anna forgot about her dream, Paulo stopped thinking about the letter he received on his return from vacation, and Robert Stone was convinced the letter was a hoax.

On Friday evening, after the children were put to bed, the family watched a movie. When it was over Assunta set up ice cream in the dining room.

"Mama and I are going out for the day tomorrow," Paulo announced. "There's some antique furniture we want to check out." Then Paulo looked straight at Assunta. "We'll be home in time for dinner. We learned our lesson last weekend. If there's a problem getting home on time, I'll give you a call. Assunta, do I have your permission to take a walk with Mama through the garden?"

Assunta tried to avoid laughing.

"As long as you're both back for nine o'clock, that'll be fine," she replied. Paulo helped Anna up from her chair. He then walked toward Assunta and whispered something in her ear. Assunta's mood became very serious.

"Okay, Papa," she muttered.

Anna and Paulo walked out the kitchen door in absolute silence. When they reached the garden, Anna stopped.

"What did you whisper in Assunta's ear?" she asked Paulo.

"I whispered to Assunta to watch her step. She was treading on thin ice."

Anna jokingly hit Paulo on the arm.

"That's not fair. Assunta has been on her best behavior and then you tell her something like that."

Paulo rubbed his arm and then looked at Anna.

"Perhaps it's also time to teach her Mama who's in charge around the Altro home."

"That's not necessary." Anna looked into Paulo's eyes. "I knew from day one who was in charge and I wouldn't want it any other way."

Before breakfast Michael and Timothy concelebrated Mass with the family in the garden chapel. Everyone was in attendance, including the children. It was times like these, in the privacy of his garden chapel, that Paulo enjoyed the most.

Before leaving, Paulo and Anna spent time out back with their grandchildren. The children would all try to get their Pop Pop's attention. In the end the one who would win out was his granddaughter. Even at the tender age of eight months she knew how to make her Pop Pop melt.

31

Paulo, however, tried not to make it so obvious.

Timothy joined the family out back.

"Look at that. Anna already knows how to wrap her Pop Pop around her finger." Seeing Michael coming, he began to laugh. "Here comes Michael, watch what happens when the children see their Uncle Michael."

Timothy was correct in his assumption. As soon as the children saw Michael they all became excited. Antonio and Paulo automatically crawled toward Michael. Anna climbed off Paulo's lap trying to follow the boys. She hesitated momentarily and then crawled back. Paulo beamed from ear to ear.

Before long, everyone joined them on the lawn in the back of the house. Some time around ten, Paulo and Anna left for the day. Paulo could see his children and grandchildren all waving good-bye in his rear view mirror.

"Anna, God has surely blessed us."

Anna moved closer to Paulo and he put his arm around her. It was a beautiful day without a cloud in the sky. This was one of the few times they were alone since their marriage.

Assunta called for a meeting once the children were napping.

"Mama and Papa are gone for the day. Let's do the seating arrangements. Franco, phone your mother and check the responses; you can check it against Gino's master list."

Assunta went on with the meeting while Franco was phoning his mother.

Gino looked at Assunta in such a way she knew something was wrong.

"I'm sorry, I left the list at work."

"Gino, how dumb could you be! Now what are we going to do?"

Franco overheard Assunta while he was waiting for his mother to get the list of cancellations.

"Mama, will you excuse me for one moment."

Walking over to Assunta he turned her face toward him.

"You apologize to Gino right now!" Franco scolded her.

Assunta, realizing Franco wasn't playing games, did exactly as he said.

"I guess with the party being next Sunday I lost my cool. Please forgive me," she apologized.

Franco then resumed his conversation with Maria while Gino walked over to Assunta.

"There's nothing to forgive. It was stupid of me to leave the list at work. I'll get it and be back soon."

"Wait a minute. Why don't we all go down to the company and do the seating arrangements. Michael, what do you think?"

"I think Assunta has a good idea," Gino responded before Michael had a chance. "If Mama and Papa decide to return home they'll catch us making the seating arrangements."

Franco put the receiver down and returned to the table with a very serious look on his face.

"Who wrote the date on the invitations?" he asked.

"I did," Assunta said smiling.

Franco put down the piece of paper he was holding. "We have a problem," he said. "All the people that responded to Mama, responded for August 13th. Apparently you wrote August 13th instead of August 6th."

"That isn't possible, Franco. I distinctly remember writing in the bottom right hand corner: Date of Liturgy and Dinner - August 6th. I've a few extra invitations upstairs in our room. I'll get them."

Assunta returned to the library within a few minutes.

"Michael, I think it's best to give Papa a surprise birthday right on his birthday."

Everyone sat back in frustration. Franco asked to see the extra invitations. Instead of getting upset, he phoned the restaurant.

"Giuseppe, we have a slight problem. The invitations went out with the wrong date for Papa's dinner. Is it possible to hold the dinner on August 13th instead of August 6th? . . . Yes, I can hold . . . Will you notify the band?. . . Thank you Giuseppe."

Franco put the phone down and then spoke looking around the table.

"There's no problem. We can use the restaurant on August 13th."

"I think it's best to have it right on Papa's birthday," said Michael who had been sitting at the table, not saying a word, and finally entering the conversation.

"Assunta there is no reason for you to be upset," Gino said smiling.

Michael looked toward Gino's direction.

"Gino, if Assunta started World War III, I bet you could come up with a logical explanation why it wasn't her fault."

Everyone laughed, including Assunta. She realized that she wasn't paying attention to what she was doing when she wrote out the invitations.

"I'm sorry guys, but maybe it worked out for the best. We can still work on the seating arrangements. Franco, how many people responded?"

"I would say at least eighty percent."

"Does anyone object to us starting the seating arrangements?" Assunta looked around the room. "Okay, let's do it."

Then Assunta turned toward Michael.

33

"What do you think, should we go to the company since the list is there?

"I don't think it's a good idea to leave the children with Thomas and Marisa. If Papa returns and we're not here with the children, he won't be pleased."

"I think Papa would prefer one of us to stay with the children," Franco interrupted.

"I've got an idea. Why don't I stay home with the children?" Timothy suggested.

Franco looked at Michael.

"This is your call," he said.

"Papa had my Cardinal's vestment dry cleaned and forgot to take it home. We can kill two birds with one stone; make the seating arrangements and pick up my vestment."

The look of pleasure was obvious on Assunta's face.

Instead of everyone taking separate cars they went up in Franco's van.

# Chapter 3

## The Altro Estate Becomes An Armed Fortress

Peter, the head of the surveillance team, was in conference when he noticed Franco, Assunta, Gino, Donna, and Michael getting into the van. His heart dropped.

"Where are they all going," he thought to himself. "David, you stay here. Everyone else, follow me," Peter instructed.

Normally, the team would take separate cars and split up to follow their targets but, in this instance, Peter made the decision to follow in one car. Once they were on the road, Peter phoned Robert Stone.

"Robert, Paulo Altro's children have all left the property together and are in Franco's van heading eastbound on the freeway. I'm not sure where they're going but we're on their trail. David is at the house with Timothy and the grandchildren."

"Were there any calls intercepted before they left?" Robert inquired.

"Franco placed two phone calls out; one to his mother and one to Giuseppe's where they are holding Paulo's party."

"Peter, I don't like this! For the love of God, don't lose them!"

"Don't worry about that, boss. I'll contact you when we get to our destination."

The security men followed the van at a safe distance so as not to alarm its occupants. The assignment seemed to be going smoothly, until a few miles down the road, Peter noticed that they were being followed. He continued the pursuit with more caution as Paulo's children led them to their father's company and into the parking lot. His initial plan had been to park in the rear of the building but given the turn of events, at the last minute, he changed his mind. He thought the main road would be the best spot for surveillance, now that he suspected they had unwanted company.

"John, we were followed! Park on the main road leading to the company!" Peter instructed.

"I noticed a while back myself. I don't like the looks of it," John replied.

Peter turned to face the others in the back seat.

"Listen up, guys. A car has been tailing us for some time now. I'm not sure whether there are three or four people in the car. When John pulls over, get out of the car very casually but don't let your guard down."

Just then, the car that had been following them so menacingly passed without hesitation. Alex, one of the security men sitting in the back, wasn't concerned.

"Those poor guys are probably just lost. Why don't we get out of the car and stretch our legs?"

Peter wasn't convinced. It was disturbing to him that the car was on their tail for over half an hour and then suddenly disappeared. Peter wasted no time issuing his orders.

"Tony, I want you to position yourself in front of the main entrance. Contact me if anyone enters or leaves. John, you and Marc take a walk around back and check things out. If anything looks unusual, contact me. Alex and I will stay here and keep an eye out for the car if it should return."

Alex took his position at the back of the car looking up and down the road. Peter felt uncomfortable about the whole situation. He paced back and forth, waiting to hear from his men. Tony phoned as soon as he was positioned in the front. John and Marc never made contact.

Peter became edgy and decided it was time to phone Robert Stone. "Robert, we're outside Paulo's company. His children are all inside. I sent Tony, John and Marc to stand guard around the building, but I'm beginning to worry about them. So far, I've only been able to make contact with Tony. John and Marc aren't responding. I'm going around back myself to check things out."

Robert Stone tapped his pen on the desk nervously, fearing the worst. "Peter, get back to me as soon as you know anything! Be careful! In the meantime, I'll be planning our next move."

Robert put the phone down to look for Paulo's cell number. Holding the file in his hand, Robert felt a sudden chill. Five of his top men and all of Paulo Altro's children were in grave danger. He'd have to move quickly.

Meanwhile, Peter was making a second attempt to communicate with his men.

"Tony, any movement in the front?"

"No one has entered or exited. Do you want me to remain?"

"Keep your position. Have you seen or heard from John or Marc?"

"I haven't heard from them since I arrived. Would you like me to try and find them?"

"No, Tony, stay right where you are! I want to hear from you every five minutes, starting now."

"Will do."

Peter walked over to Alex.

"I'm going to look for John and Marc. If you don't hear from me within the next five minutes, phone Robert, then the police."

Peter painstakingly advanced toward the rear of the building. He dropped to the grass to keep himself out of sight then crawled closely alongside the garage wall. Rounding the corner, he noticed an object lying in the grass and immediately suspected its identity. He prayed he was wrong, but when he got closer, he realized it was indeed a body. Reaching the body, he found John lying in a pool of blood. To the left, he could see Marc in the same gruesome state. Peter tried unsuccessfully to find a pulse. Regaining his composure, he crawled over to Marc's body. He was dead also. Peter closed Marc's eyes then prayed silently. Tearfully, he crawled over to John's body and did the same. Now he had to focus his attention on locating Tony and keeping him out of harm's way. A feeling of relief rushed over him when he spotted Tony alive and well.

"Tony, stay low and crawl toward the car."

"Peter, did you find John and Marc?"

"John and Marc are fine now. Follow me."

Together they crawled over to where Alex was guarding the road. Tony stood up first, dusting off his suit.

"I hope you gave the guys hell for not answering you."

Alex knew by the look on Peter's face that something awful must have happened.

"Are they...?"

"I'm afraid they're both dead." Peter confirmed, placing his hand on Alex's shoulder and bowing his head. Tony and Alex were stunned while Peter was still in a state of shock over what he had witnessed. "I know how you feel but, right now, we have a job to do."

Peter phoned Robert to tell him the bad news.

"We have a major problem here. I think it's time to contact the police."

"Did you find John and Marc?"

There was hesitation on Peter's end of the line.

"John and Marc are all right, aren't they?" Robert asked but he already knew the answer. "Peter, how serious is it?"

"I'm sorry, sir, but they are dead. They were ambushed and their necks broken. I had no idea they were in trouble."

The sadness in Peter's voice was heartbreaking to hear, but Robert had to concentrate on the business at hand.

"John and Marc were very special to us all, but we have to put our grief aside temporarily to make sure no harm comes to anyone else out there. We're obviously dealing with a depraved element."

Peter tried his best to act calm.

"Robert, have you been able to contact Mr. Altro?"

"I've been trying to radio Billy, but something is wrong with the transmission. I've a call into the sheriff for assistance. Hopefully, we'll reach Paulo soon. Also, after speaking with you earlier, I phoned David at the Altro estate and advised him to be on high alert. Veronica will be joining him inside the house shortly. I requested William and his crew for backup. They are currently surrounding the house. There's a second team on its way to give you a hand. When they arrive, scout around for somewhere to set up our base command. I'm on my way to meet Sheriff DeVito now at the Altro estate"

"We'll be waiting." Peter put the phone down and leaned against the car along with Alex and Tony. No words were necessary since they all felt the loss of their friends.

Timothy felt a jolt of fear at the sight of Sheriff DeVito pulling up the driveway. He became especially worried when he noticed a second car behind him. At the same time, David came out of hiding to join them at the steps. Timothy flew to the door to see what the problem was, but Sheriff DeVito wouldn't divulge any information until they were all inside the house. Timothy nervously retreated into the house followed by Sheriff DeVito, Robert and David. He waited anxiously to hear the reason for their visit.

Sheriff DeVito started by making introductions. "Fr. DelVecchio, this is Mr. Robert Stone of Stone Security. He was hired by Mr. Altro to conduct surveillance on the family."

"Surveillance, for what?"

"Mr. Stone, I think you should be the one to explain everything to Fr. DelVecchio."

"Mr. Altro hired my agency to protect his family. He had received a threatening letter in the beginning of July. We have been monitoring each of them since then. When Mr. Altro returned from vacation, he received a second threatening letter. I doubled security from that day forward. Every time someone leaves this house, one of my men is on their trail. This morning, the Altros were escorted by two of my top men and now we can't reach them. Earlier, when the others left the house, my men immediately followed and are in the midst of a situation at the company as we speak. Two of them have already been killed and more are in great danger. It's important that as soon as you hear from Mr. Altro, you contact me. Here is the number. Sheriff DeVito, my extra men have just arrived. We can go over to the company now."

"Okay, let's get moving. I'll dispatch more officers to the scene as well."

The entire time Robert was talking to Timothy, David remained speechless. Robert suspected David was responding badly to the news of John and Marc's death.

"David, can I have a word with you? I know how you're feeling. John and Marc were like sons to me. For now, a greater problem exists. A mad man is out there hunting Paulo's children. Fr. DelVecchio and his grandchildren are in as much danger. We all have to keep our cool and be strong. I need you in charge of securing the house. Veronica will be along shortly to assist you."

Just then, the front door opened and in walked William, who was in charge of the second team, and trailing close behind was Veronica. She immediately located David then made her way over to shake his hand. David regarded her suspiciously, but ultimately extended a nonchalant smile in return. Robert, who had known for some time that David and Veronica clash when they work together, was scrutinizing their interaction. Veronica was headstrong and refused to follow David's directions. Likewise, David was too proud to allow a woman to have control. Robert found it easier to simply avoid teaming them up. However, in this case, he needed both of their unique talents in order for the rescue to be carried out successfully.

Shaking his head in frustration, Robert swiftly redirected his attention to William and his plans for securing the perimeter of the house. He walked over to the table where William was unrolling blueprints of the property. David and Veronica approached the table also and stood on either side of William.

"We have every entrance to the house covered. Don't worry about a false alarm. I'd rather be safe than sorry. Veronica, keep everyone in the family room. If it becomes necessary for one of them to leave for any reason, it's your responsibility to guard him or her until they return. Fr. DelVecchio, is there anyone else here with you beside the children?"

"Two employees, Thomas and Marisa. They went out to do some grocery shopping. I expect them back shortly."

"Where do they usually park their car to unload the groceries?"

"In the driveway near the kitchen entrance."

"What's the make and color of the car Thomas is driving?"

"It's a blue Jeep Cherokee."

"I'll keep an eye on the front of the house," William continued. "The minute I see a blue Jeep Cherokee pull up, I'll let David know. It will then be your responsibility to check through the glass in the foyer to make sure it's them. David, you let me know the instant Fr. DelVecchio identifies them. Once Thomas and Marisa are in the house, I want everyone to stay in one room."

Once William laid down the groundwork, he asked to speak to Robert and David alone for a few minutes to go over some particulars that he thought would be best said in private. He emphasized to David the importance of everyone staying together in the family room since it was the only area inaccessible from the outside because there were no windows or doors.  Next, he instructed David to move everyone to the basement if there's any indication that the perpetrators have gained entrance to the house and to remain there until someone came for them.  Before heading to his post, William asked Robert for any last minute suggestions. Robert had none due to the fact that, as usual, William had everything under control.

As soon as William, Robert and Sheriff DeVito left the house, David promptly approached Veronica in an effort to clear the air.

"I know you and I don't get along very well, but, for now, I think it's best we put aside our personal feelings.  We have an important job to do and we need to work as a team."

Veronica nodded in agreement, then, in a sympathetic tone, she changed the subject to that of his departed friends.

"David, I'm sorry about John and Marc.  They were two of the finest men I ever worked with."

David put his head down momentarily to hide his emotions.  On impulse, he quickly turned away, suggesting they get to work.

Their plan was soon under way.  David, Veronica and Timothy moved to the family room to await news while the children all napped on the floor. The rash sound of William's voice over the transmitter startled them.

"There's a Jeep pulling up the drive!  Ask Fr. DelVecchio to check and make sure that it's Thomas and Marisa!  Leave Veronica with the children! I don't want them left alone for one minute!"

It appeared to Veronica that David was uncomfortable about the task. She, too, was feeling the strain of the situation; so much so, that she was afraid she'd crack under the pressure.  Strange as it seemed, she was relying on David to maintain control.  Giving him the thumb up was her way of encouraging him to go on.  With that, David gestured to Timothy to follow him to the door.

Timothy and David approached the foyer with apprehension.  It was a relief to identify Thomas and Marisa.

"William, all is clear.  Fr. DelVecchio has identified Thomas and Marisa. I think it's best they follow the same routine as far as taking the groceries in through the kitchen."

"I agree.  Be careful and let me know when everyone is back in position in the family room."

"Will do," David promised, concluding the conversation.

So far, everything seemed routine to William, but he had a feeling things were going to get a lot worse.  He sat back contemplating the possibilities.

Meanwhile, David was informing Timothy of their next move.

"Let's get to the kitchen. I'll take cover behind the door while you greet them. I don't want Thomas and Marisa to get alarmed by my presence. As soon as they are safely inside and the door is closed, you're to signal them not to say a word. When we get back into the family room, I'll explain everything to them. Remember that the assailants may be lying in wait ready to storm the kitchen. In the event this happens, what are you going to do?"

"I'm to hit the floor."

"Great." David smiled. "Here we go."

It seemed like they'd been waiting an eternity when the door finally opened and in walked Thomas and Marisa lugging the grocery bags. Timothy's heart was pounding as he greeted them awkwardly. Almost instantly, Thomas caught a glimpse of the man with a gun hiding behind the door. Timothy quickly signaled not to scream by putting his finger to his lips. They followed Timothy into the family room where David explained the situation to them.

"I'm not here to harm you. Veronica and I work for a security company that has been hired to protect Paulo Altro's family. We have reason to suspect that kidnappers are holding Paulo's children hostage at his company at this very moment. Our concern is that they may attempt another attack here to get the rest of the family. If for any reason Veronica or I feel your lives are in jeopardy, we're going to ask you to move to a safe area as quickly as possible. Is there any place close by where we can take shelter?"

Thomas thought for a moment before remembering the wine cellar. He explained that it hadn't been used in years then proceeded to show David the way. Its entrance was located in the coat closet in the rear of the recreation room. It was the perfect spot to hide the family at a moment's notice and David was thrilled.

Everything quieted down inside the house for the time being. They were all still blissfully unaware of the criminals' intentions. Their false sense of security, however, would soon be shattered. The kidnappers were very nearby, putting together the final pieces of their plan. They had maintained constant contact with the kidnappers at the company and it was decided that they would first take Paulo's grandchildren hostage before storming the company and taking the others.

No sooner did the children wake from their naps, than David heard footsteps upstairs. Jumping up, David and Veronica quickly reached for their guns. David stared into Thomas' eyes, trying to convey the magnitude of the situation. Within minutes, they were in the recreation room. Thomas pulled the closet doors open and lifted the carpet.

"Veronica, take everyone down to the wine cellar and stay there until I tell you everything is clear!"

"David, I'm not leaving you alone!" she argued.

David grabbed Veronica's arm.

"This isn't a request, it's an order! I want you to stay with the family in the wine cellar! Do you understand? Now move!"

Veronica was frightened by the tone of his voice. Once David saw Veronica follow behind everyone down the steps, he headed for the first floor. As he opened the door leading to the kitchen he could hear footsteps in the family room. Cautiously, he made his way, checking occasionally to make sure no one was behind him. Turning quickly to the right, he spotted the intruder. Before the kidnapper could get a shot off, David charged him and knocked him out with the butt end of his gun. If there were others in the house, he wouldn't want to alarm them with gunfire. Seeing nothing else that could be used as rope, David snagged the telephone wire and tied him up with it then gagged him with a handkerchief. Suddenly, he felt another presence in the room. He dropped to the floor, gun pointed and ready to shoot, when he realized it was Veronica.

"What the hell did I tell you? You're so goddamned pigheaded! That's why I never liked working with you! You're going to be in big trouble if we get out of this mess alive."

Suddenly, out of nowhere another kidnapper appeared. Before long, David and the kidnapper were fighting fiercely on the floor. Veronica didn't fire her gun for the same reason David chose not to; if a third kidnapper were in the house, the shot would direct him to their location. Instead, Veronica picked up the crystal vase that was on the table and used it to hit the kidnapper over the head, thus knocking him out. David looked around for another telephone to use the wire to tie up the second kidnapper. When he finished, he stood up and faced Veronica.

"Thanks, Veronica. Now you can go straight to the wine cellar where I sent you in the first place!"

"That's the gratitude you show me for saving your life! You're a jerk and I'll never work with you again!"

Just as she was about to storm off, they heard footsteps on the second floor. David quickly grabbed Veronica and pushed her into the dining room and under the dining room table.

"Listen to me! I want you to stay put! No matter what, I don't want you to come out from under that table!

Veronica gave in to his request.

"David, be careful," she warned.

David couldn't believe his ears. She was actually following his orders and, on top of it, she was worried about him. He walked away confused, heading slowly from the dining room toward the stairway. As soon as he entered the hallway, a third kidnapper attacked him from behind, but he was no match for David. It wasn't long before David got the better of the kidnapper and was able to knock the gun out of his hands but a struggle ensued.

Veronica listened helplessly for a minute or so, but then couldn't stand it any longer. She came out from under the table, preparing to fire, if necessary. When she approached, David and the kidnapper were still struggling on the floor and David was finding it difficult to keep his gun under control. Without warning, the gun went off, hitting Veronica in the left shoulder. She fell to the ground, moaning in agony, but somehow managed to shoot the kidnapper in his leg. William, who was stationed outside, heard the gunshots and ordered his team to storm the house. Within seconds, they were crashing through the foyer, kitchen, dining room and library patio doors. William took control and easily subdued the kidnapper, giving David a chance to recuperate. David sustained numerous lacerations to the face and neck and his clothes were saturated with blood.

"Thanks, buddy!" David said, still lying on the floor, trying to regain his strength. Then, with a jolt, he recalled Veronica's presence in the room during the struggle but noticed that she was no longer there. He asked William where she was.

William hesitated for a moment. "Veronica has been shot. When you were struggling with the kidnapper . . ."

"I told her to stay put under the table!" David struggled to stand up. "Why didn't she do as I told her? Wait until I get my hands on her!"

William tried to calm David down.

"Veronica is in the dining room waiting for the paramedics. I think you'd better have someone take a look at your face also."

David pulled away from William and rushed toward the dining room. Seeing Veronica lying on the floor in a pool of blood was more than he could take. He fell to his knees and held Veronica in his arms.

"Why didn't you listen to me? I told you to stay put! You're a stubborn woman! I'm so furious with you, I . . ."

Just then Veronica started to regain consciousness.

"Did we get them?" she asked.

David ran his fingers through Veronica's long hair.

"Yes, we did. The house has been secured and Timothy and the children are safe."

"I guess we're a good team after all," Veronica muttered.

43

"I guess we are," David replied.

Just as Veronica passed out again, the paramedics rushed into the house. They immediately took Veronica's vital signs. She had lost so much blood that they realized they had to get her to the hospital as soon as possible or she'd bleed to death.

Riding in the ambulance with Veronica, David couldn't help but notice how beautiful she was. He said a silent prayer to God to save her life.

Hospital staff was eager to rush Veronica into the operating room as soon as they arrived. The only thing David could do now was wait. In the meantime, his face was examined and bandaged in the emergency room. The cut that caused most of the bleeding was right above the eyebrow and required a few stitches. They couldn't finish fast enough for David. He was anxious to go to Veronica. The instant they were done, he headed for the operating room. William was already there, waiting to hear the prognosis, when he saw David rushing toward him down the corridor.

"How is Veronica?" David asked excitedly.

"No news yet. Say guy, your face doesn't look so bad anymore."

"I'm all right. Everyone knows facial cuts tend to bleed more profusely. Veronica is the one I'm concerned about. If anything happens to her. . .. "

"It's not your fault Veronica was shot."

"You don't understand! I told her to stay under the dining room table and not to move. I should have taken her back to the wine cellar myself."

"Listen to me! You both did an excellent job and should be commended. When our communication was broken off, I thought we were in deep trouble."

"William, we purposely stopped using the radio because we feared that our transmission was being picked up by the kidnappers and that they would find out where I intended on hiding everyone."

"I never gave that a thought. You know what? You were right. That's probably how they were able to slip by us without being noticed. Good work, David."

David paced back and forth in the lounge. At one point, he walked over to the window and gazed up at the sky as if he was in a trance. It wasn't until Dr. Gennaro came out of the operating room that David snapped out of it. The news they'd been waiting for had arrived.

"Veronica is resting," Dr. Gennaro stated matter-of-factly. "The bullet just missed the main artery so she isn't in any immediate danger. However, there's always a chance for an infection to set in. For that reason, I've started her on antibiotics. Also, since she has lost so much blood, her heart may have been affected. We're monitoring her and will continue to do so through the night."

Dr. Gennaro hesitated momentarily, noticing David's shirt and pants full of blood. He realized just then that he must be the other security person who was injured in the attack.

"You must be the young man who was transfused in the ambulance. I was told I'd know who you were just by looking at you. The paramedics told me you looked as if you were in a war. Veronica owes you her life."

"When can I see her?"

"If you promise not to disturb her, I'll let you into her room for a few minutes. First, let's get you something to change into."

Dr. Gennaro took David to one of the dressing rooms and gave him green surgical scrubs to put on. When David emerged from the dressing room, looking like a doctor, William couldn't help but laugh.

"David, I believe you missed your calling. That color is very becoming on you."

After a few laughs, William and David followed the doctor down the long corridor to a closed door. A horrible image loomed in David's mind, making him almost too afraid to open the door. He forced himself to peek in and face the reality. There lay Veronica in bed with tubes covering her body. They were giving her more blood, intravenous fluids and medication as well.

"May I sit with her?" David asked.

Dr. Gennaro sensed David's concern and felt bad. Normally, he wouldn't permit anyone to stay, but under the circumstances, he allowed it.

"If you promise to let Veronica sleep and not disturb her, I'll pretend I never saw you here."

With that said, Dr. Gennaro left the room. William stayed for a short while longer just to be sure everything was all right. After all, ever since they'd become partners, William thought of himself as Veronica's guardian. It was Robert's idea to team them up, hoping that perhaps an older influence would have a good effect on her and it worked. He gently kissed Veronica on the forehead before leaving to report back to Robert.

"David, take care of Veronica. She's special to Robert in more ways than you know," William told him.

On his way to the phones, William bumped into Dr. Gennaro and thanked him again for allowing David to stay.

"Not at all," he replied. "It's nice to see a young couple that love each other as much as they do."

"Why do you say that?"

"Well, it's obvious how the young man feels about her and, likewise, she fretted the entire time she was in recovery, calling out David's name and asking if he was all right."

"I know you're not going to believe this but I swear it's the gospel truth. Up until today they couldn't stand each other."

"You're right, I find that hard to believe."

"So do I, doctor, so do I."

Within minutes, William was on the phone with Robert and could tell by his voice that Robert was extremely uptight. At first, he spoke roughly, ordering William to return to the Altro residence with the others and wait there for further instructions. Then, all of a sudden, his voice changed, exposing his hidden concerns, when he asked about Veronica and David.

William filled him in on all the details, starting with David. He explained that David had only superficial wounds and would be just fine but that Veronica wasn't as lucky. The bullet wound to her shoulder caused heavy blood loss, which necessitated an emergency blood transfusion. Fortunately, William proclaimed, it saved her life. Later, at the hospital they removed the bullet from her shoulder and stopped the bleeding. He told Robert that Dr. Gennaro was going to keep Veronica a few days for observation because there was the possibility of an infection setting in, as well as a small chance of a heart malfunction due to the loss of blood. Hoping to make Robert feel at ease, he assured him that David would stay by Veronica's side and notify them if there was any change.

"Thank you for arranging that," Robert said. "No one should have to wake up alone and confused in a hospital bed. At least she'll see a friendly face when she wakes up."

William wasn't so sure about that so he quickly changed the subject. "Have you heard from Paulo yet?"

"No, I haven't and I'm beginning to worry. If the kidnappers want to speak with Paulo and I can't locate him, God knows what they'll think. I learned over the years when dealing with men like this, you never want to upset them because they have no morals. If they thought we weren't permitting Paulo to speak with them, they just might kill one of his children to get his attention."

Just then, Sheriff DeVito approached Robert to tell him an APB was out on Mr. Altro's license plate and that if he were driving his car, they would be able to pick him up in a matter of minutes. That was exactly what Robert wanted to hear. He thanked the sheriff then instantly relayed the information to William, who'd been holding on the line. With that, Robert and William ended their conversation and went about their business.

One of Robert's security men walked over to him.

"Do you think the kidnappers at the company are waiting to hear from the kidnappers at the house?" Steve asked Robert.

"I'm kind of banking on it. The longer they wait to hear from them, the more time they buy us to locate Paulo."

Sheriff DeVito returned with a broad smile on his face. "We have located Mr. and Mrs. Altro. They are on their way home now. I'd say they should arrive within the next hour. One of my men picked them up on the highway. Paulo left his car there. We found your men unharmed. Someone had fooled with the car radio and it wasn't working. They had no idea since they never tried to phone you."

Robert breathed a sigh of relief.

"I hope they arrive in time."

When Robert entered Paulo's home, the first floor looked like a bomb hit it. Robert stood there trying to estimate the damage to Paulo's property.

"Steve, perhaps we should meet Mr. & Mrs. Altro outside. I think this room would put even a dead man into hysterics. Also, can you give the hospital a call to check on Veronica's condition? Meet me outside when you're through."

Heading to the door, Robert couldn't get his mind off of Veronica. He was startled when Steve arrived in less than five minutes.

"Veronica is running a low grade fever," Steve announced. "There's an infection somewhere. The doctor said that she's giving him a hard time. She's insisting that she wants to sign herself out. David's been trying to talk some sense into her but I don't think it's working because when I phoned, they were in the middle of a battle to keep her there. I think it would be best if you gave her a call."

Robert took out his cell phone and called the hospital. Dr. Cristanzio was Chief of Staff and a personal friend of his. Hopefully he could update him on Veronica's condition.

"May I please speak with Dr. Cristanzio? Robert Stone calling."

"Good afternoon, Robert. I'm glad you called. Your employee, Veronica Rico, was admitted with a gunshot wound. Dr. Gennaro operated and removed the bullet and would prefer Veronica stay a few days for observation because of the amount of blood she lost, but she's ready to sign herself out."

Veronica heard Dr. Cristanzio talking about her to someone on the phone and was getting upset. She continued to listen until she figured out who he was talking to.

"I'm Veronica's father. Under no circumstances is she to leave the hospital," Robert blurted out.

Dr. Christanzio was stunned. "I'm sorry," he said. "I didn't realize Veronica was your daughter. Now I know where she gets her stubbornness. Right now she's pacing back and forth instead of lying in bed."

"David Paladino, one of my men, is with her now! In my absence, she's to do exactly what he tells her!"

"I'm afraid you're wrong. He hasn't been doing a good job convincing her to stay. "

"Veronica isn't going anywhere! Will you please put her on the phone!" Robert heard her pick up the phone.

"What's this nonsense about you signing yourself out? You get right back in bed and that's an order! David is going to stay with you . . . "

"That's not necessary. I'm feeling. . . " Veronica suddenly lost her balance and fell backward.

Robert heard confusion on the other end until finally Dr. Cristanzio picked up the phone.

"This is exactly what I was speaking about Robert! Veronica has lost so much blood she's very weak. I agree with Dr. Gennaro that she'd be better off spending a few days here in the hospital!"

"Put David on the phone, please."

"David, listen to me. Do whatever you have to but make sure she doesn't leave or you'll answer to me!"

"How am I going to do that? She's not listening to anything I say!"

"Veronica is my daughter. After I'm through with her, I guarantee, she'll do exactly as you say. Put her on the phone!"

David handed Veronica the phone, totally amazed over the fact that she was Robert's daughter.

"Your father would like to speak with you."

The way he said it was as if he was asking if it were true or not.

Veronica pulled the phone out of David's hand so fast that she pulled him along with it.

"Give me the damn phone!"

Veronica spoke calmly to her father.

"What is it, Robert?"

"I think it's time you put your childish game aside for today and do as you're told!"

"Robert, I'm. . . "

"Don't interrupt me! I'm speaking to you as your father now, not your employer! You'd better listen to what I'm saying. You're going to do as you're told! I can't come down there right now because of the situation with Paulo's children, but I've assigned David to stay with you to make sure you don't leave the hospital. If it's a baby-sitter you need, then you've got one!"

"That's not . . . "

"I don't want to hear another word out of your mouth! I've done everything the way you wanted since you started working for me. Today it stops. I don't care who knows you're my daughter, Veronica Stone. Do what the Doctor says and get back into bed! As soon as I'm through here, I'll be up to see you."

"You're the boss."

"No, Veronica, I'm your father. Let me remind you one more time. In my absence, you're to stay in that bed and listen to David!"

"You're out of your mind if you think that I'll allow David Paladino to control me."

"David is your boss for the present time! Case closed!"

"All right, only until you get here. Then we can talk about this." Veronica looked at David sarcastically, then back to the phone.

On the other end of the line, Robert was trying to find the right words to say.

"I love you very much and don't want anything to happen to you. With everything going on over here, I'd appreciate it if you'd cooperate with David and Dr. Cristanzio. Please put Dr. Cristanzio back on the phone."

"Veronica won't give you any more trouble," Robert continued. "If she does, you've my permission to detain her whatever way necessary until I arrive. David has my cell number."

Robert put the phone down and looked blankly at Steve.

"Come on. We have work to do."

They were expecting the arrival of Paulo and Anna at any moment now and needed to prepare. They finished just in time to catch them pulling into the driveway.

Looking out the side window of the patrol car, Paulo saw two body bags carrying the remains of Robert's security men being placed in an ambulance and feared the worse. He immediately embraced Anna so she wouldn't see what was going on. When the patrol car stopped, Paulo jumped out with Anna close behind.

"How bad is it, Robert?"

"Everything has been secured here. Your grandchildren and Timothy are safe inside the house."

Anna flew by Robert to check on her grandchildren while Paulo fought to hide his emotions.

"When we were driving up, I noticed they were putting two body bags in one of the ambulances. I pressed Anna's face against my shoulder so she wouldn't witness the carnage. For a split second, I thought. . . "

Robert looked at Paulo with tears in his eyes.

"Today I lost four of my top men. Nick, Joseph, Marc, and John are dead. They were like sons to me. The two men that were tailing you had the wires in their car radio tampered with. Therefore, I couldn't reach either of them. Thank God they're alive."

"You said four men and yet I only saw two body bags."

"It's a long, horrible story. I'll fill you in later." Robert took his handkerchief out to wipe his tears. "Right now, we have a more pressing issue to discuss," he continued. "This afternoon, all of your children took a ride to the company. That's why they weren't here during the siege. However, I've a feeling the kidnappers are holding your children at this very moment. We haven't heard anything yet concerning ransom, but expect to hear from them shortly."

At that moment, the severity of the situation hit Paulo. Four people were dead and it was his fault entirely. How many more would it take, he thought. If the men who were sent to guard his children couldn't defeat the kidnappers, what chance did his children have against them?

"I'm so sorry. I can't find the words to express my sorrow for your loss."

"Thank you. They were all great men and will definitely be missed." Robert became choked up again but forced himself to concentrate on the job. "Paulo, I've a few questions for you. Do you know why your children would all go down to your company at the same time?"

"I've no idea. It doesn't make sense. Gino and I agreed he'd tell me whenever he went to the company so I could send for security to stay with him."

"Does Gino know the security code?"

Paulo nodded his head. "Of course. On occasion, we work late and are the last ones to leave the building so we have to set the alarm when we leave."

"Are there any security guards in the building over the weekend?"

"No, the alarm is activated after everyone has left for the weekend."

"Where is the alarm console located?"

"It's in a closet near the main entrance. Once it's set, we have thirty seconds to leave the building."

"The most important thing right now is to get you down there. I want you to be available in case the kidnappers try to contact you."

Paulo agreed but he wanted to make a quick trip into the house to see his grandchildren before going. Nothing could have prepared him for what he said when he stepped inside. Paulo couldn't believe the extent of damage.

"Looks like a war zone," he declared.

"That's exactly what it was, Paulo," Robert confirmed.

Paulo took a handkerchief out of his pocket to wipe away his tears.

"Let's go see my grandchildren now."

Elizabeth Quintino

The minute they heard his voice, the three toddlers' faces lit up. Paulo lifted them up one at a time and held them close to his heart smothering them with kisses all the while! When it sank in that they were all okay, he went to talk to Timothy.

"I'm glad you're all right, Timothy."

"I was never so frightened; not for myself, but for the children. The thought that..."

"Thankfully it's all over for you and the children. It's the others we must be concerned with now."

Paulo turned to Anna next.

"Come sit next to me. Darling, there's a very good possibility that our children are being held hostage at the company."

"What are you talking about? Who would want to hurt our children?"

Paulo held Anna's face between the palms of his hands.

"Listen to me, I promise you, nothing is going to happen to them. I don't have time to explain but take me at my word. It's important that I go there to negotiate their release. I want you to stay here with Timothy and the children. No one can harm you here."

Anna regained her composure.

"If our children are in trouble and it's your place to be there since you're their father then, in the same respect, it's my place to be there since I'm their mother. Please don't argue with me, Paulo, but I'm coming along with you."

Timothy, who had been listening calmly, stood up next to Paulo.

"I'd like to be there as well. They may need me."

It didn't take much convincing for Paulo to realize that they were right. It was settled; they would all go to the company. One last thing needed to be done before leaving and Paulo was dreading it. He needed to break the news to Antonio and Maria. With Anna and Fr. DelVecchio by his side, he picked up the phone to dial.

"Antonio, I want you to stay calm. They've carried out their threat. The children are being held hostage at Altro Electronics . . . No, it won't do any good if you and Maria rush out here . . . They were here at the house already; Fr. DelVecchio and our grandchildren were home . . . No, thank God everyone is safe. I've a favor to ask of you . . . I'd like to send Thomas and Marisa out to your house with the children . . . I promise to keep in touch . . . I'm not sure . . . Hold on a minute. Robert, is it all right if Thomas drives them?"

"I'd prefer that Sheriff DeVito has his men drive them. I want to be sure that there are no others waiting along the road."

"They'll be escorted by the Sheriff's department. Thomas will phone you as soon as he know the details."

Paulo hung up then turned toward Thomas.

"Thomas, you and Marisa are going to be driven to the Cordova's with the children. Pack enough for a few days. It's important that I join my children as soon as possible."

Paulo bent down and gave each of his grandchildren one more kiss. Accompanied by Anna and Timothy, Paulo returned to where Robert was waiting.

"We're ready," he announced.

And with that, they were whisked away to the company.

# Chapter 4

## Paulo's Worst Fears Become A Reality

The main road and every adjoining byway leading to Altro Electronics were lined with patrol cars and armed officers. The scene resembled something out of an action movie but considering this was real life, it was profoundly worse. In real life, an encounter such as this was terrifying to say the least. The sight tormented Paul and Anna. They gasped with horror as they surveyed the situation from the safety of the car that was transporting them to the garage where the command center was being organized.

The garage was located further down the road on the same side as the main building. It was generously sized, and could easily house ten cars, but it hadn't been used for parking in a good many years, ever since Paulo had a larger one built even closer to the company. Now, it served as a spacious utility shed. Normally, the area was very peaceful, as Rocco, the groundskeeper, was the only occupant. Today, however, the entire area was teaming with officials from every division of law enforcement. By the time the Altros arrived at the garage's entrance, they had seen enough.

Looking into the garage, Paulo saw people scurrying about in all directions. They were busy transforming the space to accommodate the rescue operation. The garage was hardly recognizable. Ordinarily, all the equipment and supplies needed to groom the property were kept in one corner. The groundskeeper, Rocco, was exceptionally neat and always made sure the equipment was cleaned and replaced in its original location. In another corner of the garage, beer and soda were stored in a large refrigerator, for use at company functions. The center of the garage was clear so Rocco could work on large pieces of equipment. When he wasn't fixing something, he'd place a folding table and six chairs in the center of the room. To the right, against the wall, stood a huge makeshift worktable. By its rugged appearance, you would never know that it was once Paulo's very first conference table. Eventually, a larger, more elaborate one was purchased for the office and now Rocco used the old one for repairing smaller pieces of equipment and storing parts. The surface of the worktable was always immaculately kept so this was where Robert Stone chose to set up his transmitting devices.

William was already on his way over to meet Robert when the car pulled up. After a short discussion, Robert introduced the two men.

"Paulo, I'd like to introduce you to William. He headed the rescue team at the house."

"There are no words I can say at this time to express how much we appreciate your assistance." Paulo reached out to shake William's hand. "Looking around my home a few minutes ago, I could imagine the struggle that took place. The outcome could've been drastically different if it weren't for your heroic actions. In the future, if I can be of assistance to you or anyone on your team, feel free to call on me."

Peter approached at this point with news for Robert. He leaned forward to whisper into Robert's ear.

"We have confirmed that they are holding Paulo's children inside. Sonia finally picked up one of their communications. They've been trying to reach the men at Paulo's house."

"I want to hear it right now!" Robert shouted as he darted off, with William and Peter in tow, to where Sonia was stationed. "Sonia, can you play that tape again?"

They waited in complete silence for Sonia to replay the intercepted message. Soon they would all know what kind of people they were dealing with and how to proceed. The message came through loud and clear.

"Charles, where are you? We have Paulo's children. Have you secured the house? Come in, Charles! Charles, answer me! If I don't hear from you in the next fifteen minutes, I'll start killing them off. Pretty boy will be the first."

Paulo saw them in a huddle and wanted to know what all the commotion was about. He joined them just in time to hear the recording of a madman threatening the lives of his children. For the first time in his life, Paulo felt helpless. His legs suddenly gave out on him and he went limp, almost falling to the ground.

The severity of the situation took everyone, except Robert, by surprise. Robert made it his business to always be prepared for the worst. He wasted no time putting his plan in motion. The first thing he needed to do was talk to Sheriff DeVito. He spotted him almost immediately and signaled for him to come over. "Sheriff, it's important that one of the kidnappers from the house reach the others in the company. Where are the men being held?"

Sheriff DeVito smiled.

"I anticipated this would happen, so I brought the kidnapper who wasn't seriously injured here with me. He is being guarded in my patrol car."

Robert grabbed the sheriff excitedly and planted a big kiss on his forehead.

"Bless your foresight! By any chance, is his name Charles? We have intercepted a message from the leader to someone by the name of

Charles. He has fifteen minutes to return his call or they'll start killing Paulo's children."

Sheriff DeVito hurried Robert to his car to speak with the kidnapper, whose name they discovered, was in fact Charles. Unfortunately, that was all he was willing to tell them. As expected, the kidnapper was very uncooperative. It seemed like they'd been talking for hours but were getting nowhere. From a distance, Paulo observed the confrontation and noticed Robert becoming frustrated with the kidnapper. He knew he had to do something quickly for his children's sake, so he regained his composure and dragged himself over to the patrol car.

"Robert, may I?" Paulo asked nervously.

With permission, he sat down next to the kidnapper in the patrol car.

"Hello. My name is Paulo Altro. Right now, my children are being held hostage. I don't know who is doing this or why; however, I do know, that as a parent, I'm concerned about my children. If I've done something so terrible to someone then it's me they should take revenge on, not my family. If you cooperate with the authorities and help me, I'll get you the best counsel available and see that you are generously rewarded for your kindness." Suddenly, the fears of losing one or all of his children shown on his face like a flashing neon sign. "Please help us. My children are in danger!"

The kidnapper looked suspiciously at Paulo then lowered his head.

"I held your grandchildren hostage. It doesn't make any sense. How can you even think of helping me after what I've just done? If I were you, I'd want me dead for all the pain and grief I caused you!"

"We all make mistakes in our lifetime. The important thing is that we ultimately make amends for the wrong we have done. I mean this sincerely. If you help me save my children, I'll personally speak on your behalf at your hearing."

The kidnapper looked up momentarily while he debated over what to do when, all of a sudden, he caught sight of Anna's face. She had been standing outside the patrol car listening to every word and crying uncontrollably. Her eyes were puffy and tear-streaked. She looked pitiful and, in the end, it was she who won his heart. He thought of his own mother, who often cried for all the pain he caused her. His mother was no longer here to comfort him but Anna was.

"Lady, please don't cry anymore, I'll do whatever you want," Charles finally blurted out, looking in Anna's direction, then instantly turning to Paulo "Mr. Altro, I'm not doing this because I'm looking for an easy way out. I'm doing this for her and for no other reason. Mrs. Altro reminds me of my own mother. Now, will someone give me a walkie-talkie to call Tony."

It was a relief to finally have his cooperation. Robert dashed toward the garage to retrieve a walkie-talkie before he changed his mind while Sheriff DeVito uncuffed Charles and released him from the patrol car. As soon as Charles stepped out of the car, he walked over to Anna and promised her that he would get her children out safely.

"Thank you, Charles, and God bless you," Anna whispered in his ear as she embraced him.

Charles entered the garage, escorted by an armed officer. He knew this wasn't going to be easy, but it soon became even more unbearable than he had imagined when he found himself surrounded by a room full of irate onlookers. A walkie-talkie was immediately handed to him to make the call and he accepted it with as much courage as he could muster. His palms were already starting to sweat. The room fell silent as he started to talk.

"Tony, this is Charles. Can you read me?"

"Charles, where've you been? I've been trying to reach you for some time now."

Charles thought for a moment and than came up with an idea.

"I was busy trying to restrain our Ace in the Hole."

"What the hell are you talking about?"

"Don't be mad, but I've done something that wasn't in our plans."

"You were told not to change any of the plans. What the fuck did you do! Tell me and get it over with!"

"Tony, I've just captured Anna Altro." Motioning to Paulo and Anna to be silent, Charles continued. "It was a struggle, but I finally dragged the bitch into the house. Right now, I'm sitting in front of Paulo Altro's wife. What do you think Paulo will give for her?"

"You're a genius! She's worth at least two million alone. How are the grandchildren?"

"Fine, so far. I sent George and Alex in the basement with everyone."

"How about Fr. DelVecchio?"

"We got him, too."

Tony screamed with joy.

"Holy shit, we have the entire family! Poor Paulo will be walking the bread lines while we'll be living it up with his money on our own private island! I guess my next move is to contact Paulo. Job well done. Over and out." Tony hesitated before hanging up. "Wait a minute! I've been so caught up in capturing our hostages that I lost track of Paulo. I don't know where he is or how to get a hold of him."

Charles thought for a minute then he signaled Paulo to get him a piece of paper and pen.

"I have an idea. Let me get the bitch to give me his cell phone number.

Wherever he is, I'm sure he has a phone with him." Then he wrote down some instructions for Anna on the paper.

*I'm going to pretend I'm beating you. I want you to scream as loud as you can into the phone. Do you understand?*

Anna nodded her head. Charles looked around for a piece of wood.

"Come here, bitch! I want your husband's cell phone number!" Charles was shaking his head side to side indicating no, as he spoke. Anna nodded again, careful not to give anything away.

"I don't know it."

"You lying bitch!"

Charles then picked up to the piece of wood and started banging it on the tabletop. He wrote down *'cry'* on the paper in front of Anna. She did exactly as he instructed her to do. It was not difficult for Anna to do since Charles was frightening her. She was so convincing that even Charles started to believe he hurt her.

"Maybe that will teach you I mean business! Now, bitch, I'm going to ask you one more time, what's your husband's number?"

Anna, still sobbing, told him the number. "I think the number is 269-3114."

"What do you mean think, is it 269-3114 or not? No more games, bitch, or you may be the first one to bite the dust."

Charles wrote down another message on the paper. *Pretend I'm pulling your hair, scream!*

Anna yelled into the phone. "No more, please! You are pulling the hair right out of my head! I swear to you, that is the phone number, 269-3114!" Charles wrote *'perfect'* on the paper:

"The bitch gave me a hard time, but I'm sure this is the right number now. Believe me, if it isn't, she will be pushing up daisies sooner than you think. The number is 269-3114."

"Good work, Charles! I knew you could do it!"

"Thanks, Tony. Talk to you later."

Charles put the phone down with a fleeting glance at Anna, and then hung his head in shame.

It was an uncomfortable situation for everyone involved so while they waited for more instructions, they all went their separate ways. Paulo expressed his gratitude to Charles for his help then took Anna to the other side of the room where there was a bench and held her in his arms.

Paulo desperately wanted to assure Anna that everything would be all right, but he wasn't even sure of it himself. He tried his best not to let on that he was worried.

"I don't want you to fret," he told her confidently. "I'm certain that the children will be fine."

Anna held on to Paulo for dear life.

"How can you be so sure?" she asked, trying to hold back the tears that were beginning to flow again.

"Because we have the best men in the business here working to rescue our children and now we have Charles on our side."

This last statement seemed to ease Anna's mind somewhat; enough to allow Paulo to leave her side for a few minutes to find out if anything was happening. Timothy was kind enough to take Paulo's place sitting with Anna and, as usual, he made her feel better. Timothy's presence had a calming effect on Anna and Paulo was grateful.

Paulo had just joined Robert, the sheriff and a few others where they were gathered near the security equipment, when his phone rang. Realizing that he wasn't prepared for the call, he froze. It wasn't supposed to be like this, he thought. They hadn't rehearsed yet and now it was too late. Robert signaled Paulo to let it ring a few times so it wouldn't seem that Paulo was expecting him.

"Hello, Paulo Altro speaking," Paulo said as casually as he could manage.

"Paulo, baby, my name is Tony. You probably won't remember me but I sure remember you. I hope you don't mind but I've made myself at home in your office. Sure looks different sitting on the other side of the desk.

I've taken your wife, children and grandchildren hostage. If you want to see any of them alive again, you'd better follow my directions. Five million dollars in small-unmarked bills is to be brought to me at your company within the next hour."

"Tony, the original ransom note asked for three million. Why has it increased to five million?"

"We now have that wife of yours included in the deal. Your wife is the icing on the cake! I also want a helicopter to take us to the airport."

"You must give me more time. I can't get my hands on that much money that quickly."

"Who are you kidding? You're worth a lot more than that! One hour, babe; no more, no less," Tony barked then hung up the phone.

The reality of the situation finally started to sink in. Robert's mind was racing.

"Charles, we need to buy more time," he stated. "What are the chances of us getting Tony to agree to three hours, instead of one?"

"Only if you can sweeten the pot."

"Give us an idea of how we can do that."

Charles suggested that they offer Tony and his guys' new birth

58

certificates, social security numbers, and passports so they could leave the country.  He knew Tony would jump at the offer because he'd expressed concern on a number of occasions about how they would flee the country undetected after the job was done.

As far as Paulo was concerned, it was well worth it, if it would spare his children's lives.  Without hesitation, he agreed and was back on the phone with Tony to make the offer.  All eyes were on Paulo as they waited for Tony to pick up the line.

"Tony here," he announced in a deep rough voice.

As though he was handling a routine business transaction, Paulo was assertive yet charming in his presentation.

"Tony, I want to run something by you.  I can have the money and helicopter for you in two hours but I have a suggestion that might be helpful. I figured out a way for you and your men to get out of the country without any red tape.  If you give me four hours, I can provide all of you with new identifications.  The only condition is that no harm comes to my children. Consider it and get back to me."

Before Tony could respond, Paulo promptly hung up.  Instantly, he felt sick to his stomach with fear; worried that Tony saw through his bravado.

Robert looked at him strangely.

"We only needed three hours."

"If we were to ask for three hours, we would probably only get two. That's why I asked for four; knowing he would refuse and hopefully offer us three."

"If you ever need a job, look me up."

There was total silence in the garage while everyone waited and hoped for the best.  Anna sat motionless, praying the Rosary repeatedly until, finally, Charles' walkie-talkie beeped.

Paulo closed his eyes as Charles answered.  *"Dear Lord, please let it be good news,"* he prayed.

"Yeah, Tony," replied Charles.

"Charles, I've received a proposition from Paulo.  He wants four hours so he could get all of us new identification along with the money and helicopter.  What do you think?"

"It's a good idea, but four hours is crazy.  I'd only give him three.  That should be plenty of time but you're the boss and I'll go along with whatever you say."

"Okay, I'll give Paulo three hours and that's all.  If he doesn't come through, then we'll wipe out his whole family and burn the house and company to the ground."

Charles saw the pain in Anna's face at the very mention of harming her children. He felt he had to say something to calm Tony down.

"I doubt very much if Paulo will let it get that far," he continued. "Give him the three hours and I bet he gives you what you want. He has to realize by now that you're not joking and that, as the brains of the operation, you have everything under control."

"Charles, you're smart to see I'm making the right decision. I'll get back to you later. By the way, how are things at the house? It seems quiet."

"The children are sleeping and I have the servants, the priest, and Paulo's wife tied up."

"Keep up the good work, Charles. I'll get back to you soon."

In a matter of minutes, Paulo's cell phone started to ring. This was it, the call from Tony with an answer to his offer. Paulo's heart began beating rapidly and his perspiration was becoming visible as he picked up the phone. Everyone stood by, listening intently to the speakerphone.

"Paulo, baby, your first hour is almost up, but you're lucky, because I've decided to give you the extra time you wanted. You have thirty minutes to show you're sincere by giving us one of the things we agreed on. To refresh your memory, there's five million dollars in unmarked bills, a helicopter to take us to the nearest airport where there will be a private jet ready to take us to an undisclosed location and new identifications for my men and me. What will you have for me?"

Paulo didn't know what to say, so he asked him to hold for a minute. Placing his hand over the mouthpiece, he quietly conferred with Robert. Unfortunately, Robert didn't know either so Paulo took it upon himself to make the decision.

"We have a helicopter on its way as we speak. It should be there a little after two. You have my word."

"Paulo, baby, it better be here by two o'clock or that 'pretty boy' son of yours, Cardinal whatever his name is, will no longer exist. You have my word!"

The line went dead and Paulo gasped. He was momentarily taken back by the harshness of Tony's words but knew that he couldn't let himself dwell on it for too long. Paulo turned to Robert for assistance.

"How soon can you get a helicopter here?"

"It will take at least forty-five minutes," Robert estimated.

"Damn it, Robert, my son's life is at stake! We don't have forty-five minutes!"

Robert was trying to figure out how to speed it up but instead, Paulo came up with the solution. Picking up his cell phone, Paulo phoned his friend Quintino.

"Quintino, this is Paulo. Is your helicopter available? I don't have time to explain, but it's a matter of life and death that I get a helicopter to the company immediately!"

"I can have it there in about forty minutes."

"That's too long, it must be here before two o'clock!"

"I'll have my pilot take me there as soon as I can locate him, but I can't promise it'll be before two o'clock."

"It must be here before two o'clock! There is a man holding my children hostage! He's threatened to execute Michael, if the helicopter isn't here before two o'clock, and kill the others, if I don't give in to all of his demands. Quintino, I'm begging you for the life of my son! Please get here as quickly as possible."

"I'll be there by two, come hell or high water!"

Paulo closed his cell phone and by this time, the tears were streaming down his face. His nerves were getting the best of him.

"I suggest you get the other demands ready," he told Robert. "I don't like playing Russian roulette with my children's lives! I'll make the arrangements to get the money from the bank. You make the arrangements to have it delivered by armored car."

"You can't give into their demands!"

"My children's lives are at stake! Money is no object!"

"I know how you must fee. . ."

"Do you? How could you sit there and honestly tell me you know how I feel? My wife is being torn apart fearing that her children may die! I love my wife more than anything else in this world and I'll not allow her to suffer, no matter what the cost! All the money in the world will not replace one of her children."

Robert directed his eyes away from Paulo momentarily.

"I, too, am a father," he declared. "I don't envy the position you're in for one moment and, to be honest with you, I would probably react the same as you, but there is something I think you should know. In most cases, even when the demands are met, the kidnappers still kill the hostages."

"I'm quite aware of that fact, Robert. It's been in the back of my mind since the beginning of this whole ordeal and it's eating me alive, but what else can I do? For now, all I can do is give him what he asks for. Do me a favor and don't mention any of this to Anna."

Remembering that Anna went to sit in one of the patrol cars, Paulo decided to go tell her the news.

"We have to meet one of the kidnapper's demands soon. They want a helicopter to bring them to the airport, so I've asked Quintino for the use of his helicopter and it should be on its way here now," he assured Anna. "We're working on the other demands. I have already contacted the bank to prepare the ransom money and the new identifications are being processed as we speak. I promise by five o'clock this will all be over."

Anna laid her head on Paulo's shoulder sobbing uncontrollably. "If anything happens to them . . . "

Paulo placed his hand under Anna's chin and lifted it up until their eyes met.

"Listen to me! Nothing will happen to our children because I'm going to meet all their demands and then some, if necessary!"

Anna had never been so scared in all her life, but she trusted her husband. Paulo continued to hold Anna tightly in his arms.

"Anna, I need you. Hang in there with me and don't give up."

Sheriff DeVito came over to the patrol car and told Paulo that Tony wanted to speak with him. Paulo looked at his watch and was surprised to see that it was already one fifty-five; only five minutes to the first deadline. He kissed Anna good-bye and closed the door behind him. On his way back to the garage, he stopped to scan the sky, hoping for a glimpse of the helicopter. He prayed it would arrive before it was too late.

The phone was handed to him as soon as he entered the garage.

"Yes, Tony?"

"I'm glad you've arrived. I take it that you're not alone either since someone else picked up your phone. Oh well, it doesn't matter as long as you come through for me. Now, back to business, where is the helicopter? I think pretty boy is getting nervous. I'd sure hate to kill such a handsome guy!"

"Tony, it's on its way here! I swear to you!"

"You have five minutes or he dies! As a matter of fact, I think I'll take him outside so you can watch me execute him! Maybe then you'll know I mean business!"

Just as expected, Tony walked through the front door with a gun pointed toward Michael's temple. He continued to talk to Paulo as he marched Michael outside.

"May I come forward and speak with you?" Paulo asked.

"Come forward with your hands in the air. Maybe I'll let you kiss your son good-bye before I execute him."

Paulo handed the phone to Robert.

"Make sure Anna doesn't get out of the car!" Paulo made the sign of the cross then cautiously proceeded. He got within two feet of Michael before Tony stopped him.

"Stop there! That's close enough!" Tony warned.

"Are you all right, son?"

"I'm fine, Papa. I love you. In case something happens, I want to thank you for giving me a good life."

"Nothing is going to happen."

Tony laughed.

"Two minutes to go!"

"For the love of God, give me a few more minutes! I know it will be here shortly!"

"Ninety seconds!" Tony pushed Michael to a kneeling position on the ground. "Start praying, Cardinal. Maybe your God will save you."

Michael prayed the Our Father as Tony called out the seconds. When he reached five, he cocked the trigger on the gun. Paulo and Michael closed their eyes to avoid making eye contact. They were preparing for the worst when they heard a loud noise overhead. The helicopter was circling, trying to make a landing. Tony, distracted by the sound, slowly disengaged the trigger and picked Michael up by his right arm.

"Very good, Paulo, baby! That was a close call! I thought for sure that I would have to kill pretty boy. You have one hour to bring me the five million dollars in unmarked bills. If you don't, I'll then come out with that arrogant bitch you call your daughter. It'll be a pleasure to blow her brains out. Don't be late or I'll do just that!"

He retreated into the shadow of the huge building. Moving backward slowly, he continued to hold the gun to Michael's temple.

Once Michael was safely inside, Paulo straightened up and drifted back to the garage in a daze. The first person he saw when he reached the garage was Quintino and his emotions got the better of him. Paulo leaned against him and broke down.

"How can I thank you for saving Michael's life?"

"You don't have to thank me. You know I would do anything for you and your family. How is Anna holding up?"

"Anna is over there in the patrol car with Timothy. Let's go see her," he answered pointing in Anna's direction.

The stress of the day was taking a toll on Anna. Paulo noticed how fragile she looked as soon as he opened the car door. He didn't know how much more either of them could take. If anything could cheer her up right now it would be knowing Quintino arrived on time, so Paulo asked Anna to come outside to get a breath of fresh air. The instant she stepped out of the car, she saw Quintino and realized everything was all right.

"We've met the first demand. Tony is satisfied," Paulo explained to Anna.

She jumped into Paulo's arms and squeezed him with joy then reached over to Quintino and hugged him tightly.

"Thank you for helping us in our hour of need. You are a true friend."

"Anna, knowing your family has changed my life," Quintino declared. "From the moment we met, even though I was a total stranger, you have embraced me in friendship. Your son, Franco, saved me from the embarrassment and humiliation of bankruptcy. He gave me back the respect of my associates. My debt to you can never be repaid."

Anna held Quintino a little bit longer, all the while expressing her gratitude, then, once again, took comfort in Paulo's arms. Her body was trembling so much that Paulo became concerned. He suggested she go to the rectory with Timothy where she could rest until the children were freed. Of course, she refused.

"I told you before, I'm not leaving! They're my children too and I want to be here with them. Please don't try to send me away."

Paulo realized she had just as much right to be there as he did, but couldn't help feeling that she would be safer somewhere else.

"All right, I'm going to hold you to your word that you'll stay put until I tell you otherwise." Paulo kissed Anna then left with Quintino to go talk to Charles.

"Charles, I'm concerned about my daughter Assunta. She has a way of saying the wrong things sometimes. I'm afraid she's making Tony angry. He remarked earlier that if I don't meet his second demand the 'arrogant bitch, I call my daughter', will be next. He warned me not to be one minute late or he will blow her brains out. Do you think he may have hurt Assunta already?"

Charles was sure he had, but didn't want to tell that to Paulo so he told him not to worry then asked for the walkie-talkie.

"Come in, Tony. This is Charles."

"Charles, is something wrong?"

"Everything's fine. There's no problem on my end. How did you make out with the demands?"

"We have our helicopter. When I see the five million, I'll know we're well on our way. It was a close call. The helicopter almost didn't get here and I thought I would have to waste the Cardinal. In the end, it arrived right on the dot!"

The instant he completed his sentence, Tony fumbled with the walkie-talkie until it went crashing to the floor. A situation was developing with the hostages and it could be heard loud and clear.

"You dippy son of a bitch! Who do you think you are, trying to escape? I'll teach you a lesson you'll never forget!"

Tony beat Assunta while the others watched in horror. They were helpless with their hands tied behind their backs.

At one point, Franco tried to get up, but Michael stopped him, explaining that he might make it worse for Assunta. Michael told Franco to close his eyes but with every sound, Franco's insides quivered to the point of almost vomiting on the floor.

"Now, bitch, stay in that corner and don't move. The next move will be your last. Do you understand?"

There was no reply. All they could hear was Assunta crying from the second beating she was taking at the hands of her kidnapper.

"When I ask you a question, you answer me! Do you understand?" Assunta's frail voice could barely be heard.

"Yes."

"Yes what, bitch?" Tony grabbed Assunta by the hair and picked her up off the floor. She cried out in pain.

"Yes, sir."

"That's better. Now face that corner because I don't want to see your ugly face!" Then turning toward one of his men he screamed out. "Kill her if she makes one move."

"I'm sorry, Charles." He got back on the walkie-talkie. "I have taken enough of that bitch's shit since we walked in the door. I'd like to waste her right now."

"You did the right thing. Sometimes women leave you no choice but to kick the hell out of them. Then they know who's in charge. I bet she won't give you any more shit from now on."

Tony laughed.

"Yea, Charles, come to think of it, you're right. Now she knows who's in charge. I should've beaten the shit out of her from the very start. It would have avoided a lot of aggravation."

"You're doing a great job, Tony. I'm glad I hooked up with you. You know exactly how to take a situation and straighten it out. Any other guy wouldn't be able to put that bitch in her place the way you just did. I bet she'll just sit there now with her mouth shut. You are the best. Listen, I don't want to cut you short, but I want to make sure everyone's behaving themselves. Talk to you later, boss."

Charles finally shut the Walkie-talkie off, but the damage was already done. Everyone was in shock over the disturbing confrontation they'd just heard. Charles felt partially responsible for this mess, so he felt he had to say something to Paulo.

"I'm sorry about your daughter. I did my best to calm Tony down."

"Thank you for your help. Someday I hope to repay you," Paulo replied.

Paulo turned to Robert, suddenly furious, and demanded to know when the armored car would arrive and he wasn't going to accept any excuses.

It was obvious that Paulo was at his wit's end so Robert assured him that it would be there soon and that Tony would get his money at three o'clock sharp. Suspecting what Paulo had in mind, Robert added that it was important to keep the deadline at four o'clock. He thought that if Tony got the money any earlier than three, he might want the identification by three-thirty and that might not be possible.

Paulo nodded in agreement, but what he really wanted was to give Tony everything he wanted right now so he could have his children back safe and sound. The waiting and wondering was pure torture. It would be a while longer before it was over so Paulo used the remaining time to rest. He found a quiet corner where no one could see him and curled up like a little boy.

At ten-of-three, Tony made a call to Paulo asking for his second demand. This time, as he walked out of the building, he dragged Assunta behind him with a gun pointed to her head. Paulo did the same as with Michael. He walked toward Tony until he was within two feet. Paulo was horrified at the sight of Assunta's face. Assunta stood before him with two black eyes and blood trickling out of each corner of her mouth. Her face was swollen and bruised. Assunta's clothing was torn and tattered. Her hair was sticking out in every direction. She looked like a rag doll that had been dragged through the mud. It took all Paulo's might not to reach out and grab her. She had been through hell and his heart was breaking.

"Uncle Tony had to teach your little girl how to do what she was told," Tony said smiling. "Perhaps, if her Papa had done a better job raising her, she wouldn't look this way. Down on your knees, bitch." Tony pulled Assunta to the ground by her hair.

Paulo couldn't wait any longer.

"Bring me the money now!"

Robert heard Paulo's demand and threw his hands up in disgust.

"I told him not to rush it. Damn it, I don't want him to look too anxious! There's still five minutes to go before three o'clock."

Robert quickly picked up the briefcase and brought it to Paulo. He too couldn't bear to look at Assunta's face. Handing Paulo the briefcase, he turned around and rushed back to the garage. As soon as he was inside, he cringed thinking about the pain Assunta had suffered. He banged the wall with his fist out of frustration.

Paulo handed Tony the briefcase.

"Please leave my daughter with me. You have your money and your helicopter. At least release one of my children. I have been keeping up my end of our bargain. Now it's time for you to give me something. I hate to think you're playing me for a fool and intend to kill them all at the end."

Tony thought for a moment.

"This bitch is mine," he claimed. "I'll send one of your other children out to you."

Paulo watched as Tony and Assunta disappeared into the building. Before she was totally out of sight, Assunta managed to point to her heart and blow her Papa a kiss, whispering 'I love you'. With tears in his eyes, Paulo responded in the same manner. He waited a few minutes to see if Tony would keep up his end of the bargain.

It seemed like he had been waiting forever, when Donna made an appearance at the front door of the company. Paulo hesitated momentarily and then, with arms outstretched, he ran to retrieve her from this nightmare.

"Papa, is that you? I'm glad to see you. I thought I'd never see you again," Donna uttered before passing out in Paulo's arms. Carefully, he carried Donna back to the garage.

When she came to, she opened her eyes and smiled.

"Please get the others out," she pleaded.

Paulo smiled back at her, thankful that she was alive.

"I have every intention of doing just that, sweetheart."

Robert couldn't wait to ask Donna a few questions but Paulo put him in his place quickly.

"Right now, Donna needs to be taken to the hospital. The questions will have to wait."

Sheriff DeVito offered to have one of his men take her to the hospital and that was just what Paulo was thinking. Still holding Donna in his arms, he walked over to the patrol car Anna had been waiting in and opened the door. When Anna saw Donna, she couldn't control herself any longer. She leaped out of the car and pulled Donna close to her chest.

"Thank God you're all right! I've been so worried!" Anna kissed her on the forehead. "Your Papa and I love you very much."

"I love you too," Donna said softly.

Anna was beginning to feel confident that she would see all of her children safe again. For the first time today, she felt hopeful. Soon, Donna was in the patrol car between her and Timothy and they were heading for the hospital.

The third demand was the toughest. For some reason, Paulo felt that Robert was only bluffing when he said he could have all the new identifications before four o'clock. Paulo hoped he was wrong.

"How are the cards coming along?"

"I'm working on them. It takes time."

"I don't want to hear that kind of talk!" Paulo banged his fist on the table. "I told you before, don't play Russian roulette with my children!"

"I'm doing the best I can. There isn't a printing press here for me to use, remember. I'm not a miracle worker!"

Robert almost lost it, but quickly regained his composure. "I'm sorry. I guess everything is finally taking its toll on me. Losing four men who were like sons to me, seeing your daughter's face when I delivered the brief case and wondering about my daughter giving Dr. Gennaro a hard time at the hospital."

"Robert, you never told me your daughter was sick in the hospital. Has she been in there a long time?" Paulo expressed surprise.

"The young lady who was wounded during the attack on your house is my daughter, Veronica."

Paulo was beside himself. He had no idea and suddenly felt terrible for acting so hostile toward him.

"Robert, I'm sorry about your daughter and about the way I spoke to you earlier. I guess we're in the same predicament; we're both just worried parents."

# Chapter 5

## Let The Rescue Begin

For the next few moments, each man was consumed in his own thoughts. Coming back to reality, Robert broke the silence.

"Paulo, for now, let's concentrate on what's happening inside your company. I'd like to get my men into your office quickly. Is there any way this can be done without Tony knowing?"

"I keep the blueprints of the building in the top drawer of the desk near the doorway. There's a small window over that desk. A thin person should be able to slip in through the window."

Looking around, Robert recognized that there was only one person fitting that description and it happened to be Charles. He was a lanky sort of fellow, standing only about five feet-seven inches and weighing approximately one hundred forty pounds.

Charles overheard their conversation and volunteered for the task before they even asked.

"If you direct me to the window, I'll get in and out without a trace. I actually have a lot of experience doing this sort of thing."

Paulo smiled awkwardly at his revelation, thanked him once again for his help, and then directed Charles to the window.

Charles cautiously crawled toward the window praying it would be unlocked. Slowly, he opened the window and lifted himself up, then dropped himself to the desk, as quiet as a mouse. Opening the top drawer, Charles immediately spotted the floor plans. They were exactly where Paulo said they would be. He scooped them up and closed the drawer in one full swoop. Carefully, he climbed out the window, making sure to close it behind him, and began the harrowing trek back to the garage on his hands and knees.

Everyone was on pins and needles waiting for his return. It seemed Charles was gone a rather long time and Paulo was becoming concerned. All sorts of crazy thoughts ran through his mind; the worst being that Tony saw Charles and realized what he was up to. Paulo was sure Tony would kill Charles for his betrayal. He voiced his concerns to Robert hoping he would be able to do something to help Charles if need be.

Robert had other concerns, however, he thought there might be the possibility that Charles defected back to Tony's side. Since there was no proof of this, Robert decided not to mention it just yet. Rather, he announced that if Charles didn't show up soon, he would send someone to check it out.

Instead of entering through the front door of the garage, Charles unexpectedly came in through the back door and heard every word that they said.

"I'm back," he declared nonchalantly from the other end of the room, trying to conceal his surprise at their concern.

Startled by the sound of his voice, Paulo jumped and then instinctively whirled around to the direction from which the voice came. He and Robert dashed for Charles to make sure he was okay. It was a relief to see him return unharmed. Not only did it mean that Tony wasn't on to their plan, but that they were closer to rescuing his children. Paulo gave Charles a bear hug to show his delight.

"Glad to see you made it, son. You had us worried, " Robert said as he put his hand on Charles' shoulder.

Caught off guard by their actions, Charles stood motionless for a moment. When he recovered, he pulled a rolled-up piece of paper out of his back pocket and handed it to Robert.

"I believe this is what you wanted," he said.

It was exactly what Robert was waiting for, so he immediately brought it over to the table and laid it out in front of everyone. Paulo pointed out the location of his office while Robert studied the plans thoroughly to get a better idea of how to proceed.

"My men will need to enter your office the quickest and safest way possible. Is there a way to get into your office aside from the door?"

Paulo shook his head at first until he remembered one of Michael's many adventures at the company when he was a small child. He smiled at the memory and began to explain to Robert that there just might be another way into the office.

"When Michael was a boy, he discovered a crawl space leading from my office to the front of the building. He had gotten into trouble at school, so they sent a note home for me to report to school the next day with him. Michael placed the note on my desk then tried to find a place to hide. Noticing the vent in the bathroom, he climbed on the radiator and hoisted himself onto the window ledge. The vent is located directly in front of the window. Once on the window ledge, it didn't take much to remove the grate and climb into the ceiling."

Robert interrupted Paulo, "Is the bathroom near your office?"

"Right over here. It's my private bathroom," he answered, pointing to its location on the blueprints.

"Then what you're saying is once we get into the bathroom, through the grate, we'll have access to your office."

"The door from the bathroom leads directly to my office. There's also a storage area located at the top left corner of my office. The door from the storage area leads directly into my office as well."

"Is the grate removable from inside and outside in both locations?"

"Yes, that's how Michael was caught. I started to phone the police when I noticed the grate move. I put the phone down and stood in the corner hoping it was Michael."

"Was it?"

"Yes, and he climbed right into my arms." Paulo smiled. "That's one day I bet Michael never forgot."

This information was music to Robert's ears.

"Now we're cooking with grease! This means that we have three direct entryways into your office: one from the bathroom, one from the storage area, and the office door. Someone will need to go in and take a look at the crawl space."

Charles volunteered once again.

"What the hell, I'm in this far so I might as well go all the way," he reasoned.

Before too long, Charles was on his way back to the window to take a look at the crawl space. The grate was within arms' reach of the window ledge. He carefully lifted the grate out of its framework and pushed it to the side in the ceiling. Then he lifted himself into the crawl space. Once inside, he placed the grate back in position. It was exactly as Paulo described. Actually, it was large enough for an adult to crawl through without any problem. Charles was amazed at the short time it took to get from one end of the crawl space to the other. It took less than ten minutes crawling very quietly. He confirmed there was one grate over the bathroom area and one grate over the storage area. When he was sure he had seen enough, he turned around and crawled back toward the front. He was just about to remove the grate when he spotted Tony standing by the double doors in the front of the building. Charles waited nervously for Tony to return to Paulo's office so he could escape. Thankfully, it was only a matter of minutes before Alex called Tony to come back to the office. As soon as the door slammed behind Tony, Charles pulled the grate aside and climbed to the window ledge. He replaced the grate before exiting the window, turning to make sure he closed the window. Once outside on the grass, he prayed that Tony wouldn't see him crawling across the grass to the garage.

Charles entered the garage through the back door again, but this time it was expected. They were all waiting for him and right away, Paulo could tell by the look on Charles' face that it wasn't as easy as his first trip.

"What happened?" Paulo asked with utmost kindness and affection.

"You were right. The grate's accessible from the window ledge. I pushed it to the side and climbed into the crawl space, carefully replacing it in position. It took me less than ten minutes to pass both grates. I knew I was near your office because I could smell those damned cheap cigars Tony smokes. When I got back to the front, I spotted Tony standing in the doorway and I almost died. I had to sit in the crawl space for two or three minutes before Alex called Tony back to your office. I got out of there like a bat out of hell. If Tony hadn't been there, it would have been a piece of cake."

Robert patted Charles on the back showing his approval then turned to Paulo to outline his intentions.

"Now we can move ahead with our plans. The birth certificates, social security numbers, and passports will be arriving within minutes. When Tony calls for his third demand, tell him that you'll bring them into the company personally and hand them to him only after you see that your children are safe. Now, all I need to do is figure out a way to get my men into the building quickly."

Charles hesitated momentarily in order to get his thoughts together before making a suggestion.

"I'll remove the window from the frame so your men can get into the building. Once the last person is in, I'll replace the window on the frame.

"Tony is no dummy. If he should decide to walk toward the front to check on things he just might notice the window removed from the frame."

It was certainly a possibility but Robert declined his offer on the grounds that Charles may not be able to pull it off. If he were to be caught by Tony this time, the mission would be jeopardized. Paulo, on the other hand, thought it was worth a try. He wasn't ready to refuse just yet.

Charles sensed his impatience and tried to convince him it could be done successfully.

"Mr. Altro, it's a piece of cake. All you have to do is keep Tony talking on the phone to distract him from any noise we might make."

Paulo agreed and Robert gave into the idea. He thought it might just work after all. He interrupted at this point.

"I'll instruct Quintino to start the helicopter when everyone is in position. The noise will draw attention away from any movement in the crawl space."

Having everything well thought out, Robert felt it was time to fill William in on the plan. After all, he would be the one heading the rescue team. He called William over and explained the situation in detail.

"We're going to make an all out effort to save Paulo's children. Paulo is going to enter the building and personally hand the new identifications to Tony. While Paulo is doing this, you and your men will be in a bathroom and a storage area adjacent to Paulo's office. Charles will share information with you concerning the crawl space and the best way you and your men will be able to get in and out."

Robert eagerly escorted William to the table, where he laid out the floor plans and began his briefing. They discussed every scenario and potential obstacle. It soon became clear that they didn't have enough men to do the job properly.

"We need six men to climb through the crawl space, and three on either side of Paulo's office doorway. We need another team stationed along either side of the building just in case one of the kidnappers tries to take off," Robert explained to William as he assessed the situation. Then, he abruptly paused to concentrate on a solution. Within seconds the answer came to him and he darted across the garage to talk to the sheriff. "Sheriff, how many men do you have here?"

"I have at least twenty men on the property as we speak. They're waiting for my instructions. Why?"

"We need more men. Come with me and I'll explain."

They walked to the table where William was going over the strategy one last time with a few of his men.

"Our problem is solved," Robert announced. "Sheriff DeVito has twenty men ready to go. Sheriff, can you stay here with William and he'll tell you what we have in mind while I go see how Paulo is holding up."

The look of desperation on Paulo's face was haunting. Robert couldn't bear to witness it any longer so he encouraged Paulo to remain hopeful.

"Fifty minutes, Paulo, and your children will be free."

Paulo made the sign of the cross, praying to God that Robert was right.

A short time later, while Paulo was still moping around, William and Charles approached to give them an update.

"Everyone is ready," announced William. "My men have all been briefed and Quintino has been instructed as to when to start the helicopter."

Then Charles interrupted to give his news.

"Mr. Altro, I'm going to contact Tony and try to convince him that he should call you about the new IDs."

"Paulo, when he calls you, make idle chat and keep him on the phone as long as possible. We need at least twenty minutes to get everyone into the building and into position," Robert advised.

They all shook hands and wished each other good luck before embarking on the final stages of the rescue. The first step was for Charles to radio Tony over the walkie-talkie. It was a simple task yet Charles was finally starting to feel the pressure. He was extremely nervous, which showed by the way that his hands shook when he reached for the walkie-talkie.

"Come in, Tony. This is Charles."

"What's up, Charles? Is there a problem?"

"Not at all. I just wanted to check in with you about the IDs. Have you called to see how they're coming along?"

"Not yet. Maybe I should give Paulo a call now. If you don't hear from me, it means everything is going according to plan," Tony said, and then abruptly hung up.

Charles laid the walkie-talkie down on the table and faced Paulo. It was up to him now to deal with Tony. As Paulo waited for the call, William led Charles and his team out of the garage. Robert watched through his binoculars as the men slithered along the ground toward the window, ready to signal Quintino to start up the helicopter, as soon as he saw Charles removing the window.

In a flash, the window was out and the men were filing through one by one. The team to occupy the crawl space went first, followed by the men who were to be posted on either side of the doorway outside of Paulo's office. The last team to enter consisted of the Sheriff's men, who were to station themselves in strategic locations throughout the building. There were additional men guarding the exterior perimeter of the building. Thirty-two men in all were involved in the rescue.

Paulo was already talking to Tony when the engine of the helicopter started to roar.

"Why is the helicopter starting up?" Tony shouted.

"There's no need to get upset. The pilot is performing a routine inspection of the controls to make sure the helicopter is operational. He isn't going anywhere. It's just a precaution we're taking to make sure he can get you to the airport without delay."

Robert noticed a pause in their conversation and signaled for Paulo to keep talking by moving his arm in a circular motion.

"I hope my children haven't given you any trouble," Paulo blurted out in an effort to make small talk.

"Nah, they're pretty good except for that bitchy daughter of yours."

"Some people say that the only way to control a woman like her is to beat her, but Franco, her husband, is a real mouse. He believes that a man should never hit his wife. That's why she's so out of control."

"He looks like a tough cookie."

"Believe me, he's a real pussy cat when it comes to his wife. Actually,

74

she'd have been better off marrying a man like you. I bet after living with you for a month, she'd get her act together."

"Paulo, baby, you're right. I would know how to handle her."

Robert continued to wave his arm but Paulo was running out of things to say. It was killing him to be nice to this man who was torturing his children. It was hard to think of the right words, but he managed a few more compliments.

Finally Robert saw the white handkerchief from the window. It was his signal that everyone was in position and Quintino's signal to stop the helicopter.

Robert gave Paulo the thumbs up indicating it was time to end the conversation. Paulo was grateful and immediately came up with an excuse to cut Tony short.

"I hate to hang up but I want to check on the new identifications. As soon as they arrive, I'll let you know."

"Paulo, baby, fifteen minutes to go. They better be here or I'll waste all of your children one by one in front of your eyes."

Tony hung up, then without a moment's delay, he radioed for Charles. They weren't prepared to hear from him so quickly. If Charles didn't answer soon, Tony might become enraged and do something stupid. Robert quickly crawled in the grass to reach Charles. He told him to make a dash for the garage to answer Tony. Charles' eyes opened wide and his jaw dropped with fear. He rushed back and, gasping for air, picked up the walkie-talkie

"Yes, Tony." Charles said.

"Where have you been? I've been calling you for the past five minutes. I thought something happened to you."

"Sorry, Tony. I was in the bathroom taking a crap. How did you make out?"

"According to Paulo, the new identifications should be here shortly. We had a long conversation about his daughter. I think he likes me. I bet he'd even accept me as his son-in-law if Assunta weren't married to that jerk off. I know what I'll do. Franco will be the first one I execute. With him out of the way, I'll have Assunta for myself. As for Gino, I'll waste him before we leave, but hold onto Michael. If we have a priest on board, they'll think twice before shooting us down. Michael is our insurance until we arrive at our destination. Then I can waste him there. What a pity, I've grown to like the guys. What the hell, a man's got to do what a man's got to do. What do you think?"

"Sounds good to me, boss. You're a genius and I want to thank you for giving me the opportunity to work with you."

Tony beamed from ear to ear. "Keep your walkie-talkie next to you at all times from now on. After I take care of everyone here, you can take care of everyone there. Don't forget to waste the grandchildren. I don't want to leave any of the Altro family behind to give him strength to go on. I want Paulo Altro to die a slow agonizing death, constantly reliving the execution of his family. We'll meet you at the airport near the terminal entrance at five o'clock. The only pity of it is, I won't be there to see Paulo's face when he identifies the bodies. Better yet, maybe I'll bump off Paulo when he brings me our new identifications. Just imagine, in less than one hour we can wipe the entire Altro family off the face of the earth. When he's dead, maybe then, he'll regret not keeping me on my job. Talk to you later."

Paulo went outside and stood under the weeping willow tree, feeling as if his heart was being torn from his chest. Robert followed him out.

"Come on Paulo! Don't give up on me now, not when we're this close to saving your children. Charles did a great job. All the men are in position. I need you to finish the job. You have to bring the new IDs to Tony in ten minutes. I've just heard from the office. They are on the way here as we speak! Hang in there with me!"

Paulo lowered his head.

"You don't understand. I remember now. I had an employee named Tony Drino, who I had to let go for the safety of the other employees. One day he came to work, high as a kite, and started a commotion on the floor threatening the other employees, and it wasn't the first time. He had been written up on four separate occasions for the same reason. I offered him counseling but he refused. We had to get security to escort him out because of the disturbance he caused. On his way out, he told me he'd get his vengeance on me no matter how long it took. I never believed he'd do something like this to my family. The last thing I remember before they took him away was the look in his eyes. They radiated pure evil, like the devil himself."

"Paulo, you can't blame yourself for letting Tony go. He's using that as an excuse to act out his hostilities. This isn't your fault, but the fault of a sick mind."

"I've been a fool from the very start. You kept telling me they intended to kill all my children no matter whether I met their demands or not. What a fool I was."

"You weren't a fool. You were a father grasping at straws to save his children. No one could have asked more of you."

As Paulo contemplated what lay ahead, a man appeared at the door with an envelope in his hands.

"Okay, gentlemen, the moment of truth has arrived."

Robert jumped up, but Paulo got to him first and snatched the envelope out of his hand.

"Not so fast! We have a few more minutes until four!" Robert urged.

The phone rang and everyone's heart stopped.

"Paulo, baby, do you have them?"

It was Tony, right on time.

"Yes I do, Tony, and since this is the final demand, I'd like permission to bring them to the office myself. I want to make sure my children are all safe before I give you the envelope."

Tony welcomed the thought of wiping out the entire Altro family in a matter of minutes, including Paulo Altro.

"That's a good idea, Paulo, baby! Only on one condition - you come in alone. I don't want anyone else walking through that door with you."

"You have a deal. I'm on my way right now."

Paulo put down the phone then shook hands with Sheriff DeVito and embraced Robert.

"Let's go save your children," Robert said.

Back at Our Lady of Lourdes Medical Center, Donna was resting peacefully and Anna felt so exhausted that she eventually fell asleep as well. All was quiet until Dr. Cristanzio entered the emergency room to check on Donna and happened to startle Anna. She suddenly started screaming at the top of her lungs, sending a chill up the doctor's spine.

Timothy gently shook Anna awake to calm her fears. He figured that she was probably having a bad dream and the sudden disturbance frightened her. Anna awoke crying and gripping Timothy with all her might. When Dr. Cristanzio came over to see if he could be of assistance, Anna grabbed on to his arm as well and started begging him to help her children. She told them that she had a feeling that they were all in grave danger.

"Anna, Paulo is there. Everyone will be free soon. There's nothing to worry about!" Dr. Cristanzio responded.

Anna started sobbing again. "You don't understand! My dream is coming true! Please, you must help my children! In my dream, I saw people lying in a room with blood all over. Please, send ambulances with blood. I beg you, please, before it's too late!"

It was an unrealistic request, but to ease her concerns, Dr. Cristanzio phoned the blood bank in the hospital.

"This is Dr. Cristanzio, there is a situation at Paulo Altro's company that may require a few ambulances. Please have them ready to roll shortly. They will also need a couple of units of O-positive blood and O-negative blood ready to go as well. I'll meet you at the ER entrance in five minutes."

Dr. Cristanzio put down the phone and for the first time considered that the possibility of bloodshed might be real. He peered out the window, wondering why this was happening to such good people.

Dr. Cristanzio considered himself a close family friend as well as the family doctor. He made it his personal business to take care of the family, hence he had knowledge of their blood types. It was especially easy to remember that Paulo and Franco shared the same rare blood type. Hopefully, his early intervention would prove advantageous. He would never forgive himself if he let them down in any way.

Anna went to the window and stood by his side to thank him for his help. If there was anyone on this earth who could help, she knew it would be Dr. Cristanzio. She asked him to return as soon as he had any news.

Before Dr. Cristanzio left, he paged Dr. James Gennaro and Dr. Samuel Schiavo to his office. He filled them in as soon as they arrived.

"There's a strong possibility that we may have many wounded people showing up in the ER very shortly. I've just received word that at any moment they are going to storm Paulo's company to try and rescue his children. I'm worried that they'll be arriving during the change of shifts and we won't be properly staffed. Sam, I need you in the ER to oversee the situation. James, I would like you to be on stand-by in case emergency surgery is required."

Dr. Gennaro and Dr. Schiavo assured him that they were willing and able to stay. They also offered to notify their teams and make sure there would be enough personnel to handle any problem that may arise.

Dr. Cristanzio left his office for the ER with a positive outlook and renewed confidence in his staff. He knew they wouldn't disappoint him. He was met at the ER entrance by one of the paramedics.

"Dr. Cristanzio, four ambulances are ready to leave as soon as you give the word."

"Good! Let's roll," he instructed as he charged out the door.

Dr. Gennaro and Dr. Schiavo strolled out into the hallway, realizing they were going to have a few tough hours ahead of them. They began discussing their strategy.

"Dr. Cristanzio was right; everyone will be coming in smack in the middle of the change of shift. I'm going to round up some volunteers to man the ER," Dr. Schiavo announced.

Dr. Gennaro nodded in approval.

"While you're doing that, I'm going to check with my surgical team about staying on after their shift ends."

Outside, Dr. Cristanzio was giving orders to the crew.

"Listen up everyone! No sirens! We'll have a police escort to get us there quickly. The last thing I want to do is alarm the kidnappers. Let's go, we have a job to do."

The ambulances arrived just after Paulo disappeared into the building with the IDs. Robert let out a sigh of relief at the sight of them and immediately began to flag them down. He ran over to Dr. Cristanzio as soon as he spotted him. "You're a sight for sore eyes. How did you know we would need your help?"

"Anna convinced me we should be here in case there's a problem. How are things going?"

"Hard to say. The leader, Tony, is a real maniac. I haven't said as much to Paulo because I didn't want to worry him, but I know he's a mental case. This guy's rap sheet reads like a horror novel. He has been arrested for burglary, armed robbery, attempted murder, arson, child abuse, assault and battery, drug dealing and God knows what else. You name it and Tony has dipped his fingers in it with horrific results. Right now there are twelve of my men, ten of Sheriff DeVito's men, four of Paulo's children, Paulo, and five kidnappers held up in the building. There are ten additional men surrounding each of the exits from the building and Paulo's office window. There's no doubt we'll need your medical assistance before this is over."

"I'll do anything I can to help. By the way, I had no idea Veronica was your daughter. When I treated your wife for depression, she spoke of a daughter, but never told me her name."

"How's she doing?"

"Veronica was very lucky. If the bullet had hit a little to the left, she'd have been a goner. Also, luckily, David Paladino has the same blood type as Veronica. If they didn't have David to transfuse Veronica on the way to the hospital she may have bled to death. I left David with her to make sure she doesn't leave the hospital."

Peter called Robert over.

"I don't like it, Robert. It's too quiet."

Robert stood still for a moment to evaluate the scene and found that Peter's assessment was correct. He could almost feel the eerie silence but he was helpless to do anything about it.

Inside the company, the plot thickened. Paulo anxiously tread down the long hall leading to his office. To his surprise, Charles was standing near his door motioning to him not to say a word. Paulo continued down the hall to the door, hesitating briefly before knocking.

"Paulo, is that you babe?"

"Yes, it is, Tony. I have the new identifications."

"Push them under the door and then leave the same way you came in."

"Not this time! Now it's your turn to show your good faith and release

79

my children."

There was a choking silence and then Tony came to the door.

"Stay right where you are. You can see your children from there."

"Tony, that isn't the deal. Before you get this envelope, I want my children released."

"Who the fuck do you think you are? I'm the fucking boss now, not you." Tony pulled a gun out of his shirt and held it up to Paulo's face.

"Did you really think that any of your children were going to make it out of here alive? What a pity, now I have to shoot you, too."

The instant the words came out of his mouth, pandemonium erupted. The men in the crawl space broke through the bathroom and storage entrances to the office. At first the kidnappers were caught off guard, but quickly regained control by taking aim at Paulo's children. Franco broke free and jumped in front of Paulo to shield him from gunfire. In the chaos, Tony's gun went off, hitting Franco in the back and sending him crashing to the ground. Franco struggled to sit up but his body went limp, as there was no feeling in his legs. He went into shock when he realized he couldn't move. The room went dark as he passed out. It would be hours before they discover the extent of his injuries.

In the meantime, Assunta realized that she too was struck by one of the bullets. A second bullet almost caught her in the chest, but miraculously lodged in the medal of Saint Michael that she always wore around her neck. Michael acted quickly, dropping the kidnapper to the floor, but not before the gun went off and a bullet hit him in the shoulder. Oblivious to his injury, Michael continued punching the kidnapper's face until one of Robert's men interceded.

Realizing the first two shots didn't kill Assunta, another kidnapper made a third attempt at her. Fortunately, Gino realized his intentions and pushed Assunta out of the way. A member of the rescue team subsequently tackled the kidnapper.

Gino gently helped Assunta off the floor, guiding her to a safe location while the struggle continued. Across the room, Charles was concentrating all his energy on keeping Franco clear of any more gunfire. By this time, Tony realized that Charles turned on him and decided to make him pay. Just as Tony was about to fire, Peter jumped on him from behind and fought with him until the gun went off. Tony fatally shot himself. While lying on the floor dying, Tony stared at Charles in disbelief. His lips were moving as if to say something to Charles, but no words came out. In the end, all five kidnappers, including Tony, met their untimely demise.

With the kidnappers out of the way, Michael's attention was drawn to Franco, who was stretched out on the floor. He rushed to his side and knelt down in front of him.

"Hang in there, little brother," Michael urged him. "You're Paulo Altro's son. You're a survivor."

He removed a medal of Our Lady of Lourdes from his pocket and placed it in Franco's hand, closing his fingers tightly around it. Then Michael administered the sacrament of the Anointing of the Sick; something he had done many times in the past, but this time it was different. It was personal.

Gino was still guarding Assunta at this point and she seemed to be fine until she noticed blood on his shirt. She started screaming and then nervously broke away from him. As she broke free from Gino, her eyes scanned the room for Franco. To her horror, she caught a glimpse of his body sprawled out on the floor. It was more than she could bear so she ran for cover.

As the commotion settled down, Paulo began seeking out his children. He immediately noticed Michael kneeling in front of Franco and feared the worst. He broke loose from the security men and ran to their side. Seeing Franco in this condition, Paulo couldn't hold back the tears any longer.

"Hang in there, son. I'm not ready to give you back yet. I love you."

Just then, the paramedics rushed in and took over. Dr. Cristanzio determined that Franco's condition was serious enough to be attended to first. He watched as the paramedics prepared Franco for the ambulance. Somehow, Quintino managed his way into the building behind the paramedics and was aghast at what he saw. The office was a shambles. The walls were riddled with bullet holes, the furniture was strewn about haphazardly, and everything else was destroyed. Worst of all was seeing Franco's pale, limp, bloody frame lying on the floor near the doorway. Quintino's heart sunk. Franco was like the son he never had. They had grown very close and he couldn't bear the thought of losing him. He squeezed through the crowd hovering around Franco to hear of his fate. "Doctor, how bad is it?"

"Franco is losing a lot of blood. If we don't get him into the operating room soon, I . . ."

"I have my helicopter right outside. What are we waiting for?"

"Quintino, you're a life saver!"

Within minutes, Dr. Cristanzio had informed the paramedics of the change in plans and instructed them to start blood transfusions using the O-negative blood that he had requested earlier. To ensure a smooth transition, he also phoned ahead to the hospital and informed Dr. Gennaro that Franco would need emergency surgery for a possible spinal injury.

When the helicopter was ready for take-off, the paramedics carefully hoisted Franco up into the passenger compartment where they immediately started the blood transfusion. Within minutes, Franco was on his way to Our Lady of Lourdes Medical Center.

By the time the helicopter landed on the hospital roof, there was less than one-quarter unit of blood remaining. Fortunately, Dr. Gennaro and his team were waiting ready to take over and had prepared for the worst.

Back at the company, the paramedics were still examining the rest of the family and the security men. Two ambulances were promptly loaded up with those men who were most in need of medical attention. Dr. Cristanzio was working along side the paramedics to get the situation under control when he realized Assunta was nowhere in sight and became alarmed. His first instinct was to advise Paulo, and then together they would organize a search of the premises.

Paulo's concern for Franco was so overwhelming that he hadn't yet gotten around to checking on the others. It wasn't until Dr. Cristanzio brought it to his attention that he noticed Assunta was missing. They frantically began searching every nook and cranny of the building. Running down one of the long halls, it suddenly dawned on Paulo where she might be hiding. He dashed back to his office and headed straight for the desk. Peeking underneath, he found Assunta curled up in the corner in a fetal position.

"It's all over now, Princess," he whispered to her. 'No one will ever hurt you again."

Paulo bent down to help Assunta out, but she was reluctant. She didn't want him to see her face; if it looked as bad as it hurt, it would be a horrific sight. Paulo softly turned her face toward his and looked deep into her eyes.

"It's time for us to go home."

"Papa, is everyone all right?"

"Everyone made it out safely. The boys are on their way to the hospital to be checked out. Now, it's your turn."

"My face feels horrible. How bad does it look?"

Paulo smiled and gently kissed her on the forehead.

"Assunta, you're the most beautiful daughter a father could ask for."

Sweaty and exhausted from running, Dr. Cristanzio finally made it back to the office. Seeing Assunta in pain brought tears to his eyes, yet, at the same time, he was relieved. He decided to make a joke to lighten the mood.

"Assunta, if you wanted to get out of a few days volunteer service that badly, you should have just told me. It wasn't necessary to go to these extremes."

Everyone laughed and for a very brief moment, it seemed as if nothing was wrong, but when Assunta joined in the laughter, her face hurt so badly that she shrieked in agony. It became clear to Dr. Cristanzio that her injuries may be worse than they knew.

"We should get Assunta to the hospital," he suggested.

On the way to the hospital, Paulo coddled Assunta as if she was a frightened child. He was powerless to make her pain go away so he did the next best thing; he held her hand and stroked her hair lovingly. It took all his might not to break down and cry.

At one point, Assunta's pain had become so intense that Dr. Cristanzio injected her with a sedative so she could relax. Only when her pain diminished, did he attempt to survey the damage to her face. That's when he noticed a bullet lodged in the medal of Saint Michael that she wore around her neck.

"There doesn't appear to be any major breaks," he assured Paulo. "It's a miracle that she was spared worse damage."

"What do you mean?" Paulo questioned his opinion.

"Normally, I would expect to find a broken nose or broken jaw bone on a patient who had been beaten so brutally but after examining her, I can conclude that she has neither. In addition, the only gunshot wound she sustained is on her wrist. The bullet that could have made Assunta a fatality never entered her body. I believe that your faith in Saint Michael has served Assunta well. Not only did he protect Assunta's face, but her body as well."

Paulo was confused. "What are you trying to say?"

"Paulo, can I see Assunta's medal of Saint Michael up close," Dr. Cristanzio asked. Paulo proceeded to remove it from around her neck and hand it to him, still unaware of the bullet. "You have to tell me where you bought this medal. First thing tomorrow morning, I'm going to place an order for four of them for my children," Dr. Cristanzio said as he handed the medal back to Paulo.

Paulo took another look at the medal, wondering why Dr. Cristanzio was acting so strangely. It took a minute but he finally saw the bullet. His hands started to shake as he came to terms with its significance and pondered the idea of divine intervention. He prayed all day to Saint Michael to guard his children and this was proof that he did. His children had been given a second chance at life. Placing the medal back on Assunta's neck, he realized how fortunate he was.

That day, Michael, Gino, and Assunta escaped with only minor cuts and bruises and were all well on their way to full recovery, at least physically. It would be a long time before their emotional scars were healed. Franco was the only one who sustained serious injuries requiring aggressive treatment. He would received the best medical care money could buy and subsequently given a favorable prognosis. Things could have turned out much worse but luck was on their side this time.

# Chapter 6

## Picking Up The Pieces

Word of the abduction spread rapidly throughout Our Lady of Lourdes Medical Center. It became the topic of conversation because it involved the Altro family, well known to the staff for their dedication to the hospital. Paulo was the hospital's biggest benefactor. His generosity, especially when it came to the children, was unmatched. Michael and Timothy were highly respected members of the hospital's volunteer staff. They devoted a great deal of time to the patients; making themselves available to administer the Anointing of the Sick or simply spend a few encouraging minutes with the patients. Assunta was known for her volunteer work with Dr. Cristanzio, as well as for the work she had been doing in the children's unit, and the kitchen staff knew Franco from his daily delivery of fresh bread and rolls. On Fridays, his donation included pizza for the children.

As word spread that the Altro's were in danger, the entire staff flocked to the Emergency Room, eager to lend a hand. The crowd of doctors, nurses, and orderlies prepared the ER for an onslaught of victims, hoping for the best.

Since Franco was airlifted, he was the first to arrive. Dr. Gennaro, who was already aware of Franco's status, greeted him at the helicopter and swiftly transported him to the ER. There was no time to lose considering Franco had been unconscious for such a long time. As soon as they stepped foot into the ER, a team of doctors and nurses sprung into action, checking his vital signs and starting IV lines for his impending trip to the operating room.

Anna had been nervously pacing the halls waiting for word of her family's rescue, when she heard the commotion. She reached the emergency room just as Franco was being wheeled inside and couldn't believe her eyes. It appeared that Franco was in serious trouble so she ran to his side and took hold of his hand.

"Franco, can you hear me? I love you. Hang in there for Mama. I'll be right here when you wake up."

Anna had only enough time left to give him a peck on the cheek before they whisked him away to the operating room. From across the room, Quintino quietly watched and could tell that she was about to fall to pieces. He made his way over to her, gently placing his hands on her shoulders. Anna jumped at his touch then, realizing it was Quintino, fell into his arms and began sobbing. He allowed Anna to get it all out of her system before he led her over to the sofa.

"Listen to me," he said. "The others are on their way and they need you as much as Franco does. You have to stay strong for them. I think it would be best if you wait here for them before going to meet Franco in the recovery room. It'll be a while before he's out of surgery anyway."

Anna acknowledged his advice with an irresolute nod but wondered to herself if what he suggested was possible. They sat in silence for a few minutes while Anna calmed down then, when he felt she was ready to talk, Quintino asked about Timothy and Donna.

"Timothy is wonderful. He's been a great comfort to me. Donna seems to be well aside from a few bruises but Dr. Schiavo thinks it would be a good idea to have her spend a day or two here in the hospital. He's concerned about the emotional toll the ordeal might have on her." Just then, a look of concern returned to Anna's face. "How's Assunta?" she asked. "Please tell me she's OK?"

Quintino attempted to break it to her gently but before he could even get the words out, Anna suddenly began to cry even harder than before.

"If anything happens to Assunta, I swear I'll . . ."

"Everyone, with the exception of Franco, had only superficial wounds; Assunta is fine." Quintino couldn't find it in his heart to tell Anna how badly battered Assunta's face really was.

"Quintino, do you think Franco is going to be all right?" Anna asked.

Quintino held Anna's hand in his.

"Franco is a survivor. He has strength that's hard to describe. I love that boy as if he were my own son. Do you think I'd be able to sit here this calmly if I thought he wasn't going to be all right?" The sound of ambulances approaching filtered through the waiting room and within minutes the first ambulance, carrying Sheriff DeVito's men, arrived. More sirens could be heard blaring in the distance, which meant the others were on their way. Dr. Schiavo started to worry that they wouldn't be able to accommodate everyone when all of a sudden the twelve interns, who were studying under his supervision, showed up asking to help.

Their willingness to cooperate was a source of pride to Dr. Schiavo. He happily provided them with assignments, noting their professionalism and competence. The interns were clearly very serious about their jobs. They went right to work in the examining rooms, treating Sheriff DeVito's men.

Fortunately, by the time the second ambulance arrived with Robert's men, some of whom were seriously wounded and in need of immediate attention, the ER was fully staffed and running much smoother. Dr. Schiavo's command of the Emergency Room staff was impeccable.

Finally, the third ambulance pulled in to the driveway. When it approached the entrance, the bustling room fell silent as everyone watched nervously to see who was inside. As instructed, two of Dr. Schiavo's interns ran out to assist and carefully removed Michael and Gino from the ambulance. To everyone's relief, they appeared to be unscathed. Judging by their expressions, it was a relief for Michael and Gino as well.

Anna ran to them as soon as they appeared in the doorway. She threw her arms around Gino and gave him a big hug and kiss then did the same to Michael.

"Thank God you're alive," she proclaimed.

Her heart was pounding so hard; it felt as if it would jump right out of her chest. She stared at Gino then at Michael until she was certain she wasn't dreaming. She questioned them repeatedly about how they felt and, even after they assured her that they were fine, she insisted on pestering them. Anna wouldn't leave their side until they were wheeled off to be thoroughly examined by the doctors.

By now, the Emergency Room resembled a war zone. Some of the security men were lingering in the halls on stretchers waiting to be attended to while the more critical patients were being rushed to operating rooms and recovery rooms. Hospital staff moved quickly from person to person, bandaging wounds, administering medication and comforting the victims while trying to maintain order. Family members were also starting to arrive, causing a frenzy in the waiting room.

When things finally started to calm down, the fourth ambulance could be heard screeching to a halt in the drive. Anna froze at the sound then clung nervously to Quintino, anticipating more horror. She was surprised to discover that her fears completely vanished at the sight of Paulo. His presence made everything better. She flew across the room and jumped into his arms.

Before Anna knew what was happening, Dr. Cristanzio darted past with Assunta and disappeared into one of the examining rooms. Once Assunta was safely hidden behind closed doors, away from Anna's range of vision, and in the care of Dr. Schiavo, Dr. Cristanzio requested a full report on Franco.

In the meantime, Anna was reeling with confusion by Dr. Cristanzio's behavior. She didn't expect Assunta to be taken away so quickly without at least being able to see if she was OK. On instinct, she tried to follow them, but Paulo didn't give her a chance. He distracted her with questions about Franco. After all, he was in on the plan with Dr. Cristanzio to keep Anna from seeing Assunta's face.

The plan worked and Anna began rattling on about Franco.

"He's being operated on as we speak," she told him. "I'm so scared, Paulo. If anything happens to him, I don't know what I'll do. I can't lose Franco!" Anna threw herself into Paulo's arms and broke down.

Paulo gently lifted Anna away from his chest so he could look into her eyes.

"Anna, I don't want to lose Franco either! If I could change places with him, I'd do it in a heartbeat. Right now, all we could do is place our son in the hands of Dr. Gennaro. He's one of the best surgeons in the area and if anyone can save Franco's life, he can."

After talking for a while, they both felt a little bit better about coping with the situation. Finding the nerve, Paulo was about to excuse himself to get an update on the children, when Dr. Cristanzio appeared. They were thrilled to see him and couldn't wait to hear his news but Anna didn't even give him a chance to speak before she asked to see Assunta.

"As soon as she is cleaned up, you can see her, but first I'd like to give you a report on everyone's condition."

Once Anna and Paulo agreed, giving him their undivided attention, Dr. Cristanzio continued.

"Donna is an emotional wreck and will undoubtedly need intensive counseling. Otherwise, she is unharmed. Gino was merely grazed by a bullet just below the elbow and will be fine. Michael's bullet wound to the shoulder isn't serious so they are able to handle it here in the Emergency Room. They'll all be taken to their rooms soon to recover. Franco is still in surgery and will probably be there for another hour or so. He's holding his own for now and as soon as I know more, I'll let you know. Assunta was very fortunate. The medal of Saint Michael that she wore around her neck stopped the bullet that would have made her a fatality. Paulo, I think it's best you explain the rest."

Paulo paused briefly, allowing himself time to think of the right words.

"I'm going to be honest with you," he started, and then paused again. "Assunta's face is pretty mangled."

Before he could continue, Anna started screaming uncontrollably and had to cover her face with her hands to muffle the sounds.

"Anna Altro, you listen to me. If you think for one moment that I'll allow you to see Assunta while you're behaving like this, forget it. She feels bad enough. The last thing she needs is for her mother to make her feel worse."

Anna looked at Paulo with tears in her eyes.

"I'm sorry; it's just . . .."

Paulo didn't want to upset Anna any more than she was already, so he proceeded with caution.

"I know how you feel. I'm upset too. When I first saw Assunta's face, I was sickened. I wanted to kill Tony for what he had done to her but I couldn't. I felt helpless and that made me even angrier. You can't imagine how difficult that was for me. To make matters worse, when it was finally over, the first thing Assunta asked me was if she'd ever be pretty again. Anna, my heart was breaking for her but I had to keep my cool and assure her that she was still beautiful, no matter how many bumps and bruises were on her face. That's exactly what you must do. You can't let her battered appearance get the better of you. If you overreact, she'll be devastated."

A blood-curdling shriek coming from the direction of the examining rooms put an abrupt halt to Paulo and Anna's discussion. In a flash, they were on their feet, running frantically toward the sound. They yanked open every curtain until they found Assunta curled up on the floor in the last examining room, crying wildly.

They couldn't imagine what had set her off until a quick scan of the room revealed the problem. Apparently, the room was not entirely emptied of all items that may be used as a mirror. The staff's attempt to prevent Assunta from seeing the damage to her face had failed. As she lay there alone, Assunta's curiosity got the better of her and she reached for one of the small, brilliantly polished instruments that rested on the counter next to her hospital bed. The wrenching cry that everyone heard was her reaction to the swollen, bruised, and scarred face she saw before her.

Paulo approached slowly so as not to startle her then very gently slid down on the floor beside her. He put his arms around her delicate frame, holding her close and rocking her back and forth for comfort.

At the same time, also alarmed by the screaming, Michael and Gino ran out of their examining room, knocking over anything in their way, to get to the scene. They stopped dead in their tracks when they reached the entrance to Assunta's room and saw how traumatized she was. They watched helplessly as Paulo took control.

The next person to arrive was Dr. Cristanzio. He had been notified by the floor nurse about Assunta's bizarre behavior and immediately returned to assess the situation. Seeing Assunta rocking back and forth on the floor in a trance-like state brought back memories of their very first sessions together in which she experienced flash backs. Since Paulo had already managed to calm Assunta down, Dr. Cristanzio chose not to intervene. He was afraid she might become agitated. Instead, he motioned to Paulo from the doorway for his consent to give her a sedative. It was no surprise to Dr. Cristanzio that Paulo declined the offer. He knew Paulo was against the use of mind-altering medication except as a last resort.

To everyone's amazement, Assunta suddenly sat still and raised her eyes slightly to look at Paulo.

"Papa, my face is ruined! Oh my God, look what that man did to me! Franco will hate me when he sees my face! I'm going to lose him and then what will I do!"

Assunta put her face down in embarrassment.

"That's nonsense. Franco loves you," Paulo declared confidently. "And besides, Dr. Cristanzio is going to see to it that you leave here in the same condition you were in this morning at breakfast. I guarantee you'll be as beautiful as ever."

Sensing that Assunta was feeling more at ease, Michael finally entered the room to assist Paulo. He lifted Assunta off the floor and gave her a huge hug before laying her in bed. Acting in his usual manner, Michael proceeded to tease Assunta about her antics, being careful not to remark on her appearance. She giggled and laughed at his silliness. His camaraderie never failed to raise her spirits and that's exactly what she needed.

While Michael and Assunta chatted, Paulo pulled a chair up to the bed and sat down finally able to relax knowing that Assunta was feeling better. He covered her with the sheet then sat there holding her hand and stroking her hair. Soon, Michael excused himself to talk to Anna and Gino, giving Paulo an opportunity to be alone with Assunta for a little while. Paulo moved closer to talk to Assunta.

"Assunta, listen to me; I love you very much. You're the most beautiful daughter a man could ask for. Right now your face is badly bruised, but that's only temporary. There's something more important that I think you should know." Paulo removed the medal of Saint Michael from Assunta's neck and showed her the bullet. Assunta immediately understood the significance of the bullet's location and started weeping.

"Saint Michael protected you today." Paulo explained as he examined the medal then started to put it in his pocket.

"Papa, my medal?"

Paulo looked at the medal again before gently placing it around Assunta's neck. He turned to Anna who had been standing quietly near the edge of the bed.

"Anna, remind me when I get home to order Assunta another medal of Saint Michael. I intend to keep this one on display in the library. I already know the perfect spot for it, over the light switch. Every time I turn the light on or off, I'll be reminded of how Saint Michael protected my children."

Paulo suddenly realized that he was hogging all of Assunta's attention. When he stood up to leave, he offered Anna the chair to sit down in so she could visit with Assunta as well. He noticed that Anna squeezed her eyes closed and started to tremble as she moved toward the chair for fear she wouldn't be able to handle seeing Assunta's face up close.

Assunta hardly seemed to notice Anna; she was more concerned about Paulo leaving. She wanted him to stay with her because he made her feel safe. "Papa, where are you going?" she asked nervously.

"I'm going to make a phone call. I'll only be a few minutes," he said. "Your mother will stay here with you while I'm gone. She has been waiting patiently to spend some time with you."

Paulo leaned over and kissed Assunta on the forehead then turned to Anna with an encouraging smile to give her the strength she'd need to confront her daughter's battered face.

It took all her strength not to scream out in pain at the sight of Assunta's wounds. Her first instinct was to grab Assunta and hold her tightly in her arms. She wanted desperately to make Assunta's pain go away. They cried together for a long while.

"Mama, my face . . ."

Anna smoothed the hair away from Assunta's face before answering.

"I'm not going to lie and tell you that your face is the same face I saw this morning but in a few days this will only be a memory, nothing more."

"Will Franco still love me?" Assunta asked tearfully.

"There's no need for you to worry about Franco. Your husband will love you no matter what. Papa calls it unconditional love but I call it a blessing from Almighty God. Not many women are as lucky as you and I. Some men only look for external beauty but that isn't true of Franco or Papa. They love us for what's in our hearts."

Anna and Assunta sat quietly for a few minutes until Dr. Cristanzio returned.

"We have rooms for everyone on the fourth floor," he announced. "An orderly will be coming along shortly to escort Assunta. Dr. Schiavo has ordered a series of x-rays for her."

Paulo's jaw dropped when he returned and heard the last part of Dr. Cristanzio's news.

"What's wrong with Assunta?" he stammered.

"I could imagine what you're thinking but it's not that serious. Because Assunta has had severe sinus trouble in the past, Dr. Schiavo wants to have a look merely as a precaution."

Just as Dr. Cristanzio was finishing, Dr. Schiavo arrived to talk to Paulo

"I stopped in the operating room. They shouldn't be too much longer with Franco. Dr. Gennaro will be out to give you an update as soon as he's through." Before continuing, Dr. Schiavo looked at the floor as if searching

91

for the right words to use. His displeasure was obvious. "I seem to be having trouble convincing some of your children to stay for a few days. I think it would be best to keep them for observation. They've all been through a traumatic experience and sometimes it doesn't sink in for a day or so. When this happens I'd like them to be here so we can help them through."

Dr. Cristanzio could tell by Paulo's expression that he was not pleased. He wanted to join them to see if there was something he could do to help, but was sidetracked by the arrival of Sheriff DeVito and Robert Stone. He went over to greet them instead and fill them in on some of the developments. Naturally, Robert was most concerned about his daughter, Veronica, so he started there then moved on to the others. It was up to Dr. Schiavo now to give them more details so Dr. Cristanzio summoned him over for a brief introduction.

"Sheriff DeVito, Robert, I'd like you to meet Dr. Schiavo. He has been overseeing the care of your men tonight."

Dr. Schiavo approached and shook hands with both of them.

"I'm glad to meet you. Let's sit down so we could be more comfortable and I'll give you an update."

While they conferred, Paulo took the opportunity to talk some sense into his sons. He grabbed Michael and Gino before they could leave. At first, his anger overpowered him. His tone was uncharacteristically hostile as he berated them and ordered that they remain in the hospital for as long as was necessary. It was only after he contemplated the surprised expression on their faces that he realized he was overreacting.

Paulo was known for being tough on his children but even he knew this was too much and he instantly regretted his poor conduct. After offering a heartfelt apology to Gino and Michael, he continued with a much more subtle speech about their responsibility to their family to take care of themselves. They were reluctant but they finally agreed with Paulo. Before they left to settle into their room, Paulo gave them both a hug and told them that he would be up to see them later.

By this time, the orderly had arrived to take Assunta for the additional tests. Paulo stopped for a moment to reassure Assunta that everything would be all right before she left the Emergency Room.

"Assunta, don't worry, these are only tests to check on your sinus condition. Mama is going to stay with you and then I'll be up to see you as soon as I check in on the others." Paulo kissed Assunta on the forehead then Assunta and Anna were on their way

The only ones left were Paulo, Robert, and the two doctors. Now Dr. Schiavo could finish explaining the arrangements for the night.

"When Assunta finishes her tests, she'll be taken to a room on the fourth floor which she'll be sharing with Donna and Michael and Gino will stay together in a room just down the hall from them. Veronica has been recovering in a private room also on the fourth floor. She's been very uncooperative so David Paladino has had to guard her all day from leaving the hospital. Franco will need constant care for at least the first twenty-four hours. He'll be in a private room as well closer to the nurse's station. Once he's feeling up to it, he can join his brothers. Hopefully, they'll still be here."

Paulo felt he had to extend an apology to Dr. Schiavo.

"I must apologize for the way my children have responded to your orders. From this point forward I believe they'll be more agreeable."

There was no need for Paulo to apologize. Over the years Dr. Schiavo had seen and heard it all and wasn't offended by their behavior in the least. It was getting late so Dr. Schiavo and Dr. Cristanzio excused themselves to attend to their other patients and Paulo and Robert left to visit their kids.

On the way upstairs, Paulo asked about Charles. He wondered what would happen to him after all was said and done. After all, without Charles help he wasn't sure anything would have worked out as well as it did.

"Sheriff DeVito took him down to the Police Station," Robert answered. "He will have a preliminary hearing tomorrow morning. Hopefully, the judge will be lenient on him given the circumstances."

Paulo thought for a moment and then had an idea. "I'll make a call to Judge DeStephano. He's a personal friend of mine. Maybe he can do something to help Charles."

When the elevator stopped at the fourth floor, all talk of Charles ceased. They had to concentrate on their children now. Tomorrow morning they could worry more about Charles. The two men walked the long hall in silence, each consumed in thoughts of their children.

The boys' room was the first room they came upon so while Robert waited outside, Paulo went in to talk to his sons. He found Michael and Gino leaning restlessly against their beds engrossed in a deep conversation. He almost felt sorry to interrupt them but he had no choice.

Paulo cleared his throat to get their attention but succeeded in scaring them half to death. They both jumped and Gino went tumbling to the floor at the sound. Paulo rushed in and grabbed hold of Gino to help him back to his feet then apologized for being so brusque. Clearly, Paulo hadn't given much thought to their fragile state of mind.

Once Michael and Gino calmed down, Paulo sat between them on one of the beds to have a serious talk. He decided to go easy on them especially after the incident that just took place, however, he had to be

93

forceful enough to make his wishes clear. He picked up where he left off in the Emergency Room, stressing how important it is to follow the doctor's orders and he warned them that their defiance wouldn't be tolerated.

As usual, Michael didn't argue with his father. He had so much respect for him that he would agree to just about anything he requested. Gino felt the same and knew that staying in the hospital was the right thing to do but couldn't help worrying about his work backing up.

On his way out of the room, Paulo stopped suddenly and turned around to look at his sons.

"Maybe you don't realize it, but I love you more than life itself and I'm grateful to Almighty God that you're alive. Rest before your dinner arrives and your mother and I will be in to see you later."

Outside in the hallway, Robert was still waiting and by this time was joined by Dr. Schiavo. Together, the three men agreed to check in on the girls next. He wasn't certain but Paulo thought he noticed a hint of apprehension in Robert. In fact, it seemed that Robert would have preferred to avoid his daughter all together if possible. Only time would tell if Paulo's assumptions were correct.

At the first sign of Robert approaching, David Paladino rose to his feet and the two embraced.

"Thank God you're alright," Robert declared.

"I'm fine. I just wish I could say the same about the others," David said as he sighed deeply. "We lost a lot of good men today."

Robert placed his hand on David's shoulder as he fought back tears. "I know and I'll miss them terribly. Now tell me about Veronica."

David shook his head in disgust.

"The good news is that she's recovering from surgery like a champ. The bad news is that she has a nasty temper and a hard head. I finally had to lock her in the room to keep her from leaving."

As soon as the door swung open, Veronica jumped to her feet. In a heartbeat, she was in front of her father, wagging her finger in his face defiantly. "I don't know who he thinks he is," she hollered, pointing in David's direction, "I do know that I want him fired right now. He had no right to force me to stay here. I want out as soon as possible."

Robert's face revealed anger and embarrassment.

"I was the one who told David to make sure you didn't leave the hospital. Now, I suggest you make yourself at home because you're not going anywhere until the doctor discharges you."

Veronica stomped away angrily. For the time being, she quieted down but they hadn't heard the last of her.

Meanwhile, David was filling Paulo in on Donna's escapades. Her room was next door, so David had to deal with her as well. It seemed that she too was having a hard time following orders. She didn't want to stay in the hospital and was giving everyone a hard time.

"Why were they all so dead set against staying in the hospital for a few days," Paulo asked himself. After what they had been through, he thought they would want some rest but apparently, he was wrong. Being a parent is harder than any work he had ever done.

Paulo was growing tired of scolding his children, but in this case, it was necessary. Without another moment's delay, he went next door to Donna's room.

"I've been told that you intend to sign yourself out of the hospital in the morning. Is that true?" Paulo barked.

Donna was completely taken off guard by Paulo's outburst. The tone of his voice was so harsh that for the first time, she was actually afraid of what he might do.

"No. Not until the doctor tells me I can leave," she whimpered.

"That's what I thought," he replied. "Now, get ready for dinner; it'll be served shortly. Mama and I will be back later to say good night."

At almost the exact same moment, Paulo emerged from Donna's room and Robert emerged from Veronica's room. Once again they gathered in the hallway, both men showing signs of exhaustion. Just as they were about to leave, Assunta and Anna showed up escorted by an orderly. The testing went smoothly and now it was time for Assunta to get settled into her room.

After the orderly helped Assunta into bed, Paulo sat down on the side of the bed and held her hand. He wanted her to feel safe and comfortable but her only concern at the time was Franco. She asked about him immediately.

"He's resting," Paulo said. "He's a lucky young man."

Assunta smiled, feeling relieved. Unfortunately, however, her excitement would be short-lived. As soon as her face touched the pillow, she winced in pain and the reality of her predicament came rushing back. She was on the verge of tears before asking Paulo for more pain medication.

It was obvious that Assunta was in pain but Paulo was hesitant about giving her painkillers especially after the scene she made earlier in the emergency room. He was sure that the medication was to blame for her actions but he decided to call Dr. Schiavo anyway. He couldn't stand to see Assunta this way.

Only a few minutes passed until Dr. Schiavo arrived. After a quick examination to determine her level of pain, he was ready to administer the drug. "Give it a few minutes to take effect," he advised. "You'll feel better

*Absolution*

soon then when the pain returns, let the nurse know and she'll send for me."

The medicine took effect almost instantly causing Assunta to fall fast asleep. Paulo gently let go of her hand and straightened out her pillow before leaving her side.

Paulo and Anna quietly walked out to the hallway, to figure out what to do next. The only thing they knew for sure was that neither of them wanted to leave the hospital. It was upsetting to think of spending the night at home without the rest of their family, so they called Dr. Cristanzio and asked if it would be possible for them to stay the night.

"Of course," he answered. "You're more than welcomed to stay. I'll find a room for you right away."

"If you don't mind, I think it's best if Anna stays with the girls and I stay with the boys; just in case they need us."

A few minutes later, Dr. Cristanzio got back to them about the arrangements.

"Everything's set. You'll be given cots to sleep on."

"Thank you!" Paulo replied, then hung up.

At last, things were starting to look brighter. Paulo actually felt hopeful for the first time that day. He swung around and planted a big kiss on Anna's forehead.

"Anna, before we get a bite to eat, there's something I must do. Why don't you go spend some time with Franco in recovery? I shouldn't be too long. I'll meet you there when I'm through."

As he watched Anna stroll gracefully down the hall, an image of her on their wedding day flashed through his mind. She was as radiant today as she was all those years ago he marveled. He was profoundly grateful for every joyous day they've had together and couldn't imagine going through this ordeal without her by his side. Fond memories continued to occupy his thoughts until he reached Dr. Gennaro's office.

Earlier, when Franco came out of surgery, Dr. Gennaro remarked about the seriousness of his blood loss. At the time, Paulo didn't question him because he didn't want to worry Anna but now he wanted to find out more. According to Dr. Gennaro, there was still some concern over the amount of blood that Franco lost and it was highly possible that he would need another transfusion before the night was over. However, considering that Franco had a rare blood type, Dr. Gennaro indicated that the supply might be too low. Fortunately and incredibly, Paulo shared the same rare blood type and was prepared to donate his blood. It was the least he could do. On Paulo's suggestion they headed straight to the lab to draw Paulo's blood. The procedure was simple and painless. Afterward, Paulo laid down on the bed praying for Franco.

As soon as his blood sugar stabilized, Paulo left to join Anna. She was so upset that she didn't even notice him enter the room. It was very painful for them to see Franco in this condition but they didn't want to leave. They decided to stay with him instead of going to the cafeteria. Instead, Paulo made a call and arranged for dinner to be brought to them in Franco's room.

They picked at their trays as they talked to Franco. The only thing they could do now was will Franco to pull through by offering love and encouragement. They took turns telling funny stories about Franco, Assunta and the kids in hopes that it would stir him from his slumber.

Sometime around two a.m., Dr. Cristanzio came in to check on Franco and found Paulo and Anna sitting on either side of the bed.

"It's very late. Why don't you get some sleep? As soon as Franco wakes up, I promise I'll let you know."

Paulo gazed at Anna through sagging eyes.

"Darling, perhaps Dr. Cristanzio is right. We should get some sleep."

Although she was starved for sleep, Anna knew where her place was.

"I need to be here for Franco when he wakes up."

"Anna is right," Paulo agreed. "We should be here when Franco opens his eyes."

There was no use in arguing with them. Dr. Cristanzio knew them well enough to know he couldn't change their minds. Rather, he had the two nurses move in two lounge chairs, pillows, and blankets to make them more comfortable. By the time Dr. Cristanzio left, Anna and Paulo were both sound asleep.

At around three in the morning, Assunta was startled awake. Feeling confused and disoriented, she staggered down the hall to Michael's room. "Michael, wake up," she whispered. "Papa promised he'd come in to say good night but he never did. Do you know where he is?"

Before he could answer, she started talking again.

"Michael, please come with me to Franco's room. I have to know how he's doing."

Michael looked at his watch.

"Do you know what time it is," he asked.

Assunta didn't answer; she just stared at him sadly. It was against his better judgment but, she looked so pathetic, he couldn't refuse. "I hate when you look at me like that," he said, then started walking toward the nurse's station. "You stay put until I come back."

"Oh, please, Michael, I have to see him for myself!"

He shook his head.

*Absolution*

"I don't know how I let you get me involved.  Okay, come on, just be quiet and follow me."

The first thing they had to do was stop at the nurses' station to find out what room Franco was in.  It was a good thing that the nurse on duty understood.  Normally, visiting a patient in the middle of the night wouldn't be allowed but she made an exception for them and gave them the room number.

In a flash, they were at Franco's door and ready to go inside.  Before entering, Michael leaned against the door softly, listening for any sign of movement.  Hearing nothing, he gently prodded the door open, taking care not to cause a disturbance.  They crept in on their tiptoes and kept the light shut to avoid being detected by any other staff members.  In the darkness, all they could see was the outline of Franco's body lying in the bed.  Assunta moved closer until she was at the edge of the bed and could finally see his face.  She was glad to see him sleeping peacefully.

Just then, the light flickered on and the familiar sound of their father's voice shattered the silence.  Michael and Assunta knew they were caught and were prepared to face the music.

"What on earth are you two doing out of bed at this hour?"  Paulo snapped.

"Papa, I woke Michael up and asked him to come down here with me! I wanted to make sure Franco was out of danger.  Don't be angry with him, this was my idea."

"I should have taken Assunta back to her room when she woke me up!" Michael interrupted.  "I'm the one responsible!"

Paulo was upset with both of them.

"All of you had a very stressful day and you need your rest.  You should be in bed just as the doctor ordered."

Assunta was about to try to defend herself when all of a sudden she heard a barely audible voice in the background talking to her.

"Assunta Altro-Cordova, I suggest you watch how you answer Papa."

It was Franco; he was awake at last.

"Papa, Mama, Franco is awake," she shouted excitedly as she leaped toward the bed.

Before long, Assunta was in his arms and wouldn't let him go.  She had worried sick all day waiting for him to revive.  While Assunta and Anna cooed over Franco, Paulo went outside to alert the nurses of his status.  He returned in a few minutes with Dr. Gennaro who was anxious to check his vitals.  It didn't even occur to Dr. Gennaro to question what Assunta and Michael were doing there.

After a thorough exam, Franco's progress was found to be ahead of schedule.

"You had me concerned tonight, but no more," Dr. Gennaro stated smiling down at Franco. "I'm glad to see that you're on the mend."

On his way out, he left orders for them to spend only a few more minutes with Franco so that he could get more rest.

Paulo, Anna and Michael said their good nights and proceeded out the door but Assunta made no attempt to leave.

"Assunta, darling, Franco needs his rest tonight. Dr. Gennaro said we can spend more time with him tomorrow," Paulo said.

"If you don't mind, I'd rather stay here with Franco."

"I realize how you feel, but now is not the time. Both of you need to get some sleep."

Assunta kissed Franco and started to leave when she heard his frail voice again.

"Good night, sweetheart. I love you," Franco said.

Assunta bent down to kiss him once more.

"I love you too, sweetheart."

Assunta felt better about leaving now so she turned and followed Paulo out.

"Franco is going to be fine. I just know it."

The love Paulo saw in her eyes was heartwarming. Franco was a lucky man to have Assunta by his side. As they walked to their rooms, Paulo put his arm around Assunta's shoulders and squeezed her affectionately. He wanted her to know that he understood what she was going through. He knew all too well because he went through the same pain with his first wife Martha. It is very difficult to watch the person you love suffer.

After Assunta and Michael were back in their rooms, Paulo and Anna lingered around the nurses' station to talk privately for a while before retiring themselves. It was during this time that they met up with Dr. Cristanzio. As soon as he spotted them, he asked about Franco and was thrilled to hear he was doing better. They could always count on him for an encouraging word and Paulo really appreciated that. He wanted to thank Dr. Cristanzio for all of his care and concern and now felt like the perfect time.

"Thank you for being there for my family today. At times like these, it's good to have the best on your side."

Dr. Cristanzio thought he might collapse if he didn't sit down soon so he showed them over to the chairs in the lounge before responding.

"It's my pleasure, Paulo. I'm just glad everything worked out well. Now, if you'll excuse me, I need to get some sleep and I'm pretty sure you do too. See you both in the morning."

He walked away feeling great pride in his hospital staff. He felt like the conductor of a perfectly tuned orchestra.

The girls were sound asleep when Anna and Paulo finally went in, so they were careful not to make any noise. While Anna prepared for bed, Paulo bent down beside Assunta and Donna, made the sign of the cross on their foreheads and said a silent prayer to St. Michael. By the time he gave them one last peck on the cheek, Anna had plenty of time to observe her husband's show of affection and it took her breath away. It was obvious that he adored their children and she loved him for that.

Once Paulo was gone, Anna undressed quickly and got ready to slip into bed. The instant she touched the sheets, however, she realized someone was there. Unbeknownst to Anna, Veronica had come into their room sometime during the night, crawled into Anna's bed, and waited for Anna to return. Veronica explained that she felt scared and lonely in her room and needed some company.

Anna was exhausted but she put her desire to sleep on hold a little longer so she could talk to Veronica. There was obviously something bothering her that she needed to get out.

"Is something wrong, Veronica?" asked Anna.

"Your husband truly loves your children. I could see it in the way he attended to the girls just now. Yet, when Assunta came back from seeing Franco and told me Mr. Altro caught her and Michael, she was so fearful you'd think he had beat her."

Anna wasn't sure where this conversation was leading but she was determined to see it through if it made Veronica feel better.

"Paulo is upset with Assunta and Michael. She is right to be concerned," Anna said. "However, that doesn't mean he doesn't love her. The love in his heart for his children never ceases."

Veronica lay back on her pillow looking at the ceiling.

"I'm not as fortunate as your children. My father is a perfect stranger to me. That's why I call him Robert instead of Papa."

"How do you feel about your mother?" Anna asked.

"My mother was wonderful. She loved me and I loved her. She talked to me as if I was important and listened to me when I had a problem. She taught me right from wrong and nurtured me."

"What about your father? Didn't he do any of those things?" Anna interrupted.

"No. It felt like I didn't even have a father. He always kept his distance from me. He never took me any place or did anything with me. Robert Stone doesn't care about me at all. All he's worried about is Stone Security."

Anna was shocked by what she just heard.

"You can't really believe that! He's your father; of course, he cares about you."

"You don't seem to understand. My father regrets the day I was born. I wish it could be different, like Assunta and Paulo."

Veronica lay down and faced the wall.

"I'm sorry I bothered you," she whispered. "I think I'd like to go to sleep now."

Anna felt helpless as she listened to Veronica crying into her pillow. There was only one thing she could think to do at that moment. She decided to go wake Paulo up and ask him to have a talk with Robert. Opening the door as quietly as she could, she walked out into the hallway and headed straight for Paulo's room. She was surprised to discover Paulo peering out the window instead of asleep in bed. She joined him at the window, leaning against him to gaze at the stars.

Instinctively, Paulo put his arms around his wife.

"Isn't it beautiful!" he remarked as he looked up into the sky. "There are so many stars out tonight. It looks like there's a party going on up there. They appear to be dancing in celebration of the new day."

For a long while, Anna and Paulo remained at the window captivated by the beautiful night sky. Eventually, they diverted their eyes from the sky to each other and began talking about their many blessings. There was so much to be grateful for; friends, family, wealth and good fortune, but today they were given the best gift of all. God spared their children's lives and them a lifetime of pain.

It was almost morning now, so Anna had to move quickly. She took Paulo's hand and led him out into the lounge.

"Paulo, we need to talk about Veronica. She is in my room crying herself to sleep."

Paulo became infuriated.

"She should cry. The way she spoke to her father was outrageous. She's lucky she isn't my daughter."

Anna placed her finger on Paulo's lips.

"You are one of the wisest and most loving men I've ever met and it was you who taught me to try and walk two blocks in someone else's shoes before passing judgment."

"Even wise men have to be told right from wrong once in awhile," Paulo added. "Tell me about Veronica."

The story she told made Paulo realize he had indeed wrongly judged Veronica.

"I'll talk to her and see what I can do to help."

Anna squeezed Paulo's arm affectionately.

"Remember, under that tough exterior beats the heart of a little girl trying desperately to find her father. Help her to find him!"

Paulo smiled.

"You're an angel. How can I refuse you?"

Once Anna was safely back in her room, Paulo slouched against the corridor wall and tried to figure out a way to handle Veronica.

# Chapter 7

## Franco's Fears Overpower Him

By nine a.m., the hospital was already buzzing with activity. The lobby was full of hospital employees arriving for work and patients showing up for appointments. Throughout the hospital, janitors were busy cleaning while the kitchen crew was hard at work delivering the morning meal. The fourth floor was no exception, since it was as lively as the rest of the hospital. Most of the patients were awake and the doctors and nurses on duty had already begun making rounds.

Having had only a few hours of sleep, Paulo awoke feeling achy and tense. For a moment there, he had forgotten where he was, but a glimpse of Michael and Gino still asleep in their hospital beds brought it all back. He wondered if the girls were sleeping late as well. Surely, they were all exhausted. This might be a good time to catch Veronica thought Paulo, so he dressed quickly and headed for the girls' room.

The room was dim but there was just enough light to see that Veronica wasn't there so Paulo backed out quietly and went directly next door to Veronica's room. He peeked in the room first to make sure she was there before entering. The sight of her childlike figure curled up on the bed alone was saddening. Apparently, she had returned to her own room sometime in the early morning hours.

The mere sound of his footsteps jolted Veronica awake.

"Robert, you came," she cried out as she turned to face the direction of the sound. Excitement turned to disappointment and embarrassment when she realized it wasn't her father.

"I came to see how you were feeling," said Paulo. "Mrs. Altro told me you were crying last night and was concerned. You know, Veronica, you're wrong about your father."

Veronica shot upright in bed.

"I have no father! Robert is only my employer! My father died the day I was born!"

Paulo could sense this was going to be difficult so he pulled up a chair and moved closer to Veronica.

"If you can remain calm and tell me what's on your mind, maybe I can help you."

"Mr. Alto, you don't understand. You can't help me; nobody can. Robert simply doesn't love me. He wasn't even concerned that I was shot."

Paulo looked at Veronica sympathetically.

"He most certainly was concerned about you getting shot. He phoned in to check on your condition every chance he got and came to the hospital just as soon as he could. If you don't believe me, you can ask David Paladino or Dr. Cristanzio. I know you would've preferred that he stay at the hospital with you but he couldn't be in two places at once. While you were being treated over here, my children were still in a life-threatening situation. He felt he had to stay until everyone got out safely. Sometimes as parents we have to make decisions that don't necessarily meet with our children's approval. Yesterday was one of those days for your father."

Veronica looked toward Paulo.

"Last night you went in to say good night to your wife and daughters, did you see my father anywhere?"

Paulo tried to explain why Robert couldn't say good night to Veronica before leaving.

"Your father had to attend to an urgent matter last night that couldn't wait. That's why he wasn't here but I'm sure he wanted to be."

Veronica looked away in disgust.

"As a child, all I wanted from my father was for him to hug and kiss me, tuck me into bed, and walk me to church, or just spend some time alone with me, but he was never available. When I did something wrong and should have been punished; Robert didn't give a damn. Why should I believe that anything's changed? Now, if you'll excuse me, I didn't get much sleep last night and suddenly feel exhausted."

Paulo smiled.

"It's important that you get your rest so I'll leave you alone for now. We can talk again later."

Paulo was upset that he hadn't made any progress with Veronica and walked away feeling defeated and bewildered. To his surprise, Veronica called him back just as he was ready to walk out the door.

"All my life, I've wanted nothing more than to sit down and have a conversation with my father the way you and I just did but he never gave me the time of day. Maybe he's disappointed that he didn't have a son. Anyway, thanks for listening to me."

Later that morning, Dr. Cristanzio arrived with news for Paulo.

"Good morning. I hope you slept well. I figured you'd want to know what was happening at your house, so on the way here this morning; I stopped by to check it out. It looks pretty good considering what took place there yesterday. They've done a superb job cleaning it up so far, and by the end of the day, they expect to have all of the windows and doors replaced. It should be as good as new very soon. Of course, you're welcome to stay at hospital longer if you wish."

"Thanks, Doc, but I think we'll be going home tonight. Franco's parents are coming to spend a few days. We should be fine."

"Whatever you think is best! Just remember, we can always accommodate the four of you if necessary."

Paulo was grateful for his offer.

"After we pick up Maria and Antonio at the airport, we'll stop at the house. If I think we should spend the night here at the hospital, I'll let you know in plenty of time. I was just on my way to wake Anna so we can go down to breakfast; I'd consider it an honor if you'd be my guest."

Dr. Cristanzio liked the idea.

"It would be my pleasure," he said in agreement. "I'll meet you there after I check my messages and inform the nurses where to find me."

No sooner had they parted ways, than they heard screaming coming from one of the rooms. Both men stopped dead in their tracks, turned to look at each other then at the same time ran toward the noise. Paulo didn't think he could take much more of this as he barreled down the long hall. All sorts of crazy thoughts went through his mind in the time it took to reach the room. He was afraid Assunta's flashbacks had started again. Worrying about his children was frazzling his nerves.

By the time Paulo and Dr. Cristanzio reached the commotion, a crowd had already formed in the hallway, blocking their entrance. Paulo spotted Anna, Assunta and Donna in the crowd and was relieved that they were all right. Then it hit him; the screaming must have been coming from Veronica's room. He pushed through the crowd to get to her door then stood there listening in horror as Veronica screamed into the phone at her father.

"Listen Robert, I'm signing myself out this morning. There's no reason for me to be cooped up in this hospital any longer. I feel fine and I want to go back to work . . . Oh please, don't play the concerned father with me. You never cared about me before, why start now . . . I don't care what the doctor says, I'm out of here."

At this point, Paulo was livid. He instructed Anna to go to the cafeteria with Dr. Cristanzio and start breakfast without him while he took care of Veronica. He entered the room, shutting the door behind him, and then before Veronica knew what was happening, he grabbed the phone from her hand.

"Good morning, Robert, this is Paulo. I don't want you to worry. I'm going to see to it that your daughter doesn't go anywhere. I'll see you later. Take care."

Veronica did not appreciate Paulo's interference and told him so. When he hung up the phone, she stood in front of him with arms crossed and asked why he did that. She told him that it wasn't any of his business.

Paulo's anger was now replaced with astonishment at Veronica's attitude. Never, had Paulo been so boldly admonished by anyone that it took him off guard and he didn't know how to respond. After some thought, he decided to ignore her lashing out and concentrate on her relationship with her father. "Veronica, this feud between you and your father is at its boiling point. I think for both your sakes, you should sit down together and try to work things out. He'll be here later this morning. If you'll allow me, I'd like to help you patch up your relationship before it's too late."

"Why would you do that for us?"

"Because I like your father; he's a good man. And I realize now that beneath that tough exterior of yours, is a young lady who wants her father's love desperately."

"Mr. Alto, you're trying to accomplish the impossible. It's too late for us."

"Veronica, it's never too late to change your life for the better. Now, I don't know about you, but I sure can use some breakfast."

Veronica wasn't very hungry but she agreed to go nonetheless. While Paulo waited for her to get ready, he felt a sudden chill run up his spine, as if warning him of impending danger. He shook his head to release the feeling and tried to replace it with positive thoughts. The feeling of doom was becoming all too familiar to him and he wasn't going to let it get the best of him.

By the time Paulo and Veronica arrived in the cafeteria, Dr. Cristanzio and Anna were almost finished eating. Anna was glad to see them. After spending most of the time worrying about them, her fears were immediately put to rest when she saw the two of them looking peaceful. She offered to get their food so they could sit down and relax. At the same time, Dr. Cristanzio excused himself apologizing for having to run off so quickly.

Alone at the table, Paulo and Veronica seemed uncomfortable, both trying hard to forget their troubles. They looked forward to the distraction of Anna returning with their food and enjoying a quiet meal. They weren't seated long before Paulo's beeper went off. It was Sheriff DeVito probably calling about Charles' preliminary hearing so Paulo left the table immediately to return his call.

Watching him as he made his way through the cafeteria and out into the hall, Veronica wondered why Paulo cared so much about her relationship with her father. She wasn't accustomed to people caring about her feelings and it confused her.

Anna made small talk with Veronica to get her mind off her father. They talked about the weather, movies and anything else Anna could think of until Paulo returned and cut their conversation short.

"I'm sorry I took so long," Paulo said when he got back to the table. As he took his seat, he looked at Veronica's plate and realized she hadn't eaten anything. "You have to eat in order to build up your strength," he suggested.

With some encouragement, Veronica managed to finish all her food. It took so long however that now Anna and Paulo would be rushed to pick up Maria and Antonio at the airport and run some errands. Paulo looked at his watch and stood up.

"Anna, it's getting late, we'd better get started."

They walked in silence all the way back to Veronica's room, where they left her to rest.

The next thing Paulo had to do before leaving was talk to Michael so he and Anna headed straight for his room that thankfully was just down the hall. By this time, they were running so late that they couldn't hang around to chat. Paulo got right to the point.

"Michael, Mama and I are leaving for a couple of hours. We have to stop at the Sheriff's DeVito's office and then head to the airport to pick up Franco's parents. I didn't tell Assunta, because I know she'd insist on coming with us, so don't say anything. While I'm gone keep an eye on things for me."

"Sure, Papa. Can you do me a favor on the way out? Leave a message for Dr. Cristanzio that I'd like to talk to him about celebrating Mass in the chapel this evening."

Paulo shook his head in disbelief.

"I can't believe I forgot that today was Sunday. I have an idea. Let's see if we can arrange with Dr. Cristanzio about the whole family having dinner together after Mass."

Paulo glanced at his watch one more time indicating that it was time to go but Michael needed a few more minutes to discuss something important with him. While Anna checked in on Gino, Michael and Paulo sat down outside in the hall.

"When do you think Franco will be joining us?" Michael asked.

"Franco needs his rest. He just had a very serious operation."

Michael looked at Paulo awkwardly as he tried to find the right words to say.

"I think Franco needs his family. Perhaps being with us is all the medicine he needs."

Paulo could see his point but couldn't agree with him just yet.

"As soon as Franco is up and about, he'll be moved down here with you guys."

"Okay, I'll take you're word for it. You always know what's best."

After Michael walked away, Paulo rejoined Anna. On their way down the hall, they heard people talking loudly in Franco's room so they stopped to listen. They stood silently in the doorway for a few minutes.

"Mr. Altro-Cordova, you need to get out of bed and start walking!"

Franco screamed at the top of his lungs, "I told you before and I'll tell you again, no way in hell!"

Paulo turned toward Anna.

"Perhaps I better speak with Franco alone. Wait for me in the lounge until I calm Franco down, then I'll come and get you."

The nurses were relieved when Paulo entered and asked them to wait outside while he talked to his son. They left without argument. Slowly then, Paulo moved toward Franco's bed. Paulo pulled a chair over so he could sit down. "What's the problem, son?"

Franco snapped at Paulo.

"I'm in no condition to walk! God only knows if I'll ever be able to walk again! Why must they be persistent?"

"They are only following orders from Dr. Gennaro."

"I don't care! There's no way in hell that I'm going to walk today!"

"Listen to me, son. After an operation, they try to get a patient up on his feet as soon as possible to avoid further complications."

"I know my condition better than you or anyone else!" Franco interrupted quite abruptly. "It's my body and I know what it's capable of doing!"

Paulo didn't back down.

"Franco Altro-Cordova, since when do you know more than the doctors?"

Franco started to interrupt again, but Paulo stopped him dead in his tracks.

"If I thought for one minute you weren't ready to walk, I'd stop you myself! No parent wants to see their child suffer needlessly, however I think you owe it to Dr. Gennaro and to yourself to at least try."

Franco had tears in his eyes now.

"You don't understand. I'm scared! What if I can't walk, then what!"

"We'll cross that bridge if we come to it."

"I'll try as long as you stay by me."

Paulo smiled. He was so proud of Franco's courage.

"It's a deal, son." Paulo carefully lifted Franco out of bed, holding him up with both hands. When it came to Franco taking that first step it was almost as if he were a baby again. Very cautiously, he extended his right foot, then the left and so forth, holding on to Paulo for dear life. After the first few steps he started to feel more confident.

"I knew you could do it son!" Paulo smiled continuing to lead Franco to the door. "There's nothing to fear except fear itself."

The nurses were still waiting outside.

"Mr. Altro, we can take over now."

Franco looked at them smiling proudly.

"If you don't mind, my father is going to walk with me to the lounge; we want to surprise my mother."

The nurses were pleased. "All right but once they leave you're all ours."

Paulo laughed. "You'd better not say that too loud because his wife is down the hall and when it comes to Franco, she is very possessive."

"Oh well, can't blame a lady for trying. It's not everyday we have such a handsome gentleman in our care."

When they arrived at the lounge, Anna was so engrossed in prayer that she didn't notice them. It wasn't until they were right next to her that she lifted her head and realized that Franco had walked. It took no time at all for her tears to start flowing.

"Mama, please don't cry."

Anna jumped up and grabbed him so hard she almost knocked him down, just in case Paulo stayed close enough to catch him if he fell. Soon, they all sat down so Franco could rest because he was showing signs of fatigue.

"Mama and I will walk you back to your room and for the rest of the morning I want you to stay in bed and rest. After lunch, you and I'll take another walk."

"How's everyone else doing?" Franco asked nervously. "Assunta stopped in to see me early this morning but I haven't seen any of the others. Was anyone seriously hurt?"

Franco looked very concerned and uneasy about not knowing the fate of his brothers and sister and Paulo assured him that no one else was hurt badly. Then it occurred to Paulo that Michael might be right. Maybe being with the boys was just what Franco needed.

"Wait here a minute, " he told Anna and Franco. Before leaving, he whispered something in Anna's ear. Within minutes, he returned with a wheelchair.

"Dr. Gennaro thinks that it will be too much for you to walk back to your room," Paulo said as he helped Franco into the wheel chair. "Okay, here we go."

When Franco realized they were going in the wrong direction, he stopped the wheel chair.

"My room is the other way," he said.

Paulo ignored him, however, and continued in the same direction. When they reached Michael and Gino's room, Paulo stopped and asked Anna to open the door. Franco was confused at first, but when he saw the boys through the small opening in the doorway, he was thrilled.

Michael was facing the door so he was the first to see them enter. He moved slowly from the bed allowing time to take in the sight of Franco at the door. Michael stopped a few feet from Franco with his arms outstretched to him. Franco lifted himself up and took a few shaky steps into Michael's arms. Paulo followed closely behind in case Franco lost his balance and fell. For the first few moments, there were no words; Michael just held Franco in his arms. The feelings they had for each other were evident to everyone.

Still holding Franco in his arms, Michael reached out and touched Paulo's shoulder.

"Thank you."

Gino watched the interaction between Michael and Franco and as soon as Franco was safely in Michael's arms, he rushed over to join them. Greetings were exchanged and then Paulo helped Franco sit on one of the beds.

"Franco is going to be staying in this room now. I know you guys have a great deal to talk about, but do me one favor, let Franco get some rest this morning. He'll need it for when his parents come to visit him. Mama and I are leaving now for the Courthouse and then the airport."

"Have you told Assunta that Franco will be staying here?" Michael asked.

"No, I haven't. I know the minute she finds out he's here, she'll want to see him and that'll be the end of his sleep. When I return from the airport, I'll tell her."

Michael escorted his parents to the elevator.

"Drive carefully," he said as he hugged them goodbye. "Your children need you."

Paulo smiled in Michael's direction.

"Thank you for the advice you gave me earlier. Franco's face lit up when he saw you two. Oh, before I forget, the last Mass is at twelve-thirty. We can use the chapel anytime after that. You can work out the details for dinner with Dr. Cristanzio."

Paulo and Anna arrived at the Courthouse just in time to meet with Judge DeStephano alone for a few minutes before the hearing. Paulo looked around the courtroom to see who was in attendance before sitting down with Judge DeStephano. Paulo was surprised to see that Robert wasn't there.

"Paulo, I've given your request a lot of thought. I don't think it would be in anyone's best interest if I were to preside over the hearing for Charles. Our friendship may come in to question and will shed some doubt over my decision. Therefore, I've recommended Judge Altimaro to hear the case. He's very fair-minded and has handled quite a number of controversial cases such as this one. He isn't available to be here today, however, because of a previous engagement but has agreed to let me officiate over today's preliminary hearing and in two weeks he'll hold the official hearing." Judge DeStephano could see the disappointment in Paulo's eyes. "Paulo, this isn't a set back; it will give Charles' defense attorney time to go over all the facts of the case. Do you have someone to represent Charles?"

"I have retained Richard DelGazzio."

"Richard is a very good choice. I'm always impressed by the way he handles himself in my courtroom and his ability to defend his clients."

Just then, the side door opened and in walked Charles accompanied by Richard DelGazzio and a court officer.

"Do you think it would be all right if Anna and I had a few minutes with Charles before you begin the hearing," Paulo asked with utmost respect.

"Take your time, Paulo. I could go for a good cup of coffee. I'll be right back."

On the way there, Paulo had explained to Anna what happened at the company after she had left with Donna. He told her about Charles' role both in the kidnapping and in the negotiations with Tony that led to their children's release. Now, Anna was as anxious to help Charles as Paulo was. She never did get a chance to thank him so this would be her opportunity.

As they approached the table where Charles was sitting, Paulo smiled at Anna. "Darling, I'd like to formally introduce you to the gentleman who helped save our children, Charles Benson."

Charles stood up bashfully to shake Anna's hand. He felt very ashamed to face her and couldn't wait for this whole thing to be over. At the same time, Richard asked to confer with Paulo in private, so Paulo excused himself and went off with Richard to the corner of the room to talk, leaving Anna and Charles alone together.

Anna sat down next to Charles, reaching for his hand.

"Charles, thank you so much for all of your help. Paulo told me what you did yesterday and I'm very grateful."

Charles was even more embarrassed now.

"Mrs. Altro, I'm sorry I was ever involved to begin with. If I had it to do over, I'd never go along with Tony."

"Charles, I'm glad you went along with Tony. Had it been any other man, he may not have done what you did. You'll always have my undying gratitude."

Fortunately for Charles, Paulo and Richard returned and interrupted their awkward conversation. As his three companions discussed strategy, all Charles could think of was how different his life would have turned out with parents like Paulo and Anna. He forgot all about why he was there until Judge DeStephano banged the gavel on the desk.

Quickly Paulo and Anna took their seats behind the divider while Richard joined Charles who was nervously awaiting the beginning of the arraignment.

"Charles Benson, will you please stand."

Richard helped Charles to his feet.

"During today's proceedings, continued the judge, I will decide your bail and whether or not you will be remanded to jail until your hearing. Your formal hearing will be held two weeks from today with Judge Altimaro. After careful review of the facts in this case submitted by both Sheriff DeVito and Robert Stone, I've decided to set bail at five hundred thousand dollars. If you're able to come up with the bail and present to this court an address where you'll be residing, the court will be agreeable. However, if you cannot do so than you'll remain at the county jail until the day of your hearing."

The judge's decision hit Charles hard. Realizing he couldn't meet these requirements, he hung his head in despair. For the first time in his life, he actually worried about what would become of his future.

Richard touched Charles' shoulder before addressing the court.

"Your honor, Mr. and Mrs. Paulo Altro have offered to post bond for Mr. Benson and in the absence of appropriate living arrangements, they are also willing to sponsor his release by acting as his custodians if he is shown leniency and placed in an informal holding area until his hearing."

Charles thought he was dreaming. He raised his head exposing his tear-streaked face, and looked at Paulo and Anna in complete disbelief. It took a while to regain his composure when the judge addressed him with his verdict.

"Mr. Charles Benson, will you please face the court? Mr. and Mrs. Paulo Altro are putting up your bail and, in light of their decision to take responsibility for your actions during the next two weeks, I'm going to make arrangements for you to serve the next two weeks in the work-study program at the county detention center for juveniles. I hope that you will use this time wisely and take advantage of the Altros generosity. Mr. Benson, do you understand the decision of the court?"

Charles found it difficult to speak. Richard spoke for him.

"Your honor, Mr. Benson is fully aware of what's expected of him. He wishes to extend his gratitude to Mr. and Mrs. Altro and the court for the kindness extended him. Mr. Benson and I will return here two weeks from tomorrow for a formal hearing with Judge Gene Altimaro."

"This court stands adjourned until two weeks from tomorrow," Judge DeStephano declared with one last stroke of the gavel.

Anna approached Charles excitedly but before she could say anything, Charles began groveling.

"Mrs. Altro, I can't thank you enough. How will I ever be able to repay you?"

"One thing you can do is stop calling us Mr. and Mrs. Altro. My name is Anna and my husband's name is Paulo. That's what our friends call us. I'm glad things worked out well today. Take care of yourself and if you need anything at all, please call us. We'll be back here in two weeks to see you through the trial."

After a brief conference with the judge, Paulo approached to talk to Charles as well. Now, Richard, Paulo and Anna all stood around the table wishing Charles well, giving him advice and guidance and informing him of their strategy for the trial. It was unconventional to allow the defendant time with family and friends after a ruling, but Judge Altimaro saw no harm in it in this case since Paulo was a friend of his. Soon enough, they all bid farewell and went their separate ways.

On the way out, Paulo and Anna spotted Robert waiting near the exit at the back of the courtroom. He had arrived late and didn't want to disrupt the hearing so he took a seat in the back to listen and was satisfied with the outcome. Robert was anxious to get more details about Charles' trial so Paulo invited him along to pick up Maria and Antonio and have lunch with them. As soon as Robert accepted his offer, they made a dash for the car and left for the airport. They pulled into the airport parking lot with only five minutes to spare, which was cutting it close in Paulo's opinion.

The only thing on Maria's and Antonio's minds during the flight was Franco's recovery. They couldn't wait to see for themselves that he was all right. They worried about him so much and knew the only place for them right now was by his side but the more they thought about it, the longer it seemed to take to get there. When they finally got off of the plane and met Anna and Paulo, they immediately bombarded them with questions about the ordeal.

"Franco is coming along just fine. Given a few days rest, I guarantee, he'll be right back on his feet. As a matter of fact, he has already taken a couple of steps," Paulo exclaimed.

It was obvious that Maria and Antonio were relieved. Before they could ask any more questions, Paulo took the opportunity to make the necessary introductions.

"Maria, Antonio I want you to meet the man in charge of saving our children." Placing his hand on Robert's shoulder, he said, "This gentleman here is Robert Stone and if it wasn't for his dedication and determination, we might not have been so fortunate."

Antonio gave him a warm embrace.

"Paulo has told me all about you. You have our deepest gratitude. In the future, if there's anything you need, please don't hesitate to call on me. If it's within my means, I'll see to it that you have it."

Paulo interrupted just then.

"Antonio, if it's all right with you and Maria, we'd like to stop at Giuseppe's for lunch before heading to the hospital."

Antonio and Maria were famished so they were thankful for the offer and readily agreed. Besides, thought Antonio, it would be a good opportunity to get all of the facts once and for all.

The restaurant was crowded as usual with the lunch rush, but Giuseppe found a way to make accommodations for them. The Altros were his best customers and he was always happy to see them. He immediately escorted them to his best available table. Once seated, Paulo and Robert explained everything to Maria and Antonio. It was a relief to finally be able to discuss Franco's condition without interruptions. It took some time for them to absorb the details, but afterward they were able to relax and enjoy their meal.

While Anna chatted with them about Assunta's antics, Paulo turned his attention to Robert and tried to get him to open up about Veronica.

"Your daughter is almost as challenging as mine. Daughters are much tougher then sons."

"I wouldn't know since I never had a son," Robert sighed. "I know one thing for sure, nothing I say or do is ever right. When she phoned me this morning, she was livid but everything I said to calm her down only made things worse."

Paulo thought carefully for a minute.

"I'm concerned about the two of you and I'd like to help, if you'll let me. Why don't the three of us talk after dinner tonight?"

"Do yourself a favor and stop trying to figure her out. I stopped a long time ago."

Paulo was surprised by Robert's attitude.

"She's your daughter! You can't give up on your relationship!"

Robert's expression changed and his eyes revealed the confusion he was feeling.

"I've tried time and time again only to walk away crushed. There's only so much a parent can take before they realize it's a lost cause."

"Veronica isn't a lost cause! She's looking for love and doesn't realize she can have it with you. It's staring her in the face, but she can't see it."

"If you think it will do any good, I'm willing to try," Robert said. Then in a more serious tone, he spoke again, "I wish Veronica loved me but . . . " He stopped abruptly. He couldn't finish his sentence because the thought of their failed relationship upset him so much.

No one was in the mood for conversation during the drive to the hospital. Lack of sleep combined with a large satisfying meal left them all feeling rather sluggish. Robert occupied his time with thoughts of Veronica while Maria and Antonio distracted themselves by anticipating visiting their son. By the time they pulled in to the hospital parking lot, it was already after two o'clock.

Eager to see their children, they headed straight for the fourth floor. When Paulo opened the door to the boys' room, his heart skipped a beat seeing the room empty. He was afraid something had happened to Franco but didn't dare mention it because he didn't want to worry anyone needlessly. Instead, he told everyone to hang out there for a bit while he went to find Franco.

What Paulo didn't know was that everyone, including Franco, was in the cafeteria discussing his birthday party. Michael was trying desperately to figure out how they were going to pull it off.

"Listen, we have a real problem. Papa's dinner is scheduled for next Sunday and we still have a great deal to do. How are we going to run around to make the final preparations if Papa doesn't let us out of his sight?"

"Do you think Papa will keep that tight of a reign on us when we get home," Assunta asked innocently.

"Try to put yourself in his place. What would you do, if your children were held for ransom and almost killed?"

Assunta was horrified at the thought.

"I wouldn't let my children out of my sight."

Michael nodded his head, "There you go, exactly what I suspected. I'm open for any suggestions. How are we going to get everything done with Papa breathing down our necks?"

When no one responded, Michael sighed reluctant to continue.

"Then there's only one thing left to do. We have to phone everyone and tell them the party is off."

Up until this point, Veronica sat quietly just listening but she had an idea that she thought might work so she interrupted before anyone else had a chance to speak.

"Why don't I do all the running around for you? I'll just tell Robert that I decided to stay home and get some rest."

Assunta hugged Veronica with all her might

"That's a great idea. You're a life saver."

With everyone in agreement, they finished up just in time to see Paulo heading their way. Quickly, Michael thought up an excuse for why they were all there. He knew Paulo would want to know what they were up to. Michael stood up facing Paulo.

"Doctor Cristanzio suggested Franco take a walk so we decided to come down for a cup of coffee," Michael burst out before Paulo even asked.

Paulo smiled at Michael.

"I know. I bumped into Dr. Cristanzio at the nurses' station and he told me where to find you. How's Franco managing?"

"So far, so good. He made it here with no problem. By the way, I made arrangements with Dr. Cristanzio for the Mass at five o'clock in the chapel."

Paulo looked at his watch. "That'll work out well. Giuseppe is delivering dinner between six and six-thirty. We can set it up in one of the conference rooms on the first floor."

Paulo's attention then turned toward Franco.

"How are you feeling?"

"Not bad, actually pretty good. It's a little bit easier walking now than when I first tried with you this morning. About this morning . . ."

Paulo interrupted, "This morning is gone so let's not speak of it anymore.

We have more important things to do."

It wasn't fair to let Maria and Antonio wait any longer so Paulo hurried and helped Franco back into his wheelchair and called Assunta over to join them. He explained that he had a surprise waiting for them. Soon, Paulo, Assunta, and Franco were riding the elevator to the fourth floor. It was unusual behavior for her but somehow Assunta managed to stay quiet all the way up. Her curiosity was peaked but she didn't want to upset Paulo.

It was a wonderful surprise. Franco and Assunta were overjoyed when they saw Maria and Antonio. Likewise, the Cordovas were ecstatic. It was a joyous time for Maria and Antonio. They had come very close to losing their son and were grateful to Almighty God for his survival. Maria became overwhelmed at the sight of Franco and began crying. With every ounce of strength he could muster, Franco stood up and walked toward his parents. The three of them ended up in a long heartfelt embrace.

Assunta held on to Paulo's arm as she watched Franco with his parents. "Papa, you've made Franco very happy."

After Mass in the chapel, everyone met in the large conference room on the first floor. The table looked exquisite and the food was terrific. For the first time since the unthinkable incident, everyone actually seemed like their old selves. At about eight o'clock, after languishing over his meal, Paulo felt it was time to get Robert and Veronica together.

"Anna," he whispered, "Robert and I are going to meet with Veronica for a few minutes. I'd like you to come with us. I value your touch, especially in a delicate situation such as this."

Before leaving, Paulo talked to Michael for a minute.

"Mama and I are leaving with Robert and Veronica for a brief meeting. I'm going to try to get those two speaking again. We'll be in Dr. Cristanzio's office if you need me. Please see to it that Giuseppe sets up the dessert table soon. If we're not back by the time it comes out, let everyone help themselves and we'll join you as soon as we're through."

Paulo left Michael feeling confident that everything would work out just fine. He took Robert by the arm.

"Are you ready to talk to Veronica?"

"Is she willing to meet with me?" Robert inquired.

Paulo smiled, "Leave it to me."

Veronica was in the middle of a conversation with Assunta when Paulo approached them and asked Veronica if she could meet with him for a few minutes. She couldn't imagine what they possibly had to talk about but agreed anyway. Anna held her hand out to Veronica when she stood up then they all walked toward the door together in silence.

David noticed the three of them walking toward the door and questioned Michael.

"What's that all about?"

"Papa wants to help mend Robert and Veronica's relationship."

David nodded, "I hope he can. It certainly is the object of great stress for Robert. Veronica is like an angel from heaven sometimes, but when she throws one of her fits, she's more like the devil. She's such a complex person."

"When did you realize you were in love with her?" Franco asked shrewdly after overhearing the conversation.

"From the moment . . . Wait a minute, who said I was in love with Veronica? She's a spoiled, self-centered, arrogant witch. She makes me want to . . . "

"No need to explain. In fact, she reminds me of Assunta when we first met. She was a spoiled brat back then yet I instantly knew that she'd be my wife some day. We met the day that I interviewed at Palmieri's Bakery and it was love at first sight, for me at least. After the interview, Mr. Palmieri offered me the supervisory position and I was thrilled but when Assunta found out, she went crazy.

"Assunta made my life a living hell. She harassed me every step of the way until I warned her to back off. I let her know that she'd regret messing with me. Then one day, she pushed me too far. Her attitude changed from that day forward. It wasn't too long afterward that we started to date. The rest is history."

# Chapter 8

## Stress Catches Up With Robert

On the way to Dr. Cristanzio's office, Veronica felt comfort in the fact that Anna was accompanying her.

"I appreciate your coming in with me."

The short trip to the office seemed like an eternity to Veronica. Once they were all seated Paulo began the conversation. Paulo opened the discussion. He suggested that Robert and Veronica begin to correct their relationship.

"Veronica, you told me your father doesn't love you and he never has."

Veronica was stone-faced.

"That's absolutely correct," she said. "I'm his daughter in name only. He never wanted me from the day I was born."

Robert needed to defend himself.

"That's not true. When you were born I was so proud of you." Robert stood up. "What's the use? You won't believe me anyway."

"How can you sit there and deny what I'm saying!" Veronica's eyes opened wide. "You never cared about me when I was growing up! We never spent time together unless Mama was with us! When I went to bed you didn't come up to say good night. Instead you stayed downstairs watching television until Mama came up to bed! I can't once remember being alone with you! When you went to the store I always wanted to jump in the car and take a ride! You never asked me!"

"Your mother wouldn't have permitted me to take you."

"That's a lie, God damn it, and you know it!" Veronica banged her hand on the chair. "She'd never stop you from taking me for a ride to the store! You didn't want me in your car. You hated me and were ashamed to be seen in my company!" Veronica's facial expression changed. "I hated you Robert Stone and will always hate you as long as I live!"

Paulo walked over to Veronica and held her hand since he could see her trembling.

"Please calm down. No one is here to hurt you. I suggested this meeting so perhaps you and your father can work out your differences. Give your father a chance to speak and then you can have your say. If he can't finish telling you how he feels this meeting will be in vain. In all fairness to your father I believe you should give him a chance to explain why he reacted the way he did in your childhood."

Veronica tearfully looked to Robert.

"Will you please explain to me why you never loved me?"

Robert kept his head down not answering Veronica.

"You see, I was right! My father can't even look at me and tell me why he hates me! Had I been a boy he'd have danced in the street!"

Robert couldn't take any more.

Her accusations were the straw that broke the camel's back.

"That isn't true! The entire time your mother carried you I prayed for a daughter! The day you were born my wish became reality!"

Veronica didn't believe him.

"You're nothing but a God damn liar!"

Paulo expression was enough for Anna to know that she had to take control for Veronica's sake.

"Robert, try to understand how Veronica is feeling at this moment," she said.

"I understand, but there's nothing I can do that'll right all the wrong she feels in her heart," said Robert, feeling defeated.

Paulo gathered his thoughts before speaking.

"Veronica has a right to know why you acted the way you did toward her. What drove you to show no love for this daughter you claim to love from the day she was born?"

"I did love her from the day she was born. It was her moth . . ." Robert suddenly stopped dead.

Paulo could see his hesitation.

"Today you told me the one thing that would make you happy is if Veronica would love you half as much as you love her. Is that not correct?"

Robert nodded his head.

"Tell Veronica what drove you to withdraw from her during her childhood."

Robert lifted his head with deep emotion and began to speak.

"It doesn't matter anymore. Let's just drop the entire issue. At my age it doesn't matter."

Paulo was becoming frustrated at their lack of progress.

"Like hell! You owe your daughter an explanation and we're not leaving until you give her one!"

"It hurts too much!" Robert admitted.

"How can you sit there and tell me it hurts too much!" Paulo banged the desk. "Your daughter has been hurt her entire life and deserves an explanation!"

"You and everyone else wouldn't understand!" Robert shouted back.

"Try me!" said Paulo as he sat back waiting for an explanation.

Robert chose is words carefully. He was sure Veronica would be devastated by the truth.

"When Carol and I married I thought I had the world at my fingertips. I loved her and knew she loved me. The only thing that would have made our life more enjoyable was to conceive a child. God granted us that wish within the first three months of our marriage. We celebrated for days at the news of Carol's conception. From the very start I wanted a daughter as beautiful as her mother; Carol differed with me and wanted a boy."

Veronica interrupted angrily.

"You lying son of a bitch! That's a lie and you know it!"

Robert looked directly into Veronica's eyes with love and compassion. "Your mother had a deep seeded problem which caused her to act strangely concerning my relationship with you. We both went into counseling hoping this would cure her feelings. Nothing ever came out of it."

Veronica started to lose control of her temper.

"I won't sit here and listen to you tell me one lie after the other! He's blaming my mother now because she's dead! He didn't want me! She never kept me away from him! Why is he lying?"

Veronica turned toward Anna sobbing uncontrollably.

Paulo at the same time asked to see Robert in the outer office. After he closed the door between both offices he sat down with Robert on a sofa near by.

"You've to tell Veronica the whole truth; it's quite obvious to me you're skirting the issue."

Robert held his head down speaking in a barely audible tone.

"I've told Veronica everything I can tell her. Carol would prefer it this way." Suddenly Robert started to grab for his chest as if he were fighting for breath.

Paulo ran into the hallway and shouted for help.

"There's a man in here possibly having a heart attack."

Within seconds a couple of interns were by Robert's side. One of them called for assistance while the other started mouth-to mouth resuscitation. Before long people were surrounding Robert. Dr. Cristanzio came rushing in. "What happened?"

Paulo himself was still trying to figure out what happened.

"I'm not sure. We were talking in your outer office when suddenly Robert grabbed his chest! I ran outside and fortunately two of your interns were passing by, who came in to assist him!"

Veronica and Anna were unaware what was going on in the outer office.

"I can't stand to hear all these lies! Please take me back to the room!"

Anna held Veronica for a few more minutes trying to soothe her. As they stood up Anna could feel Veronica trembling.

"Before we leave we should let Robert and Paulo know where we're going."

When Anna opened the door she immediately noticed Robert lying on the floor. The first thing Veronica noticed was the crash cart and someone trying to shock Robert's heart. Veronica passed out at the sight. Paulo quickly ran over lifting Veronica up in his arms and laying her on another sofa. Veronica came to, she struggled to get to her father's side.

Paulo grabbed Veronica's arms to restrain her.

"Let them work on your father. There's nothing you can do to help him."

Veronica kept pulling away from Paulo with all her force.

"I caused this to happen; this is all my fault! I didn't mean all those things I said!"

Paulo put his hand under her chin and made Veronica look into his eyes.

"Veronica Stone, listen to me! This isn't your fault! I know for a fact that your father has been seeing a cardiologist here at the hospital! I know that it looks bad right now but this is only temporary."

Veronica couldn't stop the tears from flowing down her face. She leaned against Paulo's chest praying that he was telling her the truth.

Dr. Cristanzio came over to give them an update.

"Paulo, it's a good thing you were with him; he may not have survived without immediate attention. He's stable now. They'll bring him up to his room in a few minutes."

Veronica tried to get up.

"I want to go with my father! You can't stop me!"

Dr. Cristanzio insisted she stay put.

"I know you don't like following orders but this time you've no choice. They are bringing your father into a room in Cardiac Care. It's going to take them some time to get him situated. I want you to stay with Paulo and Anna until I send for you. I promise I'll take you to see your father as soon as they are through. Is it a deal?"

Veronica hesitated momentarily and then nodded her head. She was quite shaken, but was sensible enough to trust Dr. Cristanzio. Anna joined Veronica on the sofa, trying to comfort her, while Paulo and Dr. Cristanzio went to check on Robert's condition. As soon as they were alone, Dr. Cristanzio asked Paulo what happened. Paulo explained what had taken place previous to the heart attack.

The story Paulo recounted didn't seem to surprise Dr. Cristanzio. His lack of reaction led Paulo to believe that he had been aware of the situation all along.

Paulo's curiosity had peaked. He needed to know what Robert was hiding so he questioned Dr. Cristanzio.

"Do you know for sure that Robert was telling Veronica the truth?"

Dr. Cristanzio led Paulo over to a row of chairs down the hall.

"Paulo, I'm going to take you into my confidence and explain certain facts that are considered Doctor-patient confidentially. You are trying to heal the wounds between Robert and Veronica and need to hear the truth in order to help the process to begin.

"One day, Robert came in inquiring about counseling at the hospital and he was recommended to me. I treated Carol on and off for about ten years. Carol was extremely protective of her daughter and wouldn't let anyone near her especially Robert. Her father had abused her and she feared Robert would do the same to her daughter. Carol just couldn't dump the baggage of her childhood."

Paulo almost regretted asking. His heart went out to Robert and Veronica for being denied each other's love.

"That answers my questions. Now. I want to know how serious is Robert's condition?"

"That's hard to tell until all the testing is completed. My opinion, off the record, is he'll make it. The trouble with Robert is, he doesn't know how to slow down. Robert and I have talked about this for the past three years. If Robert continues at this pace he won't have a long life."

Paulo stood up.

"When Robert is on his feet I'll convince him to slow down. I should get back to Veronica."

Dr. Cristanzio walked Paulo over to where Anna and Veronica were sitting. He put his hand on Veronica's shoulder.

"I think you should get some rest. Your father won't be settled in for some time. I'll phone your room as soon as you're able to see him."

The tears were streaming down her face.

"I didn't mean all those horrible things I said about my father. If anything happens to him, I'll never forgive myself."

It was only natural that she felt this way, but Paulo wanted Veronica to understand that it wasn't her fault.

"Veronica, sometimes we say something out of anger instead of love. We're human and human beings make mistakes. The important thing is you take this lesson and learn from it. No more tears; you've cried enough for one evening. Let me take you back to your room."

Veronica didn't want to be alone. She turned to Anna for support.

"Will you please stay with me until I'm ready to see my father."

Anna smiled pulling the hair away from Veronica's eyes and said, "Of course I will."

At Paulo's insistence they proceeded to Veronica's room to await word from Dr. Cristanzio. Anna never left Veronica's side. She did everything she could to make Veronica feel safe and secure. Paulo watched Anna as she tried to comfort Veronica and felt warm inside. She was amazing and he intended to cherish her as long as he lived. Paulo decided to leave them alone to talk. He figured he could use the time to break the news about Robert to the others. When Paulo made his exit, Veronica spoke openly to Anna.

"You and Paulo have been so kind to me. How will I ever repay you?"

Anna moved the hair from Veronica's forehead.

"You owe us nothing. When Paulo and I get attached to someone as we did with you, it doesn't end there. You invariably become part of our extended family."

"But I'm a total stranger," Veronica replied obviously confused.

Anna shook her head in disagreement.

"You're so wrong. There's always room in our heart to love someone who needs love. I think it's time for you to rest. We'll talk later. I'll be sitting right here if you need me."

By the time Paulo finally returned to the conference room everyone was finishing up their desert. At first he went unnoticed, but it wasn't long before Michael spotted him. He could tell something was wrong by looking at him. He nudged Franco to get his attention before approaching Paulo.

"Papa, what's wrong?" said Michael as he helped Paulo to a chair and signaled Assunta to bring him a glass of water. The room went silent.

"Robert had a heart attack in Dr. Cristanzio's office. His heart stopped but the doctors managed to stabilize him. He isn't out of the woods yet. The next twenty-four hours will decide his fate."

Michael asked Assunta to get him his jacket. After putting it on, Michael questioned Paulo.

"Where did they take Robert?"

"Robert is in Cardiac Care, on the fifth floor."

"I believe my place is with Robert," said Michael. He checked for his oils before starting for the door.

Paulo reached him before he walked out.

"Mama and I are going to take Veronica to see Robert shortly. We'll meet you there."

Assunta interrupted her Papa.

"How's Veronica?"

Paulo's expression showed concern.

"Mama is with her now. She's upset. I think once she sees Robert she'll feel relieved."

"Do you think all the stress Mr. Stone was under yesterday caused him to have the heart attack?" Franco asked with concern.

David answered before Paulo had a chance.

"Robert has been under a great deal of stress for quite some time now. He confided in me that he had been in for a cardiac check up a few months ago. Dr. Romano advised Robert to slow down or he'd pay the consequences. When I worked in the office with him, I tried to take the pressure off him. It worked out well for a little while until Veronica started to work there. I never knew she was his daughter. The only thing I knew was he cared for her a great deal and wanted me to keep an eye on her. We worked together constantly at the beginning, but then I requested he find someone else to play nursemaid. She made my life miserable. Her greatest moments came when she'd undermine me in front of the others. Realizing I was ready to walk away from the company Robert reassigned Veronica to another partner. That lasted one week. Since that time she has had three different partners. Veronica's problem is she's head strong and refuses to follow orders."

Paulo confirmed what David said.

"David is right. Dr. Cristanzio told me Robert has been told time and time again to slow down. I guess that's where Veronica gets her temperament."

Before it got too late Paulo wanted to settle the sleeping arrangements for the night.

"Antonio, I think it best we spend the night here at the hospital. Anna and I'll probably be spending most of the night in Cardiac Care with Veronica. If anything comes up, you can reach me there."

"Don't worry about anything. See to it that Veronica and her father make amends. I knew of a boy once who never had a chance to see his father before he died. He and his father had a bitter fight that morning before his father left for work. He swore the argument caused the heart attack. The hurt stayed with him until the day of his death. The boy I'm speaking about was my brother Daniel."

Absolute silence fell over the room. Paulo thought about what Antonio had just said and then got up to leave.

In the hallway he bumped into Dr. Cristanzio, who was Chief of Staff.

"How's Robert?"

"He's settled in now. It would be a good idea for you to take Veronica to see him. If I see her getting too emotional, I'll ask you to remove her. I don't want Robert to get upset."

Dr. Cristanzio's beeper went off and he darted toward the stairs. Paulo had a feeling the emergency was Robert and shot out after him. No sooner had Paulo opened the door then he realized he was right. The room was filled with doctors and nurses trying desperately to save Robert. Watching them, Paulo prayed silently for a miracle. Finally, Robert's heart started to beat on its own. His cardiologist Dr. Romano came out to speak with Dr. Cristanzio.

"That was a close call. I think we should do a catheterization as quickly as possible. This isn't normal for Robert. Robert's problem up to now has been stress, which caused an irregular heartbeat. It's treatable by medication. Now we're in another ball game. This is the second time his heart stopped in less than two hours. I don't think his heart can take a third time."

Dr. Cristanzio nodded his head in agreement.

"John, set it up as soon as possible."

Dr. Romano immediately set out to contact his team.

Paulo could see the look of concern in Dr. Cristanzio's eyes.

"How serious is this?" he asked, but didn't wait for an answer. "Never mind, I know what I've to do. Is it possible for Veronica to see her father before they do the catheterization?"

"I'll tell Dr. Romano to hold up until you get back with Veronica. Be as quick as you can."

Paulo hurried realizing this was a life-threatening situation and he'd have to handle Veronica carefully. Paulo took the elevator to the fourth floor the entire time thinking how he'd break the news to Veronica. She had been expecting Paulo to return soon. When he entered, she sat straight up to hear the news. Veronica didn't like the look on Paulo's face.

"Please don't tell me my father is dead?" Veronica pleaded.

Paulo pulled the chair over and sat down.

"Your father has had another heart attack, this one more serious than the first. They are getting ready to take him for a catheterization. Dr. Romano is going to wait until you see him before he goes to surgery."

Veronica jumped up and started to dash for the door when Paulo stopped her.

"I'll take you to see your father if you promise me you won't get upset. If your Papa sees you upset then he'll become upset. That won't be good him before surgery. I know how difficult this is for you, but you need to be braver than you've ever been in your life. You won't be alone. Anna and I won't leave your side and I promise we'll stay in the lounge until the operation is over. Is that a deal?"

Veronica nodded her head.

They took the elevator to the fifth floor. Veronica held Paulo's hand tightly as they approached Robert's room. Michael was already by Robert's side anointing him as the nurses worked diligently preparing him for surgery.

"It's not as bad as it looks. They are simply preparing him for surgery."

Veronica made her way through the crowded room to where Robert was lying and kissed him.

"I never told you before but I love you! I know we have had a turbulent relationship but I promise it will be different once you're on your feet! Please hang in there for me!"

Veronica kissed Robert again before they whisked him off to the operating room.

Paulo, Veronica, and Anna went directly to the lounge.

"I told Dr. Cristanzio we would wait here until the catheterization is over."

Dr. Cristanzio came out and spoke with Paulo once they were settled in the operating room.

"It should take a couple of hours, Paulo. Wouldn't you rather go back to the fourth floor; I'll call when it's over."

Looking in Veronica's direction, Paulo answered: "Veronica wants to stay in the lounge and wait. Will you let us know as soon as you hear any news?"

Just then Michael appeared at the door. Paulo could see how distraught he had become.

"Come sit down, " Paulo called out to him.

Michael sat next to Paulo with his head down trying to focus.

Paulo could tell Michael was disturbed.

"Talk to me, son."

Michael remained with his head bowed.

"Sometimes, I believe I chose the wrong vocation in life. I understand that death is always a thief at one's door but when it begins to stalk someone close to you it becomes difficult to accept."

"None of us know when the Lord will call us home, but when he does you help make that final journey in life a little easier. When you're through people feel the Grace of God all around and are no longer afraid. They accept the sorrow of death and look forward to their eternal reward. I pray when the Lord calls me home, I'll have you by my side to show me the way. From the moment you were born, God chose you for his ministry here on earth. I remember a familiar quote from my early years in catholic school,

'Many are called, but few are chosen'. I knew the day Pope David, then Deacon Pollato, visited us for lunch and you put on his shirt, collar, and jacket, your destiny in life."

"I remember that day as if it were yesterday." Michael cracked a smile. "You were so angry with me for touching Deacon Pollato's things. I also remember Deacon Pollato saved me when he told me I looked good in his clothing. I thought I looked good, too. I watched your anger disappear and a tranquil look take over your face. Now I know why."

"I remember that also. A calmness came over my body I never experienced before."

Once again Michael could see that same look.

"Papa, what's wrong?"

Paulo gathered his thoughts first.

"Michael, God put you here on earth for a specific goal. Someday you'll prove to the world that his selecting you wasn't done in vain. Now tell me about Robert."

"I spoke with Robert just before they put him under. He told me to give you a message. Keep an eye on his little girl until he's able to do so himself. It has taken this long to find her and he doesn't want to lose her."

Paulo looked over at Veronica praying she wouldn't lose her father. Michael left shortly thereafter. He knew the others were wondering what was going on.

The operation started shortly after ten. Sometime around one in the morning Dr. Romano entered the lounge. He awoke Paulo to give him the news. The smile on his face gave it away.

"The operation is over. Robert is a lucky man. He has a very small clot that we'll dissolve. We also will be starting him on new heart medication. If he takes his medication, keeps up with his diet, and relaxes, he can lead a long life. The most important thing is to convince him to slow down at work."

Paulo nodded his head.

"That's gong to be my job. Let me wake Veronica up so you can speak with her."

Paulo gently nudged her on the shoulder.

"Veronica, Dr. Romano is here to speak with you."

At the sound of Paulo's voice, Veronica jumped up.

"My father, is he . . ?"

"Everything went well," said Dr. Romano as he took her hand.

"There's a small clot that we're taking care of. He must take his medication and watch his diet. It's also very important for him to avoid stress. I suggest you try to get him to spend less time at work."

Veronica could feel the adrenaline in her system building up.

"When can I see him?"

"I'll allow you to see him for a few minutes." John looked at Paulo. "No excitement."

Paulo and Anna walked Veronica over to spend a few minutes with Robert. The reunion was a touching scene. Veronica leaned over the bed and wiped Robert's forehead. Then tucked him in carefully avoiding the tubes attached to his arm.

"You're a welcome sight." Veronica smiled lovingly at Robert. "For a minute there I thought you decided to cut out on me. Papa, I don't know if you remember me telling you, so I'm going to repeat what I said before they took you into the operating room. I love you and need you in my life. In the past I was pretty mean to you, but that's over. I wish I could take back every mean thing I said or did that caused you pain, but I know that's impossible. The only thing I can do is to grow as a person from this day forward and be the best daughter I can. That's the least I can do since you've always been the best father you could have been. I realize I was totally blind to reality and ready to condemn you. I misjudged you and for this I ask your forgiveness."

A simple nod was the only thing necessary.

"Did you see that? Papa is going to be fine."

Veronica addressed Robert once again.

"It's important for you to rest now. When you're ready to come home, we're going to sit down and talk. You can't keep going at this pace. I'm going to leave so you can rest. I promise as soon as Dr. Romano tells me I can visit I'll come back." Veronica bent down to kiss Robert. "Please do as the Doctors tell you because it took me a long time to find you. I don't want to lose you now." She walked away from the bed indicating to Paulo her intent to leave.

Once the door closed, she grabbed on to Paulo and held him tightly.

"He looks so pale. What am I going to do if anything happens to him?" Paulo rubbed her back trying to comfort her.

"Nothing is going to happen," he said.

"Your father is well on the way to recovery. He'll look one hundred percent better the next time you see him. Wait and see."

Looking at his watch he realized it was three o'clock.

Paulo put his arm around Anna.

"Lets go back to the room so both of you can get some rest." Together they walked to the elevator.

Once they arrived on the fourth floor they noticed Franco, Assunta, Michael, and David sleeping in the lounge. They had decided to sit in the lounge and wait for Veronica to return with word of Robert.

Paulo looked around and couldn't believe his eyes.

"Anna, you get Veronica in bed and get some rest yourself. I'm going to the nurse's station to get some blankets and pillows for these guys rather then wake them. See you in the morning darling."

After kissing Anna, Paulo started for the nurse's station.

"Excuse me, may I've four pillows and blankets for my children who are sleeping on the sofas in the lounge."

The nurse recognized Paulo and didn't hesitate to meet his request.

"If you need anything else feel free to let us know."

Paulo lifted everything in his arms.

"This is plenty. Thank you for your kindness."

Back in the lounge he proceeded to place a pillow under each of their heads and cover them with blankets. As Paulo was covering Franco he opened his eyes.

"How's Mr. Stone?"

Paulo finished covering him.

"Fine, son, no more talk. Get some sleep."

Franco closed his eyes.

"Good night, Papa."

"Good night, Franco."

Paulo then he walked over to Michael who was clutching his rosary beads in his hand. Paulo gently lifted them out, and put them in Michael's jacket pocket. After placing the pillow under Michael's head, he covered him. He did the same with Assunta and David. Paulo then dimmed the overhead light. Paulo went into the boys' room as quietly as possible.

Antonio was a light sleeper and immediately heard Paulo. "How did the surgery go with Robert?"

Paulo unbuttoned his shirt and sat down.

"Dr. Romano was very optimistic after the surgery," said Paulo with a smile on his face. "With the proper diet, medication, and rest Robert will be fine. Good night, Antonio. Talk to you in the morning."

Antonio rolled over and fell asleep. Paulo lay on his bed looking up to the ceiling.

"Saint Michael, besides my family tonight will you keep a special eye on Veronica and Robert for me."

Paulo turned over and fell asleep from exhaustion.

Some time later, Assunta woke up wondering where her pillow and blanket came from. Michael was closet to her so she nudged him.

"Michael, where did we get the pillows and blankets?"

Michael glanced at his watch and then at Assunta.

"From Santa Claus, who else.  Go back to bed, it's only six o'clock."

Michael turned over making himself comfortable.  Assunta tried to fall asleep but couldn't.  After twisting and turning for almost twenty minutes she decided to go up to the fifth floor and see how Robert was doing.

She stopped at the nurses' station to make sure it was okay.

"Hi, Karen, I was wondering if it would be possible for me to spend a few minutes with Robert Stone."

Karen was happy to see Assunta.

"Mr. Stone is still in Cardiac Care.  Let  me phone ahead to tell them you're coming."

After Karen made the call, she led Assunta down to the Cardiac Care Unit.

The Cardiac Care Unit took up half the fifth floor.  To enter the CCU, you go through two large doors, which lead to a huge circular room.  Outlining the room are fifteen or twenty individual patients units.  The units were all constructed of clear plastic.  This would allow the nurses to view any activity without actually having to leave the station.  In the center was a station for the nurses and doctors.  There was also a massive support post where up to three nurses could be seen day and night standing guard.  Robert was situated right across from the nurse's station.  When Assunta walked into Robert's room she was amazed at the various machines surrounding him.  Each machine recorded distinct patterns displaying all vital signs both in their room and at the nurse's station.  Assunta sat down next to Robert, staring at him.  She almost felt what it would be like to be in Veronica's shoes.  She saw Robert trying to move his hand and realized he was reaching for the water.  After checking with the nurse if she could give him water she assisted him.

Robert finished the water and then smiled at Assunta.

"Thank you, Assunta.  I've been dying for a drink of water."

"Mr. Stone, how do you feel?"

"Tired," he said.

Assunta wiped his forehead with a towel.

"My parents and Veronica were here until after your operation.  They are downstairs trying to get some rest, you should be doing the same.  I'll be back later with Veronica."

Assunta covered Robert with the blanket.

Before leaving the floor she walked over to the nurses station and thanked them for their help.  Assunta started to leave when she heard Robert calling out from his room.

Both Assunta and the nurse rushed into Robert's room.

"Mr. Stone, is anything wrong."

_Absolution_

"I'd like Assunta to stay."

The nurse looked to Assunta.

"Assunta, when you're ready to leave let me know."

Assunta sat down next to Robert's bed.

"Is there anything I can do for you?"

Robert nodded his head.

"I'd like you to call me Robert, not Mr. Stone. I admire the relationship you have with your father. You must have been the 'Princess' in the family. I didn't have a chance to do that for Veronica. We missed all those years."

Assunta held his hand.

"So did I."

"I don't understand." Robert said with confusion.

Assunta moved closer to Robert.

"I first met Papa right before my engagement. Since Franco was living with Mama and Papa, Papa agreed to pay for our engagement party and wedding. Papa is such a loving and caring man that it's difficult not to become attached. One day while I was sitting out back Papa joined me. I found the courage to ask Papa if he'd give me away. To my surprise he agreed. Shortly afterwards, Papa and Mama adopted me. That was the happiest day in my life," said Assunta smiling as she recalled.

"At first Papa spoiled me rotten. I enjoyed every minute of it. Eventually Papa realized what was happening and stopped me dead in my tracks. He can be as gentle as a kitten or as tough as a lion. The important thing is he loves me and accepts me in spite of all my shortcomings. Papa calls it unconditional love, I call it a blessing from above."

"I wish it could be like that for me and Veronica."

"It can be. Veronica is going to need you the same as I needed Papa. Papa was there for me during one of the most trying times in my life. I had to work through a problem I had during my childhood the same as Veronica. Papa attended counseling sessions with me even when they were brutal. It wasn't easy for Papa to sit there and listen to the stories of my childhood but it was a necessary part of my therapy. There were times when I'd want to stop the session, that's when Papa would shine the most in my eyes. He'd hold me and I could feel his love. It was at these times that Papa would give me the strength to continue. You can do the same for Veronica. Reach out and offer your hand to her; she'll do the rest. I really must go now. Papa doesn't know I'm up here." Assunta leaned over and kissed Robert before leaving.

When Assunta reached the lounge she was relieved to find everyone still sleeping. Walking over to the sofa she fluffed up her pillow and tried to fall back to sleep. It was then that she could feel someone else's presence

132

in the room. Slowly she turned to see Veronica sitting down in one of the chairs. "Veronica, you startled me. Is there anything wrong?"

Veronica came closer and knelt down in front of Assunta.

"I'm worried about my father."

Assunta sat up.

"He's doing well. I just left him a few minutes ago."

"How did you get in this hour of the night?" Veronica asked.

"I'm familiar with one of the nurses on duty. If you want, we can go see your father for a few minutes. You must be quiet. I don't want to wake up Michael or Franco."

Together they walked quietly out of the lounge.

When they arrived on the fifth floor, they met the head nurse in the hallway.

"Hi Assunta. I thought you just left Mr. Stone."

"I did. This is his daughter, Veronica."

Veronica interrupted. "I know visiting hours are over; however, I'd appreciate it very much if I could spend a few minutes with my father."

The nurse opened the door to the Cardiac Care Unit. Assunta knew where Robert's room was located.

"Follow me, Veronica."

When they walked in, Robert's face lit up. She ran over to him and put her arms around him. "Papa, I love you. I'm sorry for all . . . "

Robert put his fingers on her mouth.

"We can talk later. I just want to hold you in my arms so I know I'm not dreaming. I've waited a long time to hold you this way."

Assunta sat down on the chair and watched Veronica and Robert. She had a feeling that everything would work out for both of them.

Finally Veronica stood up to leave.

"We better go before we're missed."

Downstairs Paulo had awoken early and decided to check in the lounge. Everyone was still sleeping except Assunta. His heart skipped a beat. He tried to wake Michael shaking him as hard as he could.

Michael was startled when he opened his eyes.

"Papa, what's wrong? Did something happen to Robert?"

Paulo was white as a ghost.

"I can't find Assunta."

"Knowing Assunta she just took a walk," said Michael as he started to put his shoes on. "Where could she have gone?"

"You tell me," Paulo said.

Franco woke up hearing loud voices.

"Papa, what's wrong?"

133

Paulo shouted, "I can't find Assunta!"

Franco sat up.

"She probably was tired of sleeping on the sofa and went to bed. I bet that's where you'll find her sleeping."

When Paulo left the lounge Franco approached Michael.

"Papa can't go on like this. He's going to make himself sick."

Franco and Michael continued to discuss what needed to be done in order for Paulo to stop worrying as much. Franco suggested a family meeting when they got home.

Paulo walked into the girls' room hoping he'd see Assunta sleeping in bed. Assunta wasn't there and neither was Veronica. Rather than wake Anna he closed the door and went straight to the lounge.

"Veronica is gone also! Something could have happened to both of them! I'll tell you one thing, if they've left the hospital they'll regret ever doing so!"

Michael walked over to get Paulo a glass of water. "Papa, I'm sure nothing has happened to them. I doubt very much that they left the hospital. In all probability they both woke up and decided to take a walk."

David woke up in the middle of the conversation.

"What's going on?"

"Assunta and Veronica are missing. I'm beginning to worry," Paulo explained.

After yawning David had a suggestion.

"Is it possible they went up to Cardiac Care to see Robert?"

"Why didn't I think of that?" Paulo said. "You boys stay here! I'll be right back."

Paulo prayed in the elevator that Assunta was safe and sound. When the doors opened to Cardiac Care a sense of relief came over his body when seeing the two of them standing at Robert's bed. He walked over quietly and stood behind both of them for a few moments.

Assunta heard a noise and turned around to find her face in someone's chest. Lifting her head slowly she realized it was her Papa.

"I can explain."

"Not now, Assunta. There will be plenty of time to explain. Paulo walked to the other side of the bed to chat with Robert.

"Robert, you're already looking better. Did they get you out of bed yet?"

Robert shook his head. "To tell you the truth Paulo they wanted to but I refused. I'm not ready to walk yet."

Paulo looked across the bed at Assunta.

"I'm going to speak with the nurse at the nurses station. I suggest you

134

stay put."

Paulo spoke with one of the nurses. Then he made a phone call to the fourth floor lounge. He wanted to let Michael know he found Assunta and Veronica in Cardiac Care.

While waiting, Veronica thought about Robert saying that the nurses wanted her father to walk.

"Papa, all my life I wanted to take a walk with you. Will you do me the honor?"

Robert was overjoyed and at the same time fearful.

"I'm too weak. Some other time."

"I can't believe you, Robert," Assunta interrupted. "Veronica and I, two beautiful young ladies who wish to take a walk with the handsomest fellow in Cardiac Care and you're turning us down. Rejection is hard to swallow but I guess I must accept your decision."

"You're right," Robert smiled. "How could I be so dumb?"

Robert slowly sat up on the side of the bed.

A nurse on duty at the monitoring station came rushing in. "Mr. Stone, are you alright?"

Robert looked from Veronica to Assunta with a smile on his face.

"These two beautiful young ladies would like to take an old man out for a stroll."

"I think that's a great idea. Let me help you out of bed and get you set up."

She whispered to Veronica.

"We don't want your father to exert himself. I'll walk behind you with a wheelchair. As soon as I see he's getting tired, we'll make him sit down and take him back to his room."

Assunta stood on one side and Veronica on the other. Slowly they walked with Robert out of his room. The nurse grabbed on to a wheelchair and walked behind the three of them. Robert felt good as he walked around the floor. When he passed Paulo, who was talking on the phone, he called out to him.

"Paulo, before you leave stop in and spend a few minutes with me. I could use some company."

Paulo dropped the phone at the sight of Assunta and Veronica walking down the corridor with Robert.

"Michael, you're not going to believe who just walked by! It was Robert with Assunta and Veronica on either side! I don't believe my eyes! The nurses tried unsuccessfully to get him to take a few steps and now he's walking around the entire Cardiac Care Unit!"

Looking toward the entrance he now noticed Anna at the doorway

135

speaking to Robert.

"Mama has just walked in. As a matter of fact she's talking to Robert right now."

Glancing at his wristwatch Paulo was surprised to see it was already seven o'clock.

"Since Mama and the girls are up I'm going to take them to breakfast. In case Donna should wake up and look for us please let her know."

Michael put the phone down and looked at Franco and said, "Papa is taking Mama, Assunta and Veronica to breakfast."

When Michael and Paulo ended their conversation Anna joined Paulo at the nurses' station.

"I'm glad you found the girls."

Paulo and Anna joined the girls at the door of the Cardiac Care Unit. Anna and Paulo led the way to the elevator. Assunta noticed when they entered the elevator that Paulo pressed the first floor instead of the fourth.

When they exited the elevator Veronica looked at Assunta confused. Assunta shrugged her shoulders shaking her head. The girls followed Paulo and Anna wondering where they were going. Before long they were at the cafeteria. Paulo chose a table pulling out a chair for Anna to sit down.

"The girls and I are going to get some breakfast. We won't be long."

Paulo took care of his tray and Anna's while the girls took care of their own. When they returned to the table there was absolute silence. Paulo finally broke the ice.

"Veronica, I realize you're concerned about your father and understand you wanting to see him. If you felt the need to spend time with him all you had to do was wake me and I'd gladly have taken you back to the CCU. Assunta, when I woke up and didn't find you my heart dropped to my feet. I feared something happened to you. The correct thing to do would have been to leave word where you were going. I think you both realize how wrong your actions were. Now finish your breakfast so that I can walk you back to your room. You both need your strength if you're to leave this hospital."

When they finished breakfast Paulo stood up and helped Anna out of her chair. He was anxious to get back to the lounge to see the boys.

Just as they reached the lounge Dr. Schiavo showed up.

"I'm going to release all of your children as well as Veronica Stone, tomorrow morning. I'd like them all to stay home and rest for the remainder of the week. Veronica Stone should do the same thing. Knowing them as well as I do, I doubt that they are going to follow my directions."

Turning to his family, who were all gathered in the lounge, he cleared his throat before making his announcement. "Dr. Schiavo has just informed me that he'll be releasing all of you in the morning. Veronica, you'll be staying at our home until your father is released. You're all under Dr. Schiavo's direction to take off from work for the remainder of the week and rest. Do any of you've a problem with what Dr. Schiavo has suggested?"

Veronica started to open her mouth when David nudged her.

"Veronica, please don't open your mouth."

Paulo saw the interaction.

"Veronica, is there a problem?"

"No, actually I'm looking forward to spending time with your family.

Paulo looked back to Dr. Schiavo.

"Dr. Schiavo, it seems everyone agrees with you."

Dr. Schiavo was relieved. He wished Paulo good luck before going his way.

"Anna, tonight we'll go home with Antonio and Maria and figure out where everyone will be sleeping. Maria and Antonio offered to keep the children until the end of next week. What do you think?"

"If they agree I think that's a good idea," she said.

Just then Dr. Cristanzio walked into the lounge. Paulo wanted to talk to him one time before leaving the hospital.

"Dr. Shiavo decided to release everyone tomorrow morning so Anna and I are going home this evening with the Cordovas to make final preparations. I'd like David to remain here for the night.

"I'll leave a blank check with your secretary in the morning to cover the cost of Anna and myself staying at the hospital. You can fill in the amount I owe for the past few days."

"That isn't necessary." Doctor Cristanzio replied. "All you donate throughout the year more than covers the cost."

"If it weren't for the care Franco received both at the company and here at the hospital, I might not have him with me today. That boy is special to me. I'm not ready to give him up yet."

Dr. Cristanzio and Paulo shook hands in friendship.

At the point, Dr. Gennaro showed up at the nurses' station. Paulo took the opportunity to have a few words with him.

"James, can I've a minute with you."

"I always have time for you. Let's go sit down over there. What can I do for you?

"I don't know how I can ever thank you and Samuel. My children are all leaving here tomorrow because of the excellent treatment they received since their arrival."

"We were only doing our jobs. Thanks aren't necessary. Seeing your children walk out of Our Lady of Lourdes Medical Center on their own is all the thanks I want. Promise me you'll see to it that they rest. I'll be in touch toward the middle of the week."

"I'll do just that. Take care and God Bless."

The excitement was starting to get to him so he decided to spend a few minutes alone before meeting up with his family again. Paulo needed to find a secluded area where he could confront his hidden emotions. He wandered aimlessly until he found the perfect spot. Up until now, he was doing a good job being the strong one, the rock for everyone to lean on. They didn't realize just how hard it was for him. Recalling the events of the last few days, he let loose all his frustrations. He broke down remembering the horror of the abduction from its inception through its dramatic conclusion. The paralyzing fear and chaos were almost too much to bear. Paulo vowed from this day forward to protect his children with all his heart and soul. Having regained some strength he quietly came out of solitude. With a new outlook on life, Paulo reunited with his family for their journey home.

# Chapter 9

## Reclaiming Their Lives

All the lights were on throughout the Altro home. Everyone was hard at work preparing for the homecoming. They wanted to make sure that no signs of that fateful day remained. While the men busied themselves with repairs and heavy tasks, Marisa prepared an enormous lunch and tidied the bedrooms and set up the guest suite in the back wing. It became customary for Franco and Assunta to stay in the back wing when Franco's parents came for a visit. Maria and Antonio felt more comfortable in their son's room, so Franco and Assunta agreed to let them use it whenever they were in town. Besides, Franco and Assunta enjoyed the privacy of the back wing. They amorously joked about being able to make all the noise they wanted and nobody would be able to hear.

Meanwhile, on the way home, Paulo was devising a plan to distract attention from the house's appearance, fearing that the sight of the damage might be too traumatic for some of them. First, before entering the house, he would suggest a tour of the construction site. The houses were coming along so quickly that he wanted to show them off. Next, instead of waiting until morning like he originally planned, he would disclose the surprise he had been secretly arranging.

As soon as the house came into view, Paulo put his plan to work asking everyone to join him for a tour of the grounds. To his delight, they all agreed, not giving a second thought to the house's condition, so he led the way. The houses under construction for his children were already looking beautiful and everyone approved. Paulo was proud of the work and excited to see the happiness in their faces.

Finally, Paulo led the way back to the main house to unveil his surprise. Before they rounded the corner nearest the rear porch, he asked them all to close their eyes. No one was sure what to expect. After all they had been through, they couldn't imagine how Paulo found the time to plan a surprise. But when he said the word and they opened their eyes, they were all amazed. The entire back porch had been transformed into a state-of-the-art playroom, equipped with the most modern children's toys and gadgets. Best of all, it was cleverly constructed of bulletproof glass and armed with the latest security features. It was much more accessible than the old playroom, having an entryway from the library and one from the dining room, ensuring that the children would be in clear view at all times.

*Absolution*

The reaction to the new playroom was overwhelming. Anna couldn't believe how spacious it was and Assunta and Donna loved that they could keep an eye on the children from the other rooms. The guys couldn't help but talk about its construction, marveling over the workmanship and the new technology. Everyone was in agreement that the children would be thrilled with their new toys. It was some time before they settled down and headed into the house.

"I think it's great," Anna said to Paulo in private as they strolled along. "But, when they get older, I'm sure they'll prefer to play outside. You know you can't keep them enclosed in glass forever."

Paulo realized Anna knew what he was trying to do.

"I can never fool you; I just want to protect our grandchildren."

Anna put her arm around Paulo's waist.

"I agree with you, however, I don't want to suffocate them by overprotecting them. I want them to lead a normal childhood. In the future when they need someone keeping an eye on them, I know you'll take the necessary steps. Until then sweetheart, let them enjoy their childhood."

Paulo drew Anna closer.

"You're much wiser than your husband."

A tantalizing aroma of home cooking greeted them at the door. Marisa was so excited to have them home that she had prepared all of their favorite foods for the occasion. She outdid herself for the event and the result was a feast fit for a king. The spread consisted of a wide-variety of tempting appetizers, side dishes and entrees. After almost a week of hospital food, it was a welcome sight. No one could resist the banquet so they all crammed into the dining eating as if it was their last meal.

At the end of the meal, Paulo announced that there would be a family meeting in the library in a half hour and expected everyone to be there. While he and Anna prepared for the meeting, Antonio and Maria excused themselves, explaining that they couldn't wait to take a walk in the garden and enjoy some quiet time together.

Watching as they left the room, Franco expressed admiration and approval. He was witnessing a side of his father that he had never seen before, the romantic side. It felt good to see that his parents still loved each other and he hoped it would never change.

In light of Paulo's plan to hold a meeting on such short notice, the girls set out quickly to clear the dishes from the table. When they were through, it was just about time for the meeting and everyone, except for Veronica, headed toward the library.

Michael walked over to where she was sitting.

"Veronica, my father wants to meet with all of us in the library."

Veronica frowned.

"I'm not part of the family. I'm merely a guest in this house and don't think I need to sit in on some silly meeting."

"I think you should reconsider," Michael remarked sternly.

It was decided after Robert took ill that Veronica would stay with Paulo and Anna until his discharge from the hospital. The family was so large that one more wouldn't make much of a difference. There was always enough food for everyone and plenty of guest rooms to pick from. At first Veronica was hesitant but went along with the idea anyhow. What could it hurt, she had thought, but suddenly, she was starting to have doubts. She didn't know how long she could endure their peculiar ways.

For the time being, Veronica decided it best not to argue. She would attend the meeting as an observer and nothing more. Followed by Michael, she walked into the library and took a seat. Looking around the table, Veronica had to restrain herself from laughing. Before her sat a group of adults behaving like children waiting for their father to give them a lecture.

Turning in David's direction, she started to mumble about how ridiculous this was but quickly went silent when she realized the worst was yet to come. She couldn't believe what absurdity took place next. She thought her eyes were playing tricks on her. As if they didn't look foolish enough, everyone rose when Paulo and Anna made their entrance then waited until they were seated at the head of the table before sitting back down. Apparently, David was familiar with this ritual from his own childhood because it didn't seem to bother him. He even tried to get her to stand by grabbing her arm and attempting to lift her to her feet. At that, she made a mental note to have him fired. Veronica had seen enough. Who did they think they were, she thought, the King and Queen?

"Before we get started there are a few matters I wish to clear up." Paulo declared. "First, Veronica will be staying with us until Robert gets on his feet. Please welcome her and make her feel at home. Next, Dr. Schiavo has recommended that all of you take it easy for at least a week. Gino, you should give Salvatore a call and let him know that you won't be returning just yet and that if he runs into a problem, he can phone the house. Franco, you should do the same with Quintino. Emilio can call you here if he needs anything. As far as school is concerned, both of you will need to make arrangements to make-up your assignments. Michael, I'd like you and Timothy to spend the week here with the family as well. Will that be a problem?"

"I'll phone one of our neighboring parishes and make arrangements for someone to fill in for Timothy and myself for the week. I'm sure the girls in the office have everything under control. They are used to me being away from the office for days at a time. If anything comes up, they'll know to call me here."

"Veronica, Dr. Schiavo is still a little concerned about the possibility of some effect on your heart. He wants to see you for a check-up next week after you have had some time to recuperate."

Veronica was anticipating the question.

"I appreciate his concern, however, I intend to return to work in the morning. We have a lot of work to do."

"Robert and I discussed this matter earlier today. He suggested that David handle company business in his absence."

It was impossible for Veronica to hide her anger. Her face turned beet red and it looked as if she was about to kill someone, but when Paulo asked if there was a problem, she answered "no," refusing to let them make a fool out of her.

Paulo stood up.

"I think that's it for now. If any of you wish to speak with me I'll be here to listen."

Everyone started to leave the library including Veronica. Before she could safely escape, Paulo called her and David back to the table. Veronica knew she was in for it and hated the fact that David seemed to love every minute of it. When he tried to help her back into her seat, she pushed his hand away.

"I'm quite capable of handling my own chair and running my father's business for that matter."

Once David and Veronica were seated, Paulo opened the discussion by acknowledging Veronica's frustration at the situation. He told her that he understood her feelings but, out of respect for her father, she should abide by his wishes.

"My father knows what's best for his company so I'll go along with any decision he makes at this time."

Paulo was beginning to realize that taking Veronica on would be no small task. For lack of a better idea, he abruptly ended the meeting and sent Veronica and David on their way. He would have to deal with her later after giving it some more thought. Long after they were gone, he and Anna remained in the library to go over bills and important paperwork that they hadn't been able to get to over the past week. When they were finally done, the two of them decided to get some fresh air out in the garden.

From where she was sitting in the family room, Veronica had a clear view of the porch and caught a glimpse of Paulo and Anna leaving the library.

"Where are your parents going?" she asked Assunta curiously.

Assunta momentarily lifted her head and peeked over the book she was reading.

"They're going for a walk through the garden. I bet Papa is holding Mama's hand."

"How did you know?" Veronica asked in amazement.

"They often walk hand in hand through the garden. It's really quite beautiful. Sometime tomorrow I'll walk you through so you can see for yourself."

Veronica was deep in thought, wondering if her parents ever did things like that, when Franco entered and announced that he was in the mood to watch a good movie. While he searched through the videos, he had Assunta run around the house to ask if anyone else wanted to watch. Although Assunta didn't seem to mind following his orders, Veronica found Franco quite overbearing and rude and didn't understand how Assunta tolerated him.

Assunta walked upstairs and found Michael and Timothy going over the liturgy for Paulo's Mass. It didn't take long for her to convince them to take a break and watch a movie with the family. Assunta went to Gino and Donna's room next and invited them to watch the movie. A smile broke across Gino's face.

"Is it a porno?"

Assunta hit Gino over the head with a pillow.

"Gino Altro, don't be smart, young man! You know no one in the Altro house is permitted to watch pornography! If they did, they'd have to answer to 'His Majesty'! Unless, of course, they watch it while 'His Majesty' is in the hills with 'His Queen!'"

Assunta and Gino both laughed at the absurdity of that thought.

Unbeknownst to them, Paulo was eavesdropping on their conversation. Shortly after he and Anna arrived in the garden, Anna became cold and asked Paulo to get her sweater, which was hanging over the chair near her vanity. On his way to get Anna's sweater, he heard talking and couldn't help stopping to listen. At first, Paulo was infuriated. Then, picturing himself as a "King", even he found humor in it.

Anna was becoming fidgety waiting for Paulo so she went upstairs to check on him. She found him just outside the door.

"What's taking you so long," she asked.

"'His Majesty' found your sweater but couldn't find his own."

Anna couldn't make heads or tails out of his bizarre statement.

"I swear sometimes you make absolutely no sense. Right now is a prime example."

"It's a long story. Sit down and I'll fill you in," he said as he led her into their bedroom.

Anna laughed so hard at the story that she couldn't breathe.

"Please don't be upset with Assunta. She was only joking about watching pornographic movies."

Then once again, they both broke out in a fit of laughter. As Assunta, Gino and Donna were approaching the stairs, they could hear the laughter coming out of Paulo and Anna's private quarters.

Assunta smiled.

"It's good to hear Papa and Mama laughing after all they've been through."

The movie was almost over by the time Paulo and Anna returned. Even though they were engrossed in the movie, Michael and Franco stood up to offer them their seats. Veronica had never encountered such a corny family. Unfortunately, she was stuck with them for what she hoped would be a short visit. Thinking about it made her want to vomit.

The movie ended just in time for dinner and despite some underlying tension, it turned out to be quite an enjoyable meal with everyone chatting lively. Veronica, however, sat quietly trying to figure out a way to go to work the following morning. Paulo sensed that her mind was thousands of miles away from the dinner table.

"Veronica, you're not saying much this evening. I can tell your mind is wandering."

Veronica looked at Paulo sadly.

"I was just thinking about my father and how much I miss him."

Michael felt sorry for Veronica and wanted to comfort her.

"Dr. Cristanzio told me that your father should be on his feet in no time at all. I'll offer my next Mass up for him."

"Thank you, Michael."

Paulo entered the conversation.

"Michael is right, Veronica. Before you know it, your father will be home."

"I hope so."

Paulo stood up and extended his hand to Anna. "'His Majesty' would like to take 'His Queen' for a walk. Will you do him the honor?"

Assunta choked on her drink.

Paulo gave Assunta a knowing glance.

"Assunta, are you all right or would you like to lay down in the 'Royal Quarters'?"

"Papa, I . . . "

"Later, Assunta."

Gino and Assunta froze realizing that Paulo had heard their

conversation. Michael and Franco on the other hand seemed bewildered. Assunta calmly stood up attempting to appear innocent then, suddenly, she felt Franco grab her arm.

"Why do I have this funny feeling that you know what Papa means?"

Assunta continued her charade.

"I don't know what you're talking about?"

Michael nodded his head.

"For some reason I feel the same. Could we both be wrong?"

Assunta was speechless so Gino decided to explain what happened.

"When Assunta came up to see if we wanted to join you for the movie, she jokingly referred to Papa as 'His Majesty' . . . "

Franco stopped Gino and then looked toward Assunta's direction.

"What did you say?"

At first Assunta couldn't find the words.

"I was only joking!"

Franco became inpatient.

"What did you say? I want to hear it all right now."

Assunta smiled nervously and then recounted what took place. Franco and Michael looked at each other across the table and broke out laughing. Before long everyone joined in, including Assunta. Once they calmed down, Franco looked at his wife sadly and stated that he wouldn't want to be in her shoes. Then he turned his attention to Michael and asked what he thought about the situation.

Michael shook his head.

"Quite honestly, I'm glad it's her and not me."

"Franco, please talk to Papa, I was only making a joke," Assunta pleaded. "Honest, I meant no disrespect."

Assunta looked across the table at Michael for help, but he too refused to get involved.

"Don't look at me like that, Assunta. You made your bed, now you can lie in it."

"Thanks, fellows, I appreciate your help," Assunta declared on the way out of the dining room.

Paulo returned and noticed Assunta missing. He wasn't surprised but questioned Franco on her whereabouts anyway.

"Where is Assunta?" Paulo asked.

Franco responded, "She's in the family room. I think she's trying to figure out what she's going to say when the two of you meet."

"If you'll all excuse me, my daughter is waiting. It has been so long since we met privately, I almost forget how much fun Assunta and I have."

Franco interrupted Paulo at that point, "Assunta was only joking. She really didn't mean what she said to be taken sarcastically."

Michael then interjected, "Franco is right; she only meant it as a joke. Assunta never meant to be disrespectful."

"Assunta doesn't know how lucky she is. First her mother comes to her defense, then her husband, and finally her brother. I realize Assunta was only joking around. I just want to have a little fun with her, by reminding her who's in charge."

Paulo walked into the library and put the light on. Instead of closing the door, he left it open knowing Assunta would come in. Sitting down at his desk he started to go through some paperwork he had left for after dinner. Sure enough, Assunta was at the door within minutes. Paulo took his reading glasses off and laid them on the desk. Assunta entered quietly and sat down in front of his desk. Paulo could see the uneasiness in her face.

"I meant you no disrespect when I said those things to Gino. I was only kidding. I'd never make fun of you. I love you too much." Assunta was fighting to hold back her emotions.

Paulo walked around to the front of the desk and took a seat next to Assunta.

"You know what my thoughts are concerning pornographic films. The first time something like that happened, I let everyone know then what the results would be if it reoccurred in the future. Therefore, what you were telling Gino was absolutely correct. As far as me being 'His Majesty' . . . "

"Papa, I swear to you, I didn't meant it the way it sounded."

Paulo lifted her chin.

"I realized you were only joking. Actually, I sort of like the title, however, in the future please refrain from calling me as such. I prefer the name Papa if you don't mind."

Paulo helped her up and held her in his arms.

Assunta rested her head on Paulo's chest.

"I love you so very much. When I think I've angered you it tears me apart. I thought you were so angry you wanted nothing to do with me. If you ever turn me away, I swear I'll kill myself."

Paulo looked into Assunta's eyes sternly.

"Assunta, I don't ever want to hear you say such a thing again. You're my daughter and nothing you do will change our relationship. It took me all these years to find you. I guarantee you won't get away from me that easy. Let's join the others in the dining room."

By the time they returned, the group had dispersed, with the exception of Anna and Franco, who were anxiously awaiting the outcome of Assunta and Paulo's meeting. When they realized that no harm had been done,

Anna suggested the family go to the ice cream parlor for dessert and asked Assunta to gather everyone.

The only person who didn't want to go was Veronica. She was so sick of the Altro family that she came up with every excuse to get out of it but Assunta and Franco wouldn't give up. In the end she decided to go even though she detested the idea. She reluctantly got ready and joined the others downstairs in less than ten minutes.

By the time they returned home, everyone was exhausted. It had been a long day. Paulo and Anna went directly upstairs to relax. Michael, however, couldn't even think about resting. He had to break it to Paulo that he would be going to the church tomorrow and he knew Paulo would be upset. Although he hated to disturb them, he went to Paulo and Anna's room and knocked on the door.

When Michael entered, he found Paulo and Anna relaxing on the sofa. "I'm sorry to bother you but I just remembered something I wanted to discuss with you before tomorrow morning."

"Come in and sit down," Paulo offered.

Michael was searching for the right words to use.

"Timothy and I are going to Holy Spirit tomorrow to prepare for Sunday's Liturgy but I promise, I'll be back in plenty of time for dinner tomorrow evening."

Surprisingly, Paulo didn't take the news as bad as Michael expected. Michael left their room feeling positive about getting the liturgy ready in time for Sunday. He walked down to the library where he told the others to wait for him. "I just told Papa that Timothy and I are spending the day at Holy Spirit. There's a great deal to do so I want to get an early start."

Assunta couldn't resist adding her two cents.

"Michael, why don't Donna, Veronica and myself go with you to make sure the church is presentable? If it needs any final touches we can take care of it."

This was news to Veronica. She looked at Assunta as if she were crazy. She had no intentions on going to either the liturgy or the dinner and she sure as hell wasn't going to clean the church.

Michael thought about it for a minute and then responded with an abrupt "No."

Assunta wouldn't accept no for an answer.

"Please, Michael, I want everything to be perfect."

"Papa may start to wonder why I'd need the three of you to come to church with us. This time, I think it best that Timothy and I go alone to Holy Spirit."

Assunta wasn't ready to give up. She raised her voice an octave higher. "Why can't you understand? You're being completely unfair."

Franco couldn't listen to this bickering any longer. He warned Assunta to calm down before she got herself in any deeper. It didn't take her long to figure out that she pushed too far so she shut up without another word.

Having everyone's full attention, Michael continued, "Tomorrow, while we're at the church, we'll check on everything. On the way home, we'll stop by Giuseppe's to take a final look-see. "

"Is there anything else for us to discuss?" Franco inquired.

"Nothing else I can think of."

Assunta knew this was her chance to try and make things right.

"Michael, I'm sorry about the way I spoke with you. I guess I'm just a little nervous about something going wrong for Papa's party."

"I understand how you feel. I want everything to be perfect for Papa's birthday just as much as you, and it will, so stop worrying. Now smile because your favorite brother still loves you."

A smile broke out on Assunta's face.

Soon it was time for bed. Everyone turned in sometime around midnight.

Lying in bed, Anna clung to Paulo.

"It feels good to be in our own bed. I hate sleeping in hospital beds."

Paulo ran his fingers through Anna's hair.

"I agree, darling. There's no place like home. That reminds me, I'd like to meet with Thomas and Marisa in the morning. With the extra workload, I think it's only fair that we give them both a bonus."

Anna turned toward Paulo with a smile on her face.

"You must have read my mind. I was thinking the same thing when we parked the car earlier and I saw the house alive with activity."

Anna sank into Paulo's arms out of exhaustion and he didn't let her go until she fell asleep.

Breakfast was served at nine o'clock sharp the following morning and as soon as everyone was finished eating, Michael and Timothy excused themselves from the table and hurried off for the church. Somehow Assunta managed to get away in time to catch Michael on the way out and remind him to check on the centerpieces. She was worried they wouldn't be exactly what she ordered. To calm her nerves, he promised he would check and assured her once again that everything would turn out fine.

The day went by swiftly with Michael accomplishing everything he set out to do. The last stop was Giuseppe's. He phoned Assunta from the restaurant to reassure her everything was under control. He told her how beautiful it looked and that she'd be pleased when she saw it. He then asked Assunta to tell Paulo they would be home around four o'clock."

When Michael and Timothy arrived home Assunta was there to greet them. "Michael, I forgot to ask one important question when you phoned! Did the flowers arrive for the church?"

Michael felt like kicking himself. He couldn't believe he forgot. He had to say something quick before she figured it out.

"Give your big brother some credit."

Satisfied with the answer, Assunta left to get them a drink. As soon as she was out of sight, Michael picked up the phone.

"Karen, did the flowers for my father's Mass arrive yet? . . . Thank God. I forgot to check before I left today. Have a nice evening."

Michael hung up the phone.

"That was close, Timothy. I totally forgot about checking the flowers on the altar before we left. Assunta would have killed me if there were no flowers tomorrow."

After dinner Franco and Gino hit the books in the library while Paulo sorted through the mail. Anna decided to take a shower and settle down by herself with a good book and Veronica was plotting how she'd sneak to work Monday morning. Everyone else was in the family room watching a movie.

The night went by so fast that it was eleven-thirty before Paulo finally stopped to take a break.

"Boys, why don't you call it a night? You have all day tomorrow to finish up."

Franco was deep in thought when he heard Paulo.

"I'd rather get it over with tonight so we can spend time with the family tomorrow. Please let Assunta know I'll be studying for another hour or so?"

Gino chimed in, "Papa, will you let Donna know the same."

"Will do, gentlemen. Please don't study too late or Mama will have my head on a chopping block tomorrow."

The boys laughed picturing that image.

"Good night, boys. See you both in the morning."

While walking up the steps he couldn't help but marvel at how both boys had matured in such a short period of time.

Paulo awoke in the middle of the night feeling restless and out of sorts. He immediately noticed through the space under the door that the hall light was still on. This could only mean the boys never turned in. He sat on the bed, searching the floor with his feet for his slippers.

Anna woke up.

"Paulo, what's wrong?"

"It's two-thirty and the boys are still downstairs studying. I know their work is important but they need their rest.  Maybe I'm too demanding on them concerning their grades."

Anna yawned.

"I don't ever want to hear you speak such nonsense.  If you weren't demanding about their grades neither one of them would be where they are today."

Just then Paulo heard the boys walking up the stairs.

"Gino, it's much too late to stop and see Papa.  We can explain it to him in the morning.  Goodnight."

"Good night, Franco.  See you in the morning."

Paulo listened as Franco and then Gino closed their bedroom doors. "Well, my dear, it seems you know your sons better then me."

"They aren't just my sons.  They're our sons."

Anna snuggled up to Paulo.

"I feel cold.  Can you warm me up a bit?"

Paulo put his arms around Anna and kissed her tenderly.  Soon, they both drifted off to sleep.

Franco woke up sometime around seven when the sunlight fell on his face.  Walking toward the window to close the curtain he saw Paulo walking toward the garden and quickly dressed so he could join him.  He found Paulo kneeling down in front of the Blessed Mother.

"Franco, is something wrong?"

"No, Papa.  I happened to look out my window and noticed you walking toward the garden.  I hope you don't mind that I decided to join you.   I wanted to spend a few minutes with you.  We haven't spent much time together lately."

Paulo sighed.

"You're right, son.  It seems there's so much demand on my time all of the sudden, that I sometimes forget my own children.  Thank you for reminding me.  I promise to make things right."

"There's no reason for you to apologize.  I understand and I know you love me.  Everything you do for me shows how much you love me.  I just hope that you know how much I love you too."

Paulo smiled.

"Franco, love is caring, sharing, and helping.  You do that everyday."

"I have one regret though.  I don't have the same love for my own father as I have for you.  I have no problem loving my mother, but my father is different.  I always believed my father didn't love me, so I built up this wall around myself.  Whenever he'd ask to spend time with me I'd tell him I had plans.  He was extending his love to me and I tossed it in the wind."

Paulo put his hands on Franco's shoulders.

"As a child someone reinforced in your mind that your father didn't love you. It wasn't intentional, but it happened nonetheless. Yesterday is gone so we can't magically return to yesterday and make it right. Instead, we have to take the lessons we learn and grow from them. It's up to us to take that experience and allow it to make a difference in our life. In my office, over my desk, is a sign. I placed it there purposely so that when one of my employees comes in to speak with me concerning work or a personal problem they can read and grow from it. It reads as follows, 'Everyday is the first day of our lives, and we have to make everyday count.'"

"I have a two-week break between semesters; can you get away for a few days with me?" Franco asked.

"It will be my pleasure. I'm sure Mama and Assunta will enjoy coming with us."

"Would you mind if Mama and Assunta didn't come?"

"If you'd rather we go ourselves, Mama will understand. Assunta on the other hand might be another story."

"There's someone else I'd like to ask join us. I want to spend time fishing with my two fathers. With your help, I hope to find it in my heart to allow my father to love me."

Paulo wanted nothing more than to help Franco and Antonio enjoy a meaningful relationship. He told Franco not to worry. Then, once again, he reassured Franco of his love.

"I'm proud to be your father-in-law and grandfather to your children." Looking at his watch, Paulo realized it was close to eight o'clock. "Look at the time. I'd better get back to the house and wake Mama or she'll never be ready for breakfast on time."

Back at the house, Michael was opening the drapes to let the sun in and saw the two of them approaching. He always feared leaving Paulo would make him distraught. Michael prayed a special prayer every day that God would bring someone into Paulo's life that could take his place. His prayer was answered and a huge weight lifted from his shoulders. When the time came to relocate he could do so without remorse knowing that Paulo was in good hands. God allowed Michael to see his replacement and Michael approved of His choice. Looking into the heavens Michael prayed silently.

"Thank you, Father. You have made a wise choice."

# Chapter 10

## Paulo's Birthday Celebration Begins

When Assunta came out of her dressing room she found Michael and Franco in conference.

"If you guys will excuse me, I have to go down and check on the preparations for Papa's surprise after breakfast."

Franco wasn't aware of any surprise for Paulo after breakfast so when Assunta took off down the stairs, he asked Michael. He briefly explained their plan to have a private family celebration at home before going to mass.

After breakfast, Assunta casually excused herself from the table, being careful not to look suspicious, so she could prepare the birthday cake. When only a few minutes had passed, Paulo already started to wonder what was taking her so long.

"I'd better check on Assunta" he announced, "she has been gone too long."

Recognizing the look of concern on Paulo's face, Michael quickly thought up an excuse to buy her more time. He suggested that Assunta was probably just chatting with Thomas and Marisa and there was no cause for alarm.

At that very moment, the doorbell rang abruptly, startling Paulo and almost knocking him off his chair.

"Are we expecting company?"

Anna smiled.

"Not that I know of but maybe one of us should answer the door since Thomas and Marisa are tied up in the kitchen."

Franco volunteered and was thrilled when his parents and the kids greeted him at the door. He gave his mother a huge hug then told her she was just in time because Assunta was just about to take the cake out.

"Come here little man," he said to his son, "Papa has sure missed you!"

Sitting in one of the chairs in the entryway he put his arms out while Franco's mother gently sat Antonio on his lap. Antonio excitedly rubbed his hands up and down Franco's face.

Franco's father entered carrying his video camera. Maria seemed amused and quickly pointed out that he missed the silly expression on the baby's face when Franco picked him up.

"Pictures are worth a thousand words," she added.

"Don't worry, I caught it all," Antonio announced.

Monica and Carlo, Franco's brother and sister, were close behind carrying the twins. They stopped at the door to greet Franco who gave them a warm welcome then escorted them to the dining room.

Gino leaned over and whispered something in Donna's ear, "Let's see who Pop Pop picks up first; I bet its Anna."

Donna smirked, "No such luck. He'll pick up the 'Golden Haired Child' first."

"I think you're wrong," Gino argued.

Paulo immediately approached Monica and held out his arms to his granddaughter.

"Come to Pop Pop, my sweet little Anna."

She giggled and Paulo couldn't be happier. After a few minutes, he handed his granddaughter to his wife. Meanwhile, little Antonio started giving Franco a hard time. He was getting very fidgety so Franco put him on the floor, holding him up by his hands. Donna was still watching, wondering who would be next, and thought for sure that it would be Antonio. To her surprise, it turned out to be her son, Paulo. After a few minutes with little Paulo, little Antonio's squirming finally caught Paulo's attention. He handed Paulo to Anna then went to Antonio.

"Antonio, come to Pop Pop."

Antonio pulled his fingers from Franco's hands. Standing there with his hands outstretched, he realized he finally got his Pop Pop's attention. Franco tried to grab his hands again but Antonio wouldn't have it. Paulo surmised what Antonio had in mind so he moved closer and properly positioned himself in front of Antonio.

"Antonio, come to Pop Pop, I really missed you."

Antonio stood up straight waving his arms and took one shaky step followed by another shaky step right into his Pop Pop's waiting arms.

Everyone clapped and cheered but no one was more proud than Assunta and Franco. Assunta jumped up to kiss Antonio and her father.

This was all Donna needed to see. Infuriated, she stood up to leave when she felt Gino pull her back down.

"Donna, sit down and have a piece of cake. We can discuss it when we go upstairs."

Fortunately with all the celebrating going on over Antonio's first step, no one was aware of Gino and Donna's conversation. Anna however sensed some hostility. She could read the signs and decided she'd speak to them before going to Mass.

The next thing on the agenda was the cake and Assunta was proud to be the one to present it to her father. After wishing him a happy birthday, she joked about how long it took her to put all the candles on the cake, making everyone laugh.

Paulo was enjoying himself so much, laughing and chatting with his family, that he didn't want it to end. But like all good things, it had to end. Michael broke up the festivities when he announced it was time for him to leave. Michael embraced Paulo.

"Happy Birthday, Papa, and many more to come. If everyone will excuse me, I really have to get going. Papa since the children have arrived, maybe it would be a good idea if you come to the special liturgy at twelve o'clock."

'What's the liturgy for, Michael?"

"A young couple is having their marriage blessed in church. I think they would be delighted to have someone share this day with them. Both of their parents have passed on."

"Anna, is that all right with you?" Paulo asked.

"I think I'd like to attend that Mass. As a matter of fact, it would be nice if we attend as a family."

Michael quickly looked in Franco's direction with a smile on his face.

"I actually wanted to take Assunta along now if it's OK with you. There's a great deal of preparations to attend to before the Mass and Assunta will be able to help us out. Besides, I've never had a chance to show off my beautiful sister to the people at the rectory."

Assunta could hardly contain herself. She kissed Franco and baby Antonio good-bye then made a beeline to the door. Gino and Donna left the table shortly thereafter without even stopping to see the twins and Anna thought that was awfully odd. Something was wrong and she was going to find out what it was. After a few minutes, Anna excused herself so she could get ready for Mass. On her way out, she knelt in front of each of her grandchildren hugging and kissing them.

From the stairway she could hear the loud talking coming from Gino and Donna's room. She listened by the door and was outraged by what she heard. "Antonio is Papa's favorite! He loves him far more than our children! Watch and learn where you and your family stand in Papa's eyes! No where!"

Gino responded loud and clear.

"I don't agree with you and resent your saying these things about Papa!"

Donna picked up the conversation.

"Oh, I forgot that Papa is your mentor. Forgive me for seeing what your eyes are hiding from you."

155

Anna heard enough; she knocked on the bedroom door. Their loud talking suddenly turned to whisper before Gino answered the door. He was more upset than she had ever seen him. Anna asked to come in, and without hesitation, Gino let her in and showed her to the loveseat.

"I sense there's a problem starting to arise and I want to put a stop to it." Anna declared with authority. Her next comments were directed at Donna. "Donna, I don't know what has come over you. When the children arrived, you sat there miserably and stared at Paulo and I want to know why."

"No reason."

Anna knew Donna was lying.

"You can't fool me. I'm afraid if we don't discuss it, something awful will happen to this family!"

Donna became defiant refusing to talk so Anna turned her attention to Gino.

"If Donna doesn't want to tell me what's going on then it's your place to do so!"

Gino stumbled over his words.

"Mama, it's nothing, honest."

"Gino Altro, I'll not tolerate this deception from my own child! Now what's the problem?"

Gino looked at Donna and than back to Anna.

"Donna feels as though Papa favors Assunta's family over ours."

"Today is your father's birthday! I will not permit anyone, especially one of his children, to put a damper on it! To begin with, your father shows no favoritism except when it comes to Anna! She's the apple of his eye and everyone knows it! The boys are both treated equally."

Donna looked sarcastically at Anna.

"What about 'Papa's Princess'? When I heard Papa call Assunta 'Princess' the first time I wanted to vomit."

Anna turned beet red with anger. Her expression showed her displeasure.

"Papa uses the term 'Princess' when he knows Assunta is hurting. You know the delicate state of mind Assunta has been in since the flash backs of her childhood began. Aside from that, Papa treats all of you the same."

"That's a joke and you know it! Papa favors Assunta because she's his so-called daughter!"

Anna approached Donna in a rage.

"Assunta is our daughter. What are you talking about?"

Donna snickered.

"She's his daughter only because you and Papa felt sorry for the poor dear and adopted her!"

156

Anna had to do all in her power to avoid slapping Donna.

"You're never to say anything as contemptible as you just said about Assunta! She's our daughter! When we adopted her, she became part of us! You also became our daughter when you married Gino!

Donna looked in the air.

"Papa has no need for two daughters! There's no room for two 'Princesses' in one royal family!"

Gino started to quiet Donna down when Anna stopped him.

"Gino, I can handle this."

Anna looked sternly into Donna's eyes.

"Papa and I love all our children equally! No one will ever again insinuate otherwise as long as I live! I hope I've made myself clear! Now get dressed and forget this nonsense of favoritism!"

Anna slammed the door on the way out.

Then turning in haste she walked straight into Paulo.

"Anna, what's wrong?"

"Nothing, darling. I was talking with Gino and Donna and lost track of the time. When I noticed what time it was, I left quickly. My slamming the door wasn't intentional."

Paulo lifted Anna's chin until their eyes met.

"I know there must be a very good reason or you wouldn't try to deceive me. Tonight, before we go to bed, we'll talk about it."

Anna kissed Paulo on the cheek as she had done so many times before, but this time Paulo could see tears in her eyes.

As soon as Anna was settled in their bedroom with the door closed, Paulo burst into Gino's room. He wasted no time reprimanding them.

"The two of you sit down right now. There's something terribly wrong here and I don't like it. I don't know what was said or done in this room before Mama left, but I guarantee, before the end of the evening, I'll find out. I suggest the two of you get ready for Mass! I don't want to be late."

Paulo stormed out leaving Gino and Donna alone to consider his warning.

Meanwhile, at Holy Spirit Church, Michael was in the sacristy going over his sermon, anxiously awaiting his surprise guest. He was getting nervous because he was already twenty minutes late and if he didn't show up soon everything would be ruined. Just then, his assistant informed him that his visitor had arrived and was waiting in his office.

Michael set out looking for Assunta. After all, this was her surprise. He found her kneeling in front of the Blessed Mother praying silently. She looked so peaceful he almost hated to bother her. Luckily she was just about through when he approached to ask her to come with him into his office. On the way, he also asked Timothy to join them.

The man inside holding a cage confused Assunta, but instead of questioning Michael, who was already greeting the man, she looked at Timothy curiously for an explanation. It wasn't until the man opened the cage and revealed three white doves that Assunta figured it out.

She couldn't contain her excitement.

"They are so beautiful! Are they for Papa?"

"Yes. Do they pass with your approval?"

She kissed Michael on the cheek.

"Thank you, Michael."

Looking at his watch he realized the time.

"Timothy and I are going to vest. I think it would be a good idea for you to join Mama and Papa in church."

Assunta entered the sanctuary and knelt down in silent prayer once more before joining her family who were just settling into the first three pews. She greeted Paulo and Anna with a kiss on the cheek. Then she took her seat next to Franco, kissing him and Antonio. Finally, she laid her head on Franco's shoulder overcome by the intensity of her emotions.

The entire family along with all their friends had gathered for this momentous occasion. The only people missing were David and Veronica, and their absence didn't escape Franco's attention. He guessed that it was Veronica's fault and was definitely going to give her a piece of his mind when he got hold of her.

Back at the house, Veronica was being very difficult, refusing to go to the Mass. After a long, heated argument, David had no choice but to threaten her. He told her that her father would not be happy to hear what she was doing and that she would no longer have a job to go back to if she didn't wise up. It took a while but she eventually gave in to his demands.

The drive to church was awkwardly quiet. Neither of them said a word for a long time. The silence was broken finally by Veronica's abrupt shout.

"Now what's your problem?" David barked.

"Stop the car! I have to go back! I forgot Paulo's card!"

"If we turn back now we'll miss the Mass completely," he argued.

It took only a brief moment for David to come up with the solution. He suggested adding her name to his card then waited for her to respond. Unfortunately, there was no way of denying that his idea was reasonable so she graciously accepted his offer and promised to make it up to him. David was taken aback by her politeness and mistakenly took it to be a sign that she was warming up to him.

When they entered church, Michael was just taking his place at the pulpit to read the Gospel. David was relieved that everyone was standing. That way it would be less obvious that they were late. David led Veronica down the side isle to Franco and Assunta's pew where they settled in as quickly as possible in order to give Michael their full attention.

Michael chose the Gospel of the loaves and fishes. It was one of his favorites and the congregation always seemed to enjoy it. At the end of the Gospel everyone took their seats.

"Today I'm going to skip the homily," explained Michael. "Instead, I have something special planned for the end of the liturgy." As he looked around, it occurred to him that no one was upset by the exclusion of the homily. "Wow," said Michael, "I wish you could see your faces! By your expressions, you might think that I just announced that we all hit the lottery. I didn't realize how painful my homilies were."

When the laughter died down, Michael turned to face the Tabernacle and completed the Mass.

It was now time for Paulo's Birthday Tribute.

"Okay, everyone, here goes. On many occasions while Jesus would preach, a large crowd of people would gather. Keep in mind there were infants, children, teenagers, and adults mixed among the crowd. These people stayed all day and sometimes into the evening listening to Jesus speak. He was like a magnet that could draw people of all ages to stay and hear Him speak. In my eyes, Jesus was the greatest teacher that ever walked the earth. Jesus was our primary teacher of love. He loved and cared for everyone He came in contact with during His time here. Jesus always extended a hand to those in need. It didn't matter whether they were rich, poor, short, tall, fat, or thin. Looks didn't matter. What mattered was that they needed someone to love and care for them.

"Another attribute that Jesus possessed was the ability to be a fair leader and disciplinarian. In order to keep the crowds under control, He had to be able to enforce rules and set limits for His followers. Otherwise, they wouldn't have been able to hear His message of love and caring for others. By His example, His followers learned to treat one another with kindness and respect and to help those in need.

"Today, here at Holy Spirit, we're celebrating Paulo Altro's 55th birthday. Paulo is a devoted follower of Jesus' teachings and lives his life accordingly. He's loving, caring, and helpful to those in need, and a strong yet fair leader. Many of you only know him from the neighborhood. There's a part of his life that very few people know about and that's his family life. That's the one thing he keeps personal so that his children and grandchildren can lead normal lives.

"Paulo Altro, having been blessed at an early age with wealth and good fortune, realized along the way, that with success comes the responsibility of helping others, especially children."

Michael walked to the center of the Sanctuary.

"Shortly after entering into his first marriage, Paulo learned, to his dismay, that his wife wouldn't be able to carry a child full term. Their dream of having a large family was shattered. Distraught over the news, Paulo confided in Deacon Pollato hoping for some consolation. It was then that Deacon Pollato assured Paulo this wasn't a punishment from God. God had something special planned for him and he would make it known to him in the future.

"Heartbroken as they were, Paulo and his wife accepted their fate, and at the same time discovered they could share their love, with a small boy who lost both his parents to unfortunate circumstances, and facing an unknown future. Paulo and his wife eventually became his surrogate parents, finally adopting him at the age of eight. Over the years they showered the boy with as much love as if he was their biological son. The boy himself couldn't love them more if they had been his biological parents. Paulo's wife passed on, but not before realizing her dream of being a mother.

"After years of mourning his wife's death, Paulo met a wonderful woman, who later became his bride. Along with the boy Paulo adopted, his new wife took her son to their marriage. Franco, one of Gino's closest friends, joined the family shortly afterwards. Paulo opened his home and heart to both boys. His family was growing steadily now, and oh how he loved every minute of it. He became influential in his stepson's decision to go to college, and eventually he was able to convince the other boy of his potential as well.

Gino and Franco married in a double wedding ceremony on the Altro Estate, and then shortly afterward, both couples shared the good news that they were expecting. Paulo's dream of a large family came into being.

"Deacon Pollato was right when he said God had something special planned for Paulo. Over the years there would be children crossing Paulo's path that were looking for love and guidance and he would accept this responsibility willingly, considering each of them to be his natural born child.

"Each of us has been given a mission in life. Some of us accept the mission and succeed while others waver along the way. Truly, Paulo has traveled the road the Lord picked for him, never wavering in his faith and commitment to his fellow man, especially with the children he took on as his own."

Michael stepped down from the Sanctuary and walked over to the pew

Paulo was sitting in. Paulo stood and the two embraced momentarily.

"Happy birthday, Papa, and many more to come."

The enormous crowd clapped in his honor, until Timothy gave the signal to stand. As Michael walked toward the Tabernacle everyone knelt down.

Michael knelt down reverently.

"Thank you, Lord, for choosing Paulo Altro as an instrument to work with troubled children here on earth. He willingly accepted children whom otherwise may have been lost, never to find their way. I wish to thank you for all these children, but mostly, for myself, your humble servant."

There wasn't a dry eye in the church at this point. Everyone was touched by Michael's words. Before ending the Mass, Michael gave Assunta the signal to leave first. She had to be the first one out because it was her job to tell everyone to remain in front of the church for a special surprise.

Paulo and Anna proceeded to the back of the church shaking hands as they passed their friends. Michael and Timothy followed closely behind. Then the rest of the family filed out of the church ending with Veronica and David.

Outside the church was an eager audience. The main attraction was a gentleman with three white doves in a cage. One by one he would hand the doves to Paulo. Paulo was amazed by the gesture. To add a bit more excitement to the occasion, Paulo and the man arranged to have his grandchildren do the honors of releasing the doves. As he took hold of each dove, he observed the attached cards.

During the excitement, Assunta gave Michael a big hug.

"The white doves were a terrific idea. I'd never have thought of it."

"I told you no balloons and you know I'm a man of my word. I tried to think of something that would be appropriate. Then I remembered how Papa told me of his many encounters with white doves and how they seemed to bring him good luck. Ask Papa to tell you about it sometime."

Paulo read the first card. *"There's nothing to fear except fear itself."* While he contemplated the meaning of the quote, he looked around for little Paulo. As soon as he was in Paulo's arms, Mr. Johnson placed the dove in his hand. Paulo raised his grandson's arms and told him to let go of the dove. The dove soared straight up into the clear blue sky. Paulo's grandson's face glowed with exhilaration. Gino was standing close by and took Paulo from his arms when it was done.

Paulo then read the card on the second dove. *"Love your children each day for you never know when that gift may be taken away."*

Paulo then picked up his grandson Antonio. Mr. Johnson placed the white dove in Antonio's hands. Paulo raised his grandson's arms toward the sky and told him to let go of the dove. The bird sailed out of his hands and up high into the sky. His grandson's hands were outstretched in total amazement as the dove flew over them.

"Pop Pop, look!"

Paulo kissed Antonio before handing him to Assunta. Finally, he lifted Anna out of Donna's arms. Pure joy filled his soul as he held his precious granddaughter.

Paulo read the third card. *"Never harbor hatred or ill feelings. They'll eat away at your heart."*

Mr. Johnson placed the dove in Anna's hands. Paulo then raised his granddaughter's arms to the sky and told her to let go of the dove. The dove soared gracefully out of his granddaughter's outstretched hands and followed the others up into the vast sky above. Paulo looked at Anna lovingly, she was the light of his life. Instead of returning Anna to Donna, he continued holding her until the crowd disbursed. Soon however, Paulo was whisked away for dinner at Giuseppe's.

# Chapter 11

## Dinner At Giuseppe's

Assunta's nerves were finally calmed when she saw how beautiful the restaurant looked. She found Giuseppe and congratulated him on the excellent job of decorating before going to mingle with the guests. As she was making her way back to the table, she spotted Michael coming toward her. She threw her arms around him and gave him a kiss, all the while raving about how wonderful things were turning out. By this time, Franco noticed them and walked over.

At the sight of Franco, Assunta suddenly remembered to ask him something.

"Franco, did you bring Papa's gift?"

"No. I thought you did."

Assunta's anguish was obvious.

"I left it on the back porch because I didn't want Papa to see it. I need someone to drive me back to the house?"

Franco resolved not to give into her whim this time. He refused, reminding her of the last time she'd done this and how much trouble she got into.

"This is different," she explained. Then she turned toward Michael, hoping he'd understand. She begged him this time to take her.

Michael felt sorry for her but also refused.

"The abduction is still fresh in Papa's mind, can you imagine what he'll be like if we disappear now?" Michael responded.

Her disgust was obvious but more than anything else, she was disappointed in herself for being so forgetful. Nevertheless, she continued to try to win their sympathy. After all, they always came to her rescue eventually. But when Franco and Michael again declined, Assunta couldn't hide the tears in her eyes. As she slinked away from them, wearing her feelings on her sleeve, she planned her next move. She had one more ace in the hole that she intended to use. One the way to the ladies' room, she intentionally paraded in front of the receiving line, hoping to get Anna's attention.

The plan worked. Anna noticed Assunta passing by with a dejected expression on her face and decided to check on her. She followed her into the ladies' room. Opening the stalls one by one, Anna found Assunta and asked what was wrong. Assunta threw herself into Anna's arms.

"I left Papa's gift home and Michael and Franco refuse to take me home to get it. I feel so embarrassed. What am I going to do?"

Anna convinced Assunta to come out of the stall and sit with her on the sofa.

"Do you really think Papa would be upset if you didn't give him a birthday present? If you do, then you don't know him very well."

Assunta was determined to convince Anna of the need to have someone drive her home.

"I went through so much to pay for that saddle."

As Assunta cried in her arms, Anna remembered what she'd done to get the saddle and how proud she was of her accomplishment. She knew how important it was for Assunta to give it to him at the party so without further delay she suggested they get David to drive her.

The two women hurried out into the crowd to find David. Anna spotted him on the dance floor and explained the situation to him, then asked him to take Assunta back to the house. Naturally, he agreed to do what she asked. He would never consider denying Anna a request but he had no idea what he was getting himself into when he accepted the task.

On the way out, he ran into Veronica and told her where he was going. He knew she wouldn't worry about him but thought she might at least be curious of his whereabouts. It made him feel good to think she might care. He assured her he'd be back soon then unexpectedly referred to her as his "sweetheart" and planted a big kiss on her forehead.

Veronica fumed at his arrogance. As she wandered back into the dining room, she mumbled to herself about what a jerk he was. Obviously, she wasn't paying attention to where she was walking because she slammed into Franco as she turned a corner. Michael grabbed her just as she was about to fall. As he steadied her, he asked her what was wrong.

"Men, you're the most stupid beings that ever walked this earth. David just kissed me and called me 'sweetheart'. Who does he think he is? If he thinks we're going to end up together, he's crazy."

Michael laughed at her remarks and urged her to have an open mind. He told her that David really cared about her and that she should give him a chance. While Veronica blabbed on about David, Franco looked around for Assunta and didn't see her anywhere. He interrupted Michael to help him find her. He'd been holding Antonio since they'd arrived and his arms were beginning to go numb. It was about time that Assunta took over.

From where they were standing, they could see Paulo and Anna near the entranceway and it appeared that they were having a serious conversation. By the time Michael and Franco joined their parents, they had stopped talking and resumed greeting their guests.

"Mama, have you seen Assunta? I want her to hold Antonio for awhile," Franco said.

Anna reached out for the baby.

"Franco, you look tired. Let me hold Antonio until Assunta returns. I think she's in the restroom."

Anna picked up Antonio, hoping Assunta would miraculously make an appearance.

Paulo started to feel concerned that something happened to Assunta so he took it upon himself to find her. He stepped out of line to begin the search. It wasn't long before he came across Veronica and asked if she had seen Assunta.

Veronica nodded her head while sipping on her drink.

"Assunta went back to the house with David. I think she forgot something. David stopped to tell me before they left."

The thought that Assunta would leave the restaurant without telling him infuriated Paulo. Returning to the receiving line, he smiled while whispering something to Anna, which the guests couldn't hear.

"Would you believe that Assunta left the restaurant without telling anyone."

"Paulo, you shouldn't get yourself so upset. They are adults and have certain things of their own to do. Assunta is fine. She left something on the back porch and returned home to pick it up. I'm sure they'll be back shortly."

Just then, Assunta and David arrived at the front door.

"See, there she is. I knew David would get her home and back safely."

Paulo gave Anna a sharp look that didn't go unnoticed by Michael and Franco. Sensing some hostility, they headed for the front door, leaving Anna and Paulo alone.

"Paulo, let's not let this little thing ruin your day. I can explain it all to you this evening."

Paulo grabbed on to her arm.

"No darling, right now!" Then he turned to see whom he could leave Antonio with. Fortunately, Timothy was standing nearby so Paulo asked if he could take care of Antonio until Assunta or Franco returned.

Next, Paulo asked Giuseppe if they could use his private office for a few minutes. Once inside, Paulo exploded.

"Why did you allow our daughter to go home without discussing it with me first? You know how I feel since the abduction."

Anna hadn't seen Paulo this upset in a long time. She tried to calm him down by explaining what happened.

"Earlier tonight, I noticed Assunta walking toward the ladies' room and she was extremely upset. I decided to check on her, so I followed her in and got her to tell me the problem. Apparently, Assunta forgot your birthday present at home. I realized that it would have torn her apart inside if she didn't give it to you here in the restaurant. I decided, using my best judgment, to send her home with David to get it."

Paulo stood up very abruptly while Anna was still talking.

"Please let me finish," she said. "I need to get this off my chest." Without arguing, Paulo sat back down to hear what Anna had to say.

"We started our marriage with one son. Here it is, just a little over three years later and we now have three sons, two daughters and three grandchildren. Our family grew in leaps and bounds. So did my responsibility. At first, the added responsibility frightened me and I wouldn't make a decision without discussing it with you first, however, I now feel I'm capable of making the right decisions on my own. I've become stronger in dealing with the children and truly feel I'm able to help them without checking with you. They are my children as well as yours, and I, too, walk around with knots in my stomach since the abduction. Yes, we have a right to worry, but they have a right to lead a normal life."

Anna stopped a few moments to regain her composure.

"In the future we'll have to worry about our grandchildren also. Now it's easy to put them in a glass house making it impossible for any harm to come to them. In a few years however, they'll need their freedom, too. When that time comes we'll have to make the necessary arrangements."

"I'm only concerned with the safety of our children," Paulo blurted out.

Anna spoke to Paulo more seriously now than she ever did before.

"Hear me well, if anything would happen to any of our children or grandchildren, I don't know how I would survive. I do know, however, we can't put them in a glass bowl and be with them every minute of the day and night. You and I must discuss this matter further in the future."

"Yes, we do need to discuss this matter further, but for now darling, we have guests waiting for us."

Paulo helped Anna to her feet holding her in his arms and kissing her tenderly.

"Anna, nothing you say or do will change my love for you."

They kissed once more before leaving the office and once they returned to the party, they both felt peaceful and contented.

The remainder of the day turned out to be uneventful. The highlight of the night was when Assunta presented Paulo with the saddle, and he couldn't believe his eyes.

"Happy Birthday, Papa. I hope you like it."

Paulo kissed Assunta on the forehead.

"Is this what you went back home for today?"

Assunta nodded her head.

"Yes, Papa."

"It's beautiful. I couldn't have picked out a better saddle myself."

"It was worth all the trouble it has caused me by going home to pick it up."

The dinner ended at five o'clock. Although it was a wonderful day, it was exhausting and they were all anxious to go home. Paulo and Anna drove home alone as the family came in separate cars. It would be a perfect opportunity for Paulo and Anna to talk privately.

"Anna, I invited the Cordovas to stay over."

"I'm glad you did. We don't get enough time together."

Paulo sensed Anna was still feeling uncomfortable about the situation with Assunta. He wanted to clear the air and put her at ease.

"Anna, come closer. It was a beautiful affair. I must commend you and the children."

"I had nothing to do with it. I knew absolutely nothing about the liturgy or dinner until you did. Your children truly love you. About today, I wish .
. "

Paulo carefully pulled to the side of the road in order to talk without placing their lives in danger.

"I told Michael, Franco, and Assunta I'd speak with them this evening. I'd like you to be present."

Anna laid her head on Paulo's shoulder.

"The only thing I'd like to say is that everything was done innocently, not to deceive you, only to make it possible for Assunta to pick up the gift she left home. I'm sure you remember the circumstances surrounding the saddle and how hard she worked to pay it off."

Paulo stared into Anna's eyes.

"How could I forget? I can understand her going home to get the gift, but can't overlook the fact that Assunta manipulated you the way she did."

After some thought, Anna realized Paulo was right.

Paulo continued to speak.

"There's something else I'd like to discuss before we arrive home. Dr. Cristanzio told me Robert isn't doing well. Dr. Romano is considering another catherization to locate the problem. I don't want to mention anything to Veronica until we know for sure. I thought, perhaps, later on this evening, we can take a run to the hospital."

"Robert seemed to be doing so well, I thought he'd be home soon."

"These things are hard to understand at times. Robert was well on the road to recovery and then out of the blue he had a setback. Dr. Romano is also concerned about Veronica. He'd like her to get as much rest as possible so he can do some further testing at the end of the week. Something showed up in her cardiogram that Dr. Romano would like to discuss with us. It is nothing serious but may require Veronica staying with us a little longer."

"I wouldn't want it any other way. For now, I think it's best not to mention it to Veronica. I'll see to it she gets the rest she needs."

When they arrived home, they found everyone in the family room playing with the children. Paulo immediately zeroed in on Assunta.

"Assunta, Mama and I are ready to meet with you."

Assunta stood up and followed her parents into the library. Waiting for Paulo's lecture was like torture to Assunta. His silence was nerve wrecking. Finally, after a few minutes he began.

"You knew if you had told Mama you forgot my gift, she'd let you go back home. Correct or not?"

Assunta tried to defend her actions.

"I wanted to give . . ."

"I only asked you for a yes or no answer, not a story."

"Yes, Papa."

"You were being manipulative by taking advantage of Mama's love for you."

"I thought if I explained to Mama why I wanted to go home she'd ask someone to drive me. I knew they wouldn't turn her down."

"Assunta, you deliberately deceived your mother. I will not tolerate such behavior from any of my children. Anna, will you join the others in the family room. I'd like a few minutes alone with Assunta."

When the door closed, Assunta knew she was in for it. This time, however, she didn't try to shout her way out of it. For the first time, she followed Michael's advice and calmly asked to speak.

"Papa, may I say something?"

Paulo was impressed with her maturity so he let her speak.

"I'm sorry, I promise I'll never take advantage of Mama again."

"Young lady, you'd better believe you'll never do that again. Manipulating people only gets you into trouble. I must tell you I'm disappointed in your behavior, and won't stand for it again in the future."

A few minutes later they somberly emerged from the library. Instead of stopping in the family room, Assunta went straight for the stairs. She wanted to be alone to think. Assunta hated when she disappointed Paulo, and took his words to heart.

The following morning at breakfast Veronica walked down the steps dressed for work. David tried to stop her from going into the dining room for breakfast. He knew if Paulo saw her dressed for work he'd be upset.

"Veronica, just where do you think you're going?"

"To work, stupid."

Just then Paulo came up from behind. He was motioning for David not to let on he was there.

"Paulo expects you to stay home and rest. I think you're making a big mistake."

"Paulo isn't my father. I may humor him at times just to make him happy but I don't care what Paulo tells me to do. I'm my own boss. Once I'm out of here, there will be no returning. You'll see."

Paulo decided to make his presence known.

"Is that right? After breakfast you and I'll discuss your humoring me privately. Right now I suggest you join the others in the dining room."

During breakfast, Veronica carefully picked at her plate while deep in thought. Although everyone was quiet, the meal seemed to be moving along well, which suited Veronica just fine. Then as always Assunta had to open her mouth.

"Papa, have my sessions been canceled for the week or do I still have to attend them?"

"Dr. Cristanzio feels that it's important that you attend them. He doesn't want you putting any volunteer time in until next week."

"Will Franco be dropping me off?"

"I have to stop and see Dr. Cristanzio anyway, so I'll take you. As soon as I finish with Veronica we'll leave." Paulo stood up, and then kissed Anna on the cheek before leaving. "Anna, I would like you to accompany Veronica when she's through."

All eyes were on Veronica now that Paulo was gone. Assunta couldn't wait until Paulo was out of sight to find out what was wrong.

"Veronica, what did you do this early in the morning to upset Papa?"

"I haven't the foggiest idea. I was talking to David and . . . "

Franco put his hand on Assunta's hand.

"It's none of your business, so don't get involved."

Anna realized things were going to get out of control so she broke it up quickly by advising Veronica that it wasn't a good idea to keep Paulo waiting.

As soon as they left, Assunta's curiosity was at its peak.

"Aren't you just a little curious? It's only seven-fifteen and already Veronica has upset Papa."

Franco became frustrated.

"I suggest you get ready to leave and forget about Veronica."

Instead of arguing Assunta excused herself and headed to her room. Now, the only ones left in the dining room were Michael and Franco. They talked quietly a while longer then, just before leaving Michael remembered to tell Franco that Paulo called a family meeting for that evening. Franco agreed to spread the word to the rest of the family so Michael wouldn't have to worry about it while he was at the rectory. On his way out, Michael heard Paulo call out to him from the library.

"Michael, I may need you later on in the day. Will you be at the rectory or on the road?"

"I'm really not sure. Phone the rectory and Karen will be able to contact me. Anything serious?"

"No, I just want to spend a few minutes with you. Have a nice day, son."

"You too, Papa."

As Michael was walking to the car, he wondered what was on Paulo's mind. He was curious but he'd just have to wait and see.

Paulo soon returned his attention to Veronica.

"Anna, something has become known to me that I think you should hear. Veronica feels she's her own boss and as such, intends to walk out the door and not return. Her father's wishes don't mean a thing to her."

Paulo sat back in his chair trying to get his thoughts together before speaking.

"Your father wants you to remain here until he is discharged from the hospital. He feels more secure knowing you're not staying at home alone. I thought you understood that before leaving the hospital."

"I did agree to stay at your home until my father's release, but no one stated that I couldn't return to work. Had we discussed this possibility at the hospital I would have explained to you that I intended to return to work as soon as possible."

"When I picked you up from the hospital, Dr. Schiavo advised that everyone should spend a week at home resting. We discussed this in the lounge, in front of Dr. Schiavo, and everyone agreed. What has brought about the change of heart?"

"I feel much better. Staying in the house cooped up for a week will drive me crazy. I can understand if your children need rest since they were involved in a stressful situation. With me, it was a job and I can adjust rapidly."

Paulo chose his words carefully so as not to alarm her about the possibility of a problem with her heart.

"You may be able to adjust quickly as you say, but as long as you're under my care, you'll follow Dr. Schiavo's directions. If you're entertaining thoughts of sneaking off to work behind my back, I suggest you wipe them out of your mind. Now I suggest you go upstairs and get into something more comfortable for lounging around the house."

Veronica swiftly retreated to her room. He and Anna remained in the library to talk about their plans for the day until it was time for him to take Assunta to the hospital. As soon as Paulo left, Anna went upstairs to check on Veronica. Opening the door, she could see Veronica staring out the window.

"Veronica, come sit down with me for a few minutes." Anna could see that Veronica was very upset.

"I know I upset Paulo this morning, but that wasn't my intention. I don't want either of you to think I'm not grateful for your hospitality. I value your friendship. If I thought for one minute . . . "

"I'm afraid you saw the worst of Paulo this morning. He may have come off as demanding and tough, but understand that this is only out of concern for your health. I have an idea. After you've changed, we can take a walk down to the stables. I can introduce you to John. He's in charge of the horses. One day this week we can go riding."

Veronica smiled.

"I'd like that."

Anna kissed Veronica on the forehead before leaving.

On the way to the hospital, Paulo noticed that Assunta was unusually quiet. Normally, she'd be talking away, but on this day all she did was glare out the side window. She seemed to be in a world of her own. Paulo tried making small talk to relax her, but it wasn't working. The closer they came to the hospital, the tenser she became. Finally, Paulo pulled over to the side of the road to find out what was on her mind. As lovingly and gently as possible, Paulo appealed to Assunta to tell him what was bothering her.

Slowly she opened up to him.

"Papa, you said today I'm supposed to start my sessions alone with Dr. Cristanzio."

"That's correct. I thought perhaps that I was holding you back from getting the most out of your session. That's why I suggested you go alone."

"It's not because you don't love me anymore?"

"Whatever gave you that idea? If I didn't love you I wouldn't be driving you in the first place."

"In that case, would you mind coming to my sessions a little longer. When you're in the room I feel safe."

"If you feel more comfortable with me being there, so be it. As long as I live, if you need me for anything, anywhere, or anytime of the day or night,

I'll be there. You're my daughter and I love you very much."

Paulo picked up his cell phone and called the office. He told Salvatore that he was going to be late and that he would be in after one. Next, he called the house again and told Anna that he'd be home for lunch after all.

Assunta smiled leaning against his shoulder.

"Thank you for coming with me. I'm glad you're my father."

Paulo opened the car door and stepped around to the other side to help Assunta out. It was a beautiful day with just a slight breeze in the air. From the side of the road, she looked out over the valley. For miles around, all she could see were countless exquisite flowers and trees. Together they formed a collage more beautiful than anything Assunta had ever seen.

Paulo immediately realized there was something more serious bothering her and he was going to get to the bottom of it. He decided to join Assunta to take in the view.

"Breathtaking, isn't it?" Paulo remarked.

"Papa, it's so beautiful out here I could look at it forever and never tire." Assunta rested her head on her Papa's chest for a few minutes and then looked up at him with the simplicity of a young child. "Are you ashamed of me?"

"What makes you think such a silly thing?"

Assunta put her head down and didn't answer.

Paulo gently lifted her chin. "Why would you think any such thought?"

"Because I'm not as smart as the boys."

"Assunta, look out over the valley. Pick out the prettiest flower you see."

"I can't. They all look the same to me. They are all beautiful."

"Exactly my point. God has blessed me with children to love. If someone were to ask me to pick out who was the best they would be asking the impossible. In my eyes you're all equal."

Paulo looked at his watch and then gently kissed Assunta on the forehead. He warned that they would be late for her appointment if they didn't get going soon.

Assunta's session went as well as could be expected. At times she grabbed Paulo out of fear. It was obvious there was something still trapped in her mind that seemed to be hanging on for dear life. Dr. Cristanzio concluded it was so horrible that Assunta's subconscious mind wouldn't permit it to be unlocked.

At the end of the session, Dr. Cristanzio told Assunta there was someone waiting to see her. One of the little boys that she took care of when she volunteered was in today for some routine tests and was asking for her. He thought she might like to spend some time with him while he's being tested.

"Papa, do I have time," she asked.

"I have some business with Dr. Cristanzio that should take some time. When I'm through, I'll come and get you."

Assunta stood up with a smile on her face that would light up a room. As soon as she left, Paulo faced Dr. Cristanzio. He had such concern for Assunta that it was very difficult to know if he was always doing the right thing. He needed the doctor's opinion before going ahead with his plan. He wanted to know if he should enroll Assunta in a couple of classes.

"Before I say yes, let me explain something to you," stated Dr. Cristanzio. "Assunta has made outstanding progress since we started our sessions. You and your family have brought her a long way in a short period of time. The problem is that there are still some childhood memories that she has yet to let go of. It might be something trivial, but then again, it could be just the opposite."

"I understand and I agree that we have to take things slowly but I also feel that Assunta has to build up her self esteem which was destroyed by her father. I was hoping that taking some classes might help do just that. My question to you is would I be applying too much pressure to suggest that she begin a few courses this semester?"

Dr. Cristanzio gathered his thoughts before answering Paulo.

"Let's give it a shot. I do, however, suggest that Assunta continue her sessions. This will enable me to recognize if the pressure is too much for her to handle or not. I believe you should look into classes on child development. She has a great deal of potential in that area."

"Thanks for your input. Now, what would you say to having lunch with us today?"

"Love to, Paulo, but I have an Appropriations Committee meeting regarding establishing an indoor playground for the children. One day while making my rounds I noticed the children staring out the window at the playground across the street watching the children at play. They deserve to be able to join them but, unfortunately, the circumstances surrounding their health will not permit them to do so. If we can't bring the children to the playground then why not bring the playground to the children."

"At one time, this hospital wasn't equipped to treat children. You shared your hopes of someday treating children here and now we have children coming from all over. I have no doubts that the children will one day have their playground."

Paulo parted ways with Dr. Cristanzio with his mind racing. Foremost on his mind were his plans for Assunta.

# Chapter 12

## Bianca Pays A Visit To Paulo's Office

Paulo decided to stop by his office to check his mail and phone messages before picking up Assunta. On an ordinary day this would be a quick and easy task but today was different. An unexpected disturbance had arisen that would require his immediate and full attention.

The first sign to Paulo that trouble was brewing was the shouting coming from inside his office. Before storming in, he confronted Salvatore and demanded to know what was going on. In response, Salvatore simply put his head down in disgust.

Paulo instantly knew the answer to his own question.

"Is Bianca back again?"

One of Paulo's employees died while at work, but not before asking Paulo to look after his daughter, Bianca. Paulo accepted the responsibility knowing Bianca had a drug problem.

"I don't know how to keep her out. You said you didn't want the police involved so I didn't call them. Gino is trying to calm her down. He didn't go to class so he could wait for you."

"I'll handle it now," Paulo said as he walked toward his office. He prayed all the while for the right words to use. This time he had to be firm with Bianca for her baby's sake. Paulo entered to find Gino sitting behind the desk and Bianca sitting in front of the desk nervously tapping her foot. He thanked Gino for taking charge in his absence then instructed him to get to school before it was too late.

Gino did as Paulo requested without argument but wondered to himself on the way out of the company why Paulo catered to Bianca.

As soon as Gino was gone, Paulo took his seat behind the desk. Bianca waited for him to speak, but instead he stared at her in silence.

Refusing to wait any longer, she stood up and started to scream at the top of her lungs.

"You have to help me! I need money for baby food!"

Paulo shook his head in response.

"I won't give you anymore money until you sign yourself into Our Lady of Lourdes Medical Center! You can't go on destroying your body with drugs! No more!"

Bianca screamed louder this time.

"Don't you care about my baby?"

"Listen here, young lady, I'll always care about the baby and do everything in my power to see she has a good life! Where is she?"

Bianca's voice softened.

"She's with my aunt. You should see how beautiful she is. Last week I took her for a check up and she weighed in at twelve pounds. Not bad, considering she was under five when she was born. Now will you at least give me enough money to buy some formula?"

Paulo came around to the front of the desk.

"If I give you money, you'll walk out that door and head straight for your dealer! Not this time!"

An unexpected knock at the door put a halt to their conversation. Paulo briefly went to the door and spoke with his secretary in an angry tone. He didn't want to be disturbed while he was in conference.

Turning back to Bianca, he found her looking out the window. He tried again to talk some sense into her.

"Would you please reconsider and go over to Our Lady Lourdes Medical Center. I can make arrangements to have someone drive you there. Dr. Cristanzio will personally take care of you."

"Let's make a deal. I'll go as long as you give me money for food for the baby first."

Paulo banged the desk with all his might.

"No money! Not now! Not ever! Do you understand?"

Bianca stormed over to the door and then turned to face Paulo.

"Let me be the first to tell you that you're a dumb ass. I don't need your money or your shit anymore. I'll go somewhere else to get what I need. Good bye, sucker."

After Bianca slammed the door behind her, Paulo slumped down behind his desk cradling his face in his hands. He recalled the day her father had a massive heart attack on the job.

On his deathbed, he asked Paulo to keep an eye on her. Shortly after her father's death, Paulo realized she was on drugs and did everything in his power to rid her of this monkey. She was treated at the best rehabilitation center, only to resume the drug use.

One day Bianca strolled into the office looking quite radiant. To Paulo's dismay, she informed him she was pregnant. He made arrangements for her to go to a convent nearby until the baby was born. He felt in his heart that this would turn her life around. Unfortunately, he was incorrect. No sooner did she return to her home than it started all over again. Paulo realized he had failed. Not only did he fail Bianca, but he also failed her baby.

The knock at the door brought him out of the trance. Julie peered in apologetically.

"I'm sorry to bother you, Mr. Altro. They're here to pick up this month's order and I can't find it in my files."

Paulo calmly faced Julie acknowledging that he had been too abrupt with her earlier.

"I have it here in my drawer. After you give it to the courier will you please come back in? I would like a few words with you."

First, he opened his side drawer and then the top drawer noticing everything was in disarray. If Gino was looking for something, he sure made a mess.

Julie turned white at his request to return, thinking the worst. She stood quietly waiting for Paulo to find the order and hand it to her.

Julie returned after delivering the documents and stood in front of the desk.

"Mr. Altro, before you fire me, let me explain."

"Who's going to fire you? I want to apologize for the way I answered you when Bianca was in here. She's a very troubled child and I just don't know how to help her."

"Mr. Altro, you don't have to apologize for anything. Stress can bring out the worst in us. We're all guilty of it at one time or another. Is that all, sir?"

"The next time you see Gino, tell him he's lucky he wasn't here when I found the mess he left in my top drawer."

Julie looked over and seemed confused.

"Gino would never leave your drawer like that. As a matter of fact, a few weeks back I came in and found Gino straightening it out. He told me that he knew better than to move anything in your drawer without putting it in the proper place before leaving."

Paulo looked at Julie awkwardly, and then began emptying the drawers, putting everything carefully on top of the desk. He was confused by what he found and needed help so he asked Julie to bring Salvatore to him.

When Salvatore entered, Paulo questioned whether or not he knew if Gino might have written a check from the company checkbook that day.

Just as Paulo had expected, Salvatore confirmed that Gino hadn't used any checks. By this time, Salvatore became curious about Paulo's suspicions and asked, rather candidly, what was going on.

"The company checkbook is missing," he explained to his employees as he stared at his desk in disbelief. For a long while, he sat quietly considering other possibilities but, unfortunately, he could only arrive at one conclusion. It had to be Bianca who stole the checkbook.

Before accusing Bianca outright, he questioned Salvatore and Julie some more. He wanted to know if either of them had seen her leaving his office with anything unusual.

As soon as Julie proclaimed that she saw Bianca carrying a small leather wallet, Paulo ordered her to get Philip Helmi on the phone immediately.

Paulo was in a panic when he picked up the phone.

"Philip, I'm sorry to disturb you but I have a problem that needs your immediate attention. Last year, one of my most valued employees became gravely ill. On his deathbed, I promised that I would look after his daughter. To make a long story short, she has a serious drug problem and has made it very difficult for me to care for her. She was here today asking for money and I refused. Now, it appears that she has possibly made off with the company checkbook."

"Paulo, no need to worry. This is very simple to deal with. All I need to do is put a stop payment on the checks that are missing. If anyone were to come into the bank and attempt to cash one of these checks, the teller would automatically decline the transaction. If she should come into my bank, do you want me to contact the police?"

Paulo thought for a moment before making a decision.

"Follow your normal procedure. Bianca needs help! Perhaps being incarcerated will do the trick."

They closed the discussion by agreeing to meet at the bank later to sign the paperwork. Paulo had a lot to do in a short period of time.

He addressed Salvatore now to fill him in on his plans for the day.

"Salvatore, I'm afraid I'll be leaving you in charge once again. Gino will return at two o'clock. Tell him a problem came up and I'll see him later." Salvatore started to walk out the door when Paulo suddenly called him back.

"I realize you've taken on increasing responsibility in the past few months. Gino can't afford to miss any classes; therefore, I'm falling back on you more often. I want you to know how appreciative I am."

Salvatore responded modestly, "I don't mind, but honestly, I do worry sometimes about making mistakes."

Paulo smiled.

"I only know of one man who walked this earth that was perfect, beside imagine what a dull world it would be if we were all perfect."

Salvatore walked away from Paulo's office feeling good about himself. After having a childhood in which his parents destroyed his self esteem and any feelings of self worth, it was nice to hear Paulo say those words.

Not too long afterward, Paulo made an appearance on the floor.

The room fell silent as everyone waited for him to speak.

"Salvatore has been with the company for fifteen years and has done an exceptional job. However, changes must be made from time to time in order for improvement to be made. Starting today, John Lanero, will take over his supervisory position."

The crowd clapped and cheered for John while Salvatore found himself in a state of confusion. Minutes earlier Paulo had given him the impression he was pleased with his performance, and now he was removing him from his position. He froze momentarily but when the shock wore off, he attempted to retreat unnoticed to the locker to clear his things.

Paulo noticed him leaving and called him back.

"Salvatore, where are you going?"

"I'm going to my locker to pack my things. Before I go, I'd like to thank you for your kindness over the years."

Salvatore then congratulated John on his promotion and offered some advice.

"Be good to this group of people. With them by you, you'll never fail."

There wasn't a dry eye in the room as Salvatore turned to shake hands with Paulo. Salvatore wanted to exit gracefully, but he was getting choked up. He turned hastily so no one would see.

Paulo thought his behavior was rather odd and stopped him before he left again.

"Salvatore, where are you going? I didn't tell you to leave. It wouldn't be appropriate to leave early on your first day as Manager of Paulo Altro & Son."

Salvatore remained in a state of shock while everyone around him cheered with approval. When he regained his composure, Paulo finished his speech.

"Your professionalism and loyalty are to be commended. Manager is a title well deserved by you and too long in the making."

"I can't find the words to express my gratitude."

Paulo and Salvatore embraced momentarily. Their friendship and respect had blossomed over the years to the point that Paulo knew he could leave him in charge without worrying. He knew he would treat it as his own company.

John joined Paulo and Salvatore.

"Mr. Altro, how can I thank you for the promotion. I never dreamed anything like this would happen to me."

"John, you don't have to thank me for the promotion, you earned it. Ever since the day you came to work here, I have followed your progress closely. Salvatore's monthly reports indicated that you were devoted and willing to do whatever asked of you. You were quick to learn and always ready to lend a hand. You have good leadership qualities and that's what

*Absolution*

I look for in my employees.

"Now, if you'll excuse me, I have to be at Our Lady of Lourdes Medical Center shortly. If I'm late, my daughter will never let me live it down. Salvatore you can use my office until I find suitable quarters for you. Have a nice day gentlemen."

Paulo felt a huge weight lifted from his shoulders. He was confident that he was leaving his business in good hands for the future when he would be spending less time there.

Promoting Salvatore and John was the wisest decision Paulo ever made. In future months, he would see his company's expansion in terms of production and quality.

Paulo phoned the hospital and spoke with Dr. Cristanzio.

"I'm on my way to pick up Assunta. Will you please ask her to meet me in front of the hospital."

Assunta was waiting out front when Paulo arrived. She was curious to know why he showed up so early.

Without going into detail, he explained he had some unpleasant business to attend to at the bank.

When they pulled up to the bank, Assunta asked if she should wait in the car so he could have privacy.

Paulo refused, stating he had no intentions of leaving her in the car.

The Bank President, Philip Helmi, met them at the door and escorted them directly to his office. As soon as they were inside, Assunta excused herself so she could use the ladies' room.

Paulo promptly sat down to sign the paperwork then decided to give Philip some sort of explanation.

"Philip, I have had enough of this girl's nonsense. Time and time again, I've given her chances to turn her life around, but she resists every step of the way. She's too old to play games. I think it's best I let go once and for all and allow her to fall flat on her face. I tried to make things right but to no avail. It hurts me to do so, but as of today, I intend to disassociate myself from her in the future until she gets her act together."

Assunta overheard the entire conversation from the doorway and assumed Paulo was referring to her. An overwhelming sensation of dread fell upon her, causing her mind to wonder off momentarily.

Paulo's voice brought her back to reality.

"If we don't get a move on, we'll be late for lunch."

Assunta didn't say a word on the way home. After parking the car Paulo and Assunta walked out back. Assunta turned and hugged Paulo.

"Thank you for all of your kindness. I'll pack my things and be out of here shortly."

Paulo grabbed onto Assunta's arm.

"What are you talking about?"

"I realize what a burden I've been to you. I'm sorry for all the trouble I caused you."

"Sweetheart, you're not making sense. What are you talking about?"

"I overheard you tell Mr. Helmi that you had enough of my nonsense and wanted nothing to do with me."

Assunta put her head down to hide the tears.

"Is that what this is all about? I think I'd better explain to you exactly what happened this morning."

He led Assunta to the nearest bench holding her hand tenderly. He told her all about his employee that died and how he became responsible for his daughter, Bianca.

"One year later," he said, "she's using heroin everyday and, to top it off, she has a baby to care for. Instead of helping her with love and attention, I fed her money which only ignited her drug use."

The sound of an approaching car caused Paulo to hesitate. He was relieved when he realized it was Michael.

After parking his car, Michael joined Paulo and Assunta.

Looking toward Assunta he handed Assunta his jacket.

"How was your session?"

"Rough, like always, but with Papa there, I was able to get through it."

"Good, I'm glad to hear it. Now, do me a favor and let Marisa know I'm staying for lunch."

Assunta took Michael's jacket and headed for the kitchen giving Michael a chance to talk to Paulo. He sat down next to Paulo on the bench.

"I phoned the office to speak with you and Salvatore mentioned what happened with Bianca this morning."

Paulo paused momentarily.

"I have failed Bianca horribly. There must have been something I could have done differently for her."

"You didn't fail Bianca. You offered her the help she needed; more than the average person would have at their disposal."

"Drugs are destroying our youth. Someone must take control of the drugs on the street."

Michael nodded his head in agreement as he contemplated the severity of the situation.

"Have they located Bianca yet?"

"Not that I know of."

Michael, although concerned for Bianca, feared for the well being of the baby.

"Is the baby with Bianca or in someone else's custody?"

"Thank God Bianca left the baby with her aunt."

"You have done all you can do for Bianca. The rest is up to her."

Paulo kept the conversation short because they were running late for lunch. They spoke for a few more minutes and then walked toward the house.

Alone in her bedroom, Veronica could do nothing but stare out the window. She had a clear view of the garden that allowed her to witness the scene between Paulo and his children. She wondered what it would be like to have that kind of relationship with her father. That was all she wanted her entire life. She threw herself on the bed in frustration and self-pity. She hadn't realized that it was time for lunch until she heard Anna outside in the hallway.

"Veronica, what's wrong?"

"I was looking out the window a few minutes ago and saw Paulo talking to Assunta and Michael."

"It's not unusual to see Paulo and one of the children walk the grounds or sit out back to talk something out. I don't see why that would upset you."

"All my life, I wanted that kind of attention from my father. I guess I'm jealous that Assunta has what I've wanted all my life. If you don't mind, I think I'll skip lunch today."

"Paulo doesn't approve of anyone skipping lunch."

"Tell him I don't feel well. I'm sure he won't mind."

Veronica rolled over on her pillow burying her head into it.

Anna's heart went out to her and she knew she'd have to discuss it with Paulo before lunch.

Returning to the dining room, she found Michael and Paulo waiting patiently, and Assunta was in the kitchen helping Marisa prepare lunch.

"Michael, what a surprise! I'm glad you decided to join us."

"I wanted to have lunch with my beautiful mother."

"Paulo, your son is trying to con his mother. You should have a talk with him."

Paulo winked at Anna. "I think you should listen to your son. He does have a beautiful mother."

Michael laughed at the way Paulo and Anna interacted with each other. It made him feel good to see the affection they shared. When they finally stopped laughing, Michael went out to the patio to call Maria and Antonio to lunch.

Paulo looked around the room and realized Veronica was not present. "Anna, where is Veronica?"

"Veronica has decided not to join us for lunch."

Paulo sat back on his chair.

"Is she feeling ill?"

"When I went up to call her for lunch, she was crying. I'm afraid she's hurting inside. Let me tell you what she said."

After Anna finished, Paulo stood up and headed for the stairs. He went directly to Veronica's room and let himself in.

Veronica heard someone enter but never turned her face away from the wall.

"I'm not coming down for lunch. Please leave me alone."

When she didn't get a response, she slowly turned around to see Paulo.

"Veronica, are you sick?"

"No, sir, just a little tired."

"I would like you to join us for lunch."

Realizing Paulo wouldn't take no for an answer, she gave in to his request, telling him that she'd be down in a few minutes.

She quickly refreshed herself before going downstairs but she didn't expect to be there for too long. She intended to go straight back to her room after lunch.

When she was through eating, she tried to excuse herself by telling everyone she was going to lie down for a while.

"Before you go upstairs," Paulo said, "I would like a word with you. Please wait for me in the family room and I'll join you shortly."

Paulo leaned over and kissed Anna.

"I think I'll take Veronica for a walk in the garden."

Anna looked up with a smile on her face.

"She's a confused child. Be nice."

On his way out of the dining room, Paulo reminded Assunta that she was supposed to help Marissa prepare dinner that evening and that he would be very disappointed if he found out that she forgot.

He then went to meet Veronica in the family room. He was already contemplating what to say to her.

Assunta started to remove the dishes from the table and carry them into the kitchen without giving Paulo's remarks a second thought. It seemed that Donna was more bothered by it than Assunta. She became infuriated with Paulo's suggestion that she help prepare dinner.

Once Assunta was out of the dining room, Donna voiced her opinion to Anna.

"Why does Papa do that to her! She isn't the maid, and yet, he treats her like one! I think it's a disgrace Mama, and you should say something to him! I know one thing for sure, no child of mine will be doing household chores and cooking along side our maid, that's what she will be there for!

"The problem is, you never say a word to him about anything! There are times when he treats all of us like children and you approve! Not me! Gino knows better. The first time he does that he'll be out on his ass."

Michael could see the embarrassment Anna was experiencing in front of the Cordovas. He took it upon himself to remove Donna from the room.

"Donna, may I see you for a few minutes in the library?"

"You're kidding, right!"

Michael helped Donna to her feet. There was no need for words since his eyes told the tale. Once in the library, Michael directed her over to one of the chairs in front of the desk.

"Michael, just who do you think you are? I'm not that ass-kissing sister of yours who takes your abuse!"

"When we're through, you're going to apologize to Mama for the way you spoke to her! I'll not permit you, or anyone, to embarrass Mama in front of anyone, the way you just did! I don't know what has gotten into you, but I do know you're not the same girl I met five years ago."

Donna stood up with the intention of stomping out of the library.

"I'm going to my room because looking at you nauseates me to no end. Wait until my husband comes home! Then we'll see who apologizes to whom!"

Michael grabbed her arm.

"Not until you apologize to Mama and the Cordovas for causing a scene! Let's go!"

"I'll do no such thing! No one is going to tell me what to do. I think you're crazy. As a matter of fact, I think the whole family is a joke. Paulo Altro couldn't have any children so he took other people's leftovers just to satisfy his ego! You're all nothing but a bunch of pathetic orphans!

"Your parents didn't want you, so Paulo Altro, the hero of the town, came to your rescue! Three cheers for Paulo Altro, better known as Papa to his band of undesirables! Cardinal Michael Paulo Altro Roselini, I salute you!"

Donna slammed the door on the way out, leaving Michael speechless.

Michael's mind was racing as he tried to figure out what to do next. The first thing he had to do was calm Anna down and then he would discuss the matter with Gino. Fortunately, for Donna, Paulo wasn't there to witness her blatant act of disrespect. Michael knew eventually Paulo would have to be told.

Paulo was giving Veronica a tour of the grounds.

"We bought this house when Michael was four years old."

"You and Anna have lived here that long?"

"Anna and I are only married five years now.  My first wife and I purchased the house."

Veronica looked at the size of the house in amazement.

"I can't imagine anyone buying a home this size with only one child."

"I guess you could say we were out of our minds; however, in the end it turned out for the best."

They continued to tour the grounds, visiting the tennis court, basketball court, swimming pool, and stables.  They were now reaching the entrance to the garden.  Paulo always showed the garden last.  He asked Veronica if she'd like to see it and she agreed.

Veronica was impressed as she took in the view.  She noticed an unusual door.

"Does that door lead to the house?"

Instead of answering, Paulo led her to the door and with much enthusiasm, opened it wide enough, allowing her to step inside.  He waited for her reaction.

Veronica was in awe.  She immediately felt at peace, standing in the most magnificent chapel she had ever seen.  She made her way slowly to the altar.  Noticing a pamphlet with the words "The Chaplet Of The Devine Mercy."  Paulo walked over and directed Veronica to one of the pews.

"This chaplet was introduced to me by my first wife, Martha.  In a vision to St. Maria Faustina in 1935, the Lord revealed this powerful prayer that He wanted everyone to say – the Chaplet of the Divine Mercy – and He promised extraordinary graces to those who would recite it.  Over the years, I have made it part of my life."

"Can I have a copy?"  Veronica asked.

Paulo smiled handing her one.   When they exited the chapel Paulo turned toward Veronica.

"You're welcome to stop in the chapel anytime; the door is never locked."

Veronica's face lit up.

"Thank you for the tour.  I really enjoyed spending time with you."

"I want you to feel free to use all the facilities on the estate while you are staying with us.  Consider our home to be your home until your father is released from the hospital."

At this point Veronica felt she could open up to Paulo.

"I'm ashamed of the way I've been acting.  It wasn't my intention to get you upset this morning.  Can you forgive me?"

It was obvious that she was sincere.  Paulo felt sympathy for her.

"After we discussed your behavior you were forgiven.  What I did was out of love and concern for you. Someday you'll understand. Now, I suggest we both get back to the house before Anna sends for the police."

Veronica did as she had originally planned and went back to her room. When she passed by Paulo's bedroom, she heard Anna crying softly. Rather then disturb her, she decided to go down and tell Paulo something was wrong with Anna.

Paulo was in the dining room speaking with Maria and Antonio when Veronica rushed in. She told him to come quickly, that Anna was in their room crying.

Paulo jumped off the chair and ran up the stairs. Opening the door, he could see Anna crying into her pillow.

"Anna, what's wrong?"

"I guess the ordeal of the abduction has finally caught up with me. I'll be all right. Go downstairs and I'll join you shortly."

Paulo held her in his arms caressing her.

"It's all over. Our children are safe at home. I'll see to it that nothing like this ever happens again."

Paulo left Anna sitting on the bed and headed downstairs.

Waiting in the dining room, Maria was anxious to know if Anna was all right. She jumped all over Paulo as soon as he returned.

"Anna was upset but she's fine now. She should be down soon."

"I'm glad she's okay but frankly I've never witnessed anything like that before. "

Maria shook her head.

"It all happened so quickly. No sooner had you walked out of the dining room, and all hell broke loose. I've never seen anyone in this family behave in such a cruel manner. Michael was even taken back by Donna's words. My heart went out to. . ."

Paulo stopped Maria dead in her tracks.

"I'm sorry Maria, I forgot something. I shouldn't be too long. Why don't you and Antonio go outside and we'll join you there."

Paulo casually walked out of the dining room so as not to reveal his surprise.

He found Anna brushing her hair at her dressing table.

"Anna, a few minutes ago I asked what had you so upset. Your response was that you were feeling the after-effects of the abduction. The one thing you and I agreed on from the very beginning of our marriage was that we wouldn't deceive one another. I'm afraid that's what just took place before I joined Antonio and Maria. I believe you and I have something to discuss."

"I have already kept Maria and Antonio waiting for long enough.

Perhaps we can talk later."

Paulo took Anna's hand in his.

"What happened after I left the dining room earlier?"

"I don't know what you mean."

"Someone upset you today and I want to know who and why."

"I really don't know what you're talking about.   Michael left for Holy Spirit and I came to lie down since I started to feel depressed. I've already explained this to you."

"You know how I feel about being deceived. I'm going to ask you one more time. What happened after I left the dining room?"

Anna closed her eyes leaning against Paulo's chest.

"After lunch I felt depressed and decided to lie down for a few minutes and lost track of time."

Paulo reached over and picked up the phone.

"Excuse me for a moment. I want to give Michael a call."

Anna was now forced to tell Paulo the truth.  She didn't want to put Michael in the middle.

"Put down the phone. I'll tell you what happened at lunch."

Anna sugarcoated the whole story.  She didn't want Paulo to be angry with Donna.  The one fear Anna had was that Paulo would force Donna and Gino out.

"Anna, you have already lied to me three times.  For your own good, I hope you're not lying again."

"Paulo, it was no big deal; only a misunderstanding. As a matter of fact, before Donna left the dining room, she apologized."

"I'll take your word for it."

Anna breathed a sigh of relief after Paulo left.  She knew if Paulo ever found out what really happened there would be hell to pay.

Paulo walked downstairs and found Antonio and Maria out back.

"Anna will be right down."

Antonio looked toward Paulo.

"For the life of me, I can't figure out what triggered Donna. I have to tell you, no daughter or daughter-in-law of mine would speak with Maria that way and get away with it. I have spoken to Donna on several occasions before and I always found her to be pleasant.   Believe me, she was a different girl today. Something isn't right."

"I realize that and intend to get to the bottom of it quickly."

Anna arrived looking radiant as always.  Paulo held her hand while she walked toward the stables.  He decided not to confront Anna yet about what he just heard.  The one who would give him the answers he wanted was Michael.

# Chapter 13

## Family Meeting Turns Into A War Zone

Dinnertime was fast approaching and Paulo thought it would be a nice idea to get something special for dessert. On his way to the car, he noticed Assunta sitting out back relaxing.

"I'm going out to pick up some dessert. Do you want to keep me company?"

Assunta grinned from ear to ear.

"Sure. Just give me a minute to tell to Marisa, this way she can listen for Antonio."

As Assunta ran to the house, Paulo shouted after her to ask Veronica if she wanted to go also, then went to wait in the car. In no time at all, Assunta and Veronica were ready and hopped into the car. On the way to the bakery, Veronica asked Paulo how Anna was feeling.

"I spoke with her and she's feeling better," assured Paulo.

Assunta studied Paulo's face.

"You know what happened at lunch today?"

"Don't I know everything in time."

"Michael made me promise not to tell you how disrespectful Donna was to Mama. What happened to Donna? She isn't the same. Donna has this attitude about her that I can't begin to describe. Michael even tried talking to her and Donna was disrespectful to him. If that was me, Michael would have come down on me like a ton of bricks."

Paulo knew there was more to the story than he had been told. It was frustrating having to wait to speak with Michael.

At the bakery, Paulo allowed the girls to choose whatever they wanted for dessert. Of course, they went crazy and by the time they were done, there was enough cake for a month. When they arrived at home, Franco couldn't resist commenting on the huge assortment of desserts.

"I couldn't chose just one because they all looked so delicious. Do you have a problem with that?" Paulo retorted.

Franco wasn't sure what to make of Paulo's curt response. He didn't know if he was truly upset or just joking so he remained silent just in case. In the meantime, Paulo pulled Michael to the side and asked to have a word with him. They agreed to meet in the library in ten minutes so Michael used the time to help carry the cakes into the pantry. On his way back to meet Paulo, Franco stopped him to ask why Paulo was so upset. Michael denied any knowledge of the situation, and then excused himself. He didn't want to keep Paulo waiting. Michael actually did have an idea, but decided not to discuss it with Franco. This time, it was best Franco be kept in the dark.

Michael entered the library and found Paulo deep in thought. He appeared to be in a peaceful state of mind; however, his calm demeanor couldn't hide his rage for very long.

"I found Mama crying when I returned from my walk with Veronica. I know she's trying to protect someone because she blew me off when I inquired what was wrong."

Michael sat down.

"There was a misunderstanding between Donna and myself at lunch. I intend to straighten it out with Gino after dinner. No big deal."

Paulo became enraged.

"No big deal! I leave my wife smiling and enjoying herself and I return to find her crying in her pillow! No big deal! I want answers and I want them right now!"

Paulo banged the desk so hard with his fist that even Franco, who was in the family room, jumped.

Michael recounted what happened.

"After you left the table, Donna started talking crazy. I've never heard her disrespect Mama the way she did. Mama looked embarrassed so I took Donna to the library to have a few words. She did the same thing to me and refused to apologize to Mama. Papa, something isn't right. This behavior is totally out of character for Donna."

Obviously, Paulo had heard enough. He had the look of the devil in his eyes as he stood up and shouted out his instructions to Michael.

"Tell everyone I'm holding a family meeting after dinner! I intend to discuss what happened today! No one will get away with embarrassing Mama in front of company."

"I already told everyone we were having a meeting after dinner this evening; you told me so last night."

"Don't you think I remember what I told you last night? The meeting I spoke of last night was for business! This meeting is to straighten out my children! Do you have a problem with that, young man?"

"No, Papa."

Paulo sat down and started to write some notes. He heard Michael leave but never looked up. Soon he would put his pen down and lean back in his chair, contemplating the change in Donna's attitude.

Dinner that night was unusual to say the least. Paulo would normally ask his children about their day, but this night he was quiet. Assunta was always the one with the most to say. She had a way of bubbling over with enthusiasm that amused Paulo. When he didn't show any interest in the events of the day, Assunta became alarmed. Michael and Franco were already aware there was a serious problem, but the others were blissfully ignorant.

As the dishes were being cleared, Paulo asked Anna to join him in the library before the rest of the family arrived. Anna agreed and they both stood up. Then, looking around the table, Paulo spoke in a peculiar tone.

"As soon as we're through, I'll send for everyone. I suggest that you get the children ready for bed. If we're detained past their bedtime, I'm sure Maria and Antonio wouldn't mind putting them to bed."

Once inside the library, Paulo put the light on and walked over to the sofa. He wasted no time questioning Anna.

"I know one of our children did something terrible to you today. You're their mother and want to protect them, especially when you know their behavior will upset me."

Anna tried to pretend she knew nothing of what Paulo was saying but when he peered into her eyes, it was impossible to conceal her anguish.

"I know what happened, but want to hear what you have to say," Paulo continued to press on.

"It was nothing. I overreacted. Donna and I had a mother-daughter disagreement, nothing more than that. With all the stress I've been under, I blew it out of proportion."

"Correct me if I'm wrong. This wasn't the first time Donna has talked to you in this manner. Instead of leveling with me so we could figure out what caused her to react this way, you never mentioned it to me. You took the abuse and looked the other way. Am I right or wrong?"

Anna smiled nervously realizing Paulo couldn't be fooled any longer.

"Anna, I want you to level with me. No more games."

Anna put her head down.

"Donna has spoken to me this way on numerous occasions."

"I have a very good idea what the problem is. I'm interested in your observation."

"Donna's demeanor changed quite a while ago. She's exhibiting frequent mood swings. I knew how you would react if you found out. That's why I tried to hide it from you."

"You know how I feel about being deceived. Why would you hide anything this serious from me?"

"I thought I could help Donna by keeping her around me during the day and away from everyone else. The only problem is that her girlfriend Debbie visits often. I hate to admit it, but I don't like her. I think she is a bad influence."

"Anna, do you know what Debbie does for a living?"

"Not really but, by the looks of it, she has a great deal of money. She's always dressed beautifully, has expensive jewelry and a brand new car."

"Doesn't that seem odd for a girl who didn't graduate high school?"

"I asked Donna that same question and she told me that Debbie has a rich boyfriend who takes care of her."

"Did you question Donna where she was spending her time with Debbie."

"One day after everyone left the house for work, I went upstairs and found Donna getting dressed to go out. I asked her where she was going. She told me they were going shopping for the day. What seemed odd to me was that she didn't take care of the twins before she left with Debbie.

"When she came home, she could hardly stand up. Donna told me they had gone to lunch and had a glass of wine. She saw that I was upset so she promised me it would never happen again. Then she went upstairs and slept soundly until four o'clock that day. Since that day, I've been doing everything in my power to break them apart."

"This is a serious problem, however, I don't intend to confront Donna about it this evening. Instead, I'll discuss it with Gino when we return from the cabin. Tonight I will discuss what I expect of our children regarding your treatment. I intend to really storm into them and I want you to back me up."

"Haven't I always done just that?"

Paulo and Anna had much more to discuss but it was getting late. They mentally prepared themselves for what was to follow.

Paulo stepped out momentarily to let his children know he was ready to meet with them.

He looked around the room to make sure everyone was in attendance then asked Franco to close the door.

"Last night, I told Michael to inform you that we would have a family meeting this evening. I intended to give a report on the company and some policy changes that I've implemented as of today. However, I feel there's a more pressing matter to discuss.

"Today, after lunch I decided to take Veronica on a tour of the grounds. Had I known what was to occur after I walked out of the dining room, I would've never left."

Paulo's eyes did the talking as he glanced at each individual sitting in front of him. When he reached Donna, he paused momentarily.

"As your parents, we deserve the utmost respect. Today, one of you had another idea about how we're to be treated."

Paulo looked around the room.

"Not only did you show your mother disrespect but, to make matters worse, you did it in front of company! No one will ever embarrass my wife, your mother, again in this fashion. I guarantee there will be hell to pay if it ever happens again!"

Donna snickered at Michael.

Paulo was furious with Donna so he didn't hesitate to reprimand her in front of the family.

"Donna, do you have a problem with anything I just said? If so, let's hear it. We can discuss what you think is so funny!"

All eyes were on Donna. Everyone waited for her to explode as she had done so often lately. In contrast, Donna didn't say a word. In fact, she seemed to not even notice the attention. With that settled, Paulo moved on to company business.

"It has become increasingly difficult for me to spend much time at the company. Therefore, today I appointed John Lanero supervisor. He'll be replacing Salvatore Greco. John has proved to be a valuable employee and worthy of his new title. Over the past year, he has formed a good working relationship with the other employees.

"Salvatore has been supervisor for almost fifteen years now and he has proved his worth in gold. In the past few weeks, Salvatore has been running the company in my absence. He has taken on added responsibilities without an increase in salary. This kind of loyalty can't go on without recognition. As of today, Salvatore is manager of Paulo Altro & Son."

Donna interrupted raising her voice.

"You're taking a man, who has worked for you for only one year, and making him supervisor, and then you're taking a man, with little or no experience managing a company, and making him manager of our company. I think it's a bad move! If anyone should be manager, it should be Gino! In Gino's absence, I should become manager! The sign does read Paulo Altro & Son!"

"I'm well aware of what the sign reads; however, Gino is still in college and he does a great deal of studying in the evening and on weekends. This limits the time he can spend at the company. Because of unforeseen family responsibilities, my time at the company has been diminishing from day to day. Therefore, I decided to make the necessary arrangements for the company to function properly when I'm not present. I gave it a great deal of thought before making my decision."

Donna became more vocal.

"No offense, but John Lanero was hired because he was a friend of

Michael's and needed a job. I don't think that qualifies him to become supervisor of our company.

"My friend Debbie is thinking about going to work. I can set up an interview. It would be good for us to give a woman a break in climbing up the corporate ladder. By next year, Debbie may even qualify to take over Salvatore Greco's management position.

"There's another issue for us to consider. If you go ahead with your plans, the company will have to shell out considerable salary increases to these men. Our income will be greatly affected. I know it's a bad move and will not permit it."

Paulo scowled at Donna.

"Donna, let me set a few things straight for you! The sign in my company reads Paulo Altro & Son but that doesn't mean the business belongs to Gino. It's my business and, as such, belongs to Mama and myself. I have these meetings to get the family's input into the business. In reality, it's not necessary for me to do this. I do it out of courtesy to my children.

"I'm the one that controls the employee status in my company. I can hire and fire whomever I wish without the approval of anyone here. I can promote any employee with a substantial increase in salary anytime I see fit. The company is where it is due to the sweat off the brow of my brother and myself! What makes you think you should have such a huge input into it?"

"I beg to differ, we're all stockholders, and therefore, we all have a right to voice our opinion about changes made in the company! In the same respect, we also have a right not to accept any decision that will infringe on our financial status!

"It was a bad move on your part! I wish you had discussed it with us before you said anything to Salvatore or John! How will you explain to these two men that you made a mistake and they must go back to their original status?"

Michael could see that Paulo was at the boiling point and tried to calm things down before more things would be said out of anger.

"Papa, I suggest we adjourn this meeting until tomorrow evening!"

Paulo took out his frustration on Michael.

"Michael, do you think I'm not capable of running my own meeting? I'll decide when to adjourn and no one else. Sit down!"

Again, Paulo focused his attention on Donna.

"My children are stockholders in Paulo Altro & Son! Michael, Gino, and Assunta each own ten percent of company stock. The remaining seventy percent belong to Mama and myself. Therefore, we're the majority stockholders and make the major decisions in the company."

Paulo ignited a fire in Donna that would fuel a major confrontation.

"Where do I fit in? Why don't I have any stock like the others?"

It was becoming increasingly harder for Paulo to gather his thoughts as Donna was maddening him so greatly.

"Donna, listen to me carefully. The stock belongs to Mama, my three children and myself. We're the only stockholders in Paulo Altro & Son! Do you understand?"

If looks could kill, Paulo would have been dead.

"Oh, I understand alright! I'm being overlooked because you didn't adopt me! If you had, then I'd have ten percent of the company stock as well! It was the luck of the draw!"

Now it was Paulo's turn to explode.

"What do you mean by that? Get this straight, Donna, you have absolutely no right to tell me what to do with my company and my money and that's final."

Donna wouldn't let it go.

"If you picked me over Assunta, I would own ten percent of the stock! The problem was that I didn't throw myself at you the way Assunta did! She looked for your pity and I didn't! I thought it would be best if I showed you my strength rather than my weakness! If I had it to do over, I'd have played poor little sick girl and then you would have chosen me to adopt! You wanted a daughter and it didn't matter which one of us you chose! My loss was Assunta's gain!"

Franco stood up.

"Just who the hell do you think you are?"

Paulo intervened.

"Franco, stop right now! Do you hear me?"

"I hear you Papa, but I also heard enough of this person for one night!"

Gino stood up at this point and started screaming at Franco.

"Perhaps she is right! Why should I have equal stock with Michael, and Assunta when I'm the one breaking my neck studying to become an engineer! I do all the work and they reap all the rewards! Think about it for a minute!"

Franco looked at Gino wondering what happened to him.

"Gino, what the hell is wrong with you? Can't you see how out of line Donna has been throughout this whole meeting?"

Gino looked to Donna for guidance. Taking his cue from Donna he began to speak.

"I'm beginning to believe she is right about everything she said!"

Franco stood up pushing Gino against the conference table and started swinging unmercifully. Franco and Gino had a good old-fashioned brawl on top of Paulo's conference table. It took both Michael and Paulo to break them apart. There was blood everywhere as well as huge scratches in the conference table.

When everything calmed down Paulo stood at the head of the table.

"I suggest everyone leave before you see a side of me you have never seen before!"

Anna had been sitting along side Paulo trying to come to grips with the outcome of the meeting.

"I don't understand what happened this evening. Why did Donna and Gino act the way they did? I feel like I don't know them anymore."

Paulo held Anna in his arms.

"I believe I know what the problem is. Let me handle it."

Tearfully, Anna looked at Paulo questioning the repercussions Donna and Gino's actions warranted.

"Are you going to disown Gino and Donna?"

Paulo wiped the tears coming down Anna's face.

"Disown one of our children, of course not."

"What are you going to do?"

"That's hard to say. Donna has said some pretty nasty things to the two of us today. Yes, Anna, there's very little that slips by your husband. The way she acted in both instances can't be tolerated. There will be changes made. You and I can discuss the appropriate action to take. Right now, I'm convinced Donna needs professional help. I intend to discuss it with Gino. We'll do whatever is necessary to help Donna."

"I agree with you. You and I must see to it that Donna gets help."

Paulo looked at his watch.

"We have to be ready for the play in less than forty-five minutes. Will you be ready in time?"

"If you were to ask me to be ready in five minutes, I could accommodate you. I'm looking forward to a night on the town with my best friend."

"Who's that?"

"He's the last person I see before I go to sleep and the first person I see when I wake up in the morning."

"I heard he's rather handsome!"

"That he is."

Paulo and Anna embraced and kissed.

Michael, Franco, and Assunta had been sitting in the family room waiting for their parents to emerge, hoping that Paulo had calmed down. They would know by the tone of his voice when he addressed them before going to his room. However, when he walked by, he didn't say a word to them. He passed them as if they didn't exist.

When they reached their bedroom, Anna questioned him.

"Why didn't you say anything to the children when we walked through the family room? I believe they were waiting for you to say something and now they're going to think you're mad at them."

"I just need time to cool down."

As soon as he closed the door and Anna went to freshen up, he lost himself in thought. He worried that Donna would try to cause problems with the company and would sway Gino over to her side. He now had to take drastic measures to prevent any harm she might inflict on the family.

# Chapter 14

## Donna's Involvement With Drugs Surfaces

After Paulo and Anna left for the play, Michael, Franco, and Assunta remained in the family room. They had been waiting for the right time to freely discuss Donna's behavior and the predicament they were all now involved in. No matter how hard they tried, they couldn't get to the bottom of it.

Michael was ready to throw in the towel. He was certain there was a problem, but for the life of him, couldn't put his finger on it. Feeling as helpless as Michael, Assunta stood up abruptly and started to leave the room.

"Where are you going?" Franco asked curiously.

"I think I'll clean the dishes in the china closet before going to bed. I want to surprise Mama."

It was evident that Assunta was trying to hide something so Franco and Michael followed her into the dining room to confront her. By the look on their faces, Assunta knew she'd better come up with a good story. She tried to dissuade them from talking by saying that she couldn't chat because she wanted to be done before their parents returned.

At first, Michael wasn't sure that Assunta was being deceptive. But now, he started to realize that Franco was probably correct in his assumption. Neither he nor Franco intended to let her get away that easily.

Franco was losing his patience.

"Assunta, is there something you want to tell me?"

"Oh, all right! If you give me a few minutes, I'll join you in the family room."

Franco looked at his watch.

"Ten minutes, or I'll personally drag you into the family room."

Assunta replaced the dishes and then headed for the family room. It was clear that she was nervous because she was fidgeting. Without saying a word, she immediately set out to organize the family room but Franco wasn't going to give up.

"Start talking!" Franco said.

"About what?" Assunta asked innocently.

Michael decided to take control.

"Assunta, no more games! You know something and you're trying to hide it from is. I know it, Franco knows it, and you know it. We're not leaving until you spill the beans."

Franco and Michael waited for her to begin.

"For some time now, I have been catching Debbie bringing packages to Donna. We were both out back with the children the first time I saw it happen. Donna hadn't been feeling well all morning. She seemed to have the chills and was sweating profusely. I figured she was coming down with a cold. I suggested she go inside and lie down until dinner but Donna refused, explaining that Debbie was dropping off her medication.

"When she arrived with the medicine Donna paid her with a check but Debbie wasn't satisfied. She said it wasn't enough. Donna assured her she'd have the rest in a few days. Then Debbie warned her she wouldn't bring any more until she took care of unfinished business. That's it. That's all I know."

Franco couldn't believe what he was hearing.

"Michael, are you thinking what I'm thinking?"

"I think so."

Franco decided to pursue the conversation.

"Did you ever see Debbie bring Donna medicine any other time?"

"All the time. When Donna can't get down to the drugstore Debbie will pick up her medicine."

"Assunta, why would Donna need Debbie to get her medicine and why would she pay by check? We have an account at the drugstore."

"I never thought of that. If the doctor phoned in the prescription, Barco's would automatically deliver it, and bill us at the end of the month. It doesn't make sense."

Michael peered at Assunta.

"Think very carefully. Was anything else said between Debbie and Donna?"

"Debbie told Donna to expect visitors and Donna became upset."

"Anything else unusual happen?"

"The following day, two men came to see Donna. She hadn't been feeling well again that morning. When she saw them getting out of the car she panicked. She met them at the car and they talked for quite a long time."

"Do you remember the date?"

Assunta thought for a moment.

"All I can remember is that was the day Papa, you, and Gino went down to the summer camp."

Michael looked at Franco.

"That would have been in the middle of June."

Michael looked back to Assunta.

"Assunta, what happened after that?"

"They got back into the car and left. Donna came back over to me telling me she had to go out for a little while. She asked me to watch the twins. Before I knew it, Debbie arrived to pick her up. Donna returned around eleven o'clock. I asked her how she felt and she told me better than ever. She even looked better. Then she asked me if I had seen Gino. She told me she had been waiting for him in Papa's office at the company, but he never showed up. I told her that Gino went with Papa to the summer camp. She went upstairs to change and Gino arrived a short time later.

"Did Gino say anything to you or Donna?"

"Funny you should mention that. Donna saw Gino parking the car and came down to greet him. Gino told us he left the summer camp before Papa and Franco since he forgot to put something away in the safe. When he opened the door, he realized someone had been in Papa's office. Apparently, they went through the top drawer and threw everything all over the floor. Realizing Papa would be upset, he put everything back neatly. Nothing else."

Franco looked at Michael trying to put the pieces together.

"Papa never mentioned a break-in at the office."

Assunta shook her head.

"He never knew. Gino told us not to say anything. He didn't want Papa upset since nothing was missing."

Franco became enraged.

"If Gino told you to jump off the bridge, would you jump?"

"Of course I wouldn't jump off a bridge!" Assunta shouted.

"Why didn't you mention anything to Papa?"

Assunta became frightened and stood next to Michael for protection.

"Franco stop! Assunta is trying her best to help us! If Gino told you not to say something to Papa, to avoid upsetting him, what would you've done?"

"It would depend on the circumstances!" Franco answered ambiguously.

Michael looked sternly at Franco.

"Exactly! Everything was put back in place and Gino found nothing missing! Assunta presumed that there would be no harm if Papa didn't know! That was all there was to it! Assunta wasn't wrong in going along with Gino! I'd have done the same thing myself!"

Franco thought for a few minutes.

"Wait a minute. I remember why Gino left early. Papa had some checks he wanted to write out for the summer camp and forgot to do it before he left. While we were at the camp, he remembered, so Gino took a ride back to pick up the company checkbook. Gino accidentally spilled coffee on the checkbook and had to bring Papa a new one. I remember it so well because I never saw Papa laugh so hard. I myself got a good laugh."

"When Papa returns this evening, we have to tell him everything we know. The sooner he knows, the better off he'll be." Michael asserted.

Assunta wasn't following their trend of thought.

"I don't understand. What do we have to tell Papa when he comes home?"

"Everything we discussed."

Assunta looked from Franco to Michael.

"Why do I get the impression that I'm in trouble with Papa?"

Michael looked at Assunta sympathetically.

"If you explain everything to Papa the way you just did, I guarantee you won't be in trouble."

Assunta made the sign of the cross and slumped down on the sofa to await Paulo's return.

The play let out at midnight but they all had some energy left and wanted to grab a late night snack before heading home. It was just the thing Paulo needed to relax.

It was one-thirty by the time they arrived at the house. To Paulo's surprise, the light was still on in the family room. He approached cautiously and found Franco and Michael sleeping on the floor and Assunta on the sofa. He gently nudged Michael awake to send him to his room, but first he wanted to know why they had fallen asleep there.

Michael slowly opened his eyes, asking what time it was. Then, half asleep he informed Paulo that they were waiting to tell him something very important. Paulo helped Michael off the floor instructing him to go upstairs to bed. There would be plenty of time for them to talk after breakfast.

Hearing Paulo's voice, Franco woke up. Slowly, he sat up leaning against the sofa. He pleaded with Paulo to hear them out. He didn't think he'd be able to fall back to sleep with it on his mind. Finally, Assunta heard them talking. She looked distressed so Paulo agreed to listen. They went to the library for privacy. They took their usual seats around the desk.

"Now, what's so important that it couldn't wait until the morning?"

Michael spoke first.

"After you left for the play, we had a discussion about the way Donna acted at the meeting this evening. Assunta remembered something, which you may find interesting."

Paulo waited for her to start talking.

"Where do I begin?"

Then, with all eyes on her, she carefully recounted for Paulo what she had told Michael and Franco.

"Papa, if I did wrong not telling you what I saw or heard, I'm sorry. I

202

honestly thought it was medication that Debbie was bringing. If I thought for one moment anything different, you'd have been the first to know."

"Assunta, you did nothing wrong. I want to level with all of you right now. What you just told me confirms my theory about Donna. No one is to know what we talked about."

They all promised never to mention their conversation and prepared to leave. Assunta wasn't ready to go. She had something else on her mind. She spoke up to get Paulo's attention.

"I thought about what Donna said about why you adopted . . ."

Assunta put her head down.

Paulo came around to the front of the desk to sit next to her.

"I was afraid Donna had upset you. It wasn't a competition between you and Donna. You don't go about finding a daughter using a checklist. It wouldn't have mattered to me if you were short or tall, fat or thin, of average intelligence or above average intelligence. I adopted you because of what was in your heart and my heart.

"I remember the first time we had a heart-to-heart and I consoled you. I felt as if I received a sign from above and it was then that I knew that you were meant to be my daughter."

Assunta looked at Paulo strangely, then he explained.

"As I was holding you in my arms I looked out the window and saw a white dove perched on the window ledge. It was as if she was watching us. When you calmed down, I wiped your eyes and covered you. Before I left your room I went to the window to close the curtains. The white dove was no longer there. Looking toward the heavens I watched her flying off. That was my sign that you were sent to me by God to take care of. So you see, in reality, God chose you to be my daughter. Does that answer your question?"

"Knowing all my faults, if you had to do it over would you still adopt me?" Assunta 's eyes reflected her doubt.

Paulo sensed the hurt in her heart.

"I must admit, you try my patience at times. But then again, what daughter doesn't try to get the better of her father once in awhile? If I had it to do over again, would I adopt you?"

Then he looked at Assunta with such love in his heart, it could be felt around the room.

"It would only take a heartbeat for me to make you my daughter once again!"

Assunta smiled through the tears as she hugged Paulo.

"Now, I think you'd better get some sleep. I'd like to speak with Franco and Michael for a few more minutes."

Paulo got right down to business once Assunta was gone.

"I'm going to make this as brief as possible. Tomorrow afternoon I'm leaving for the cabin with Mama, Antonio and Maria for a couple days."

Paulo looked at Michael.

"Michael, is it possible for you to eat dinner here at the house and sleep here while I'm at the cabin? After the fight between Franco and Gino tonight, I don't relish the idea of them being alone. I'd prefer that you keep a handle on things while I'm away."

"I think I can arrange that. I can't be around during the day but eating dinner and sleeping over won't present a problem."

Paulo then faced Franco.

"I have a favor to ask of you. I need the company books from the safe. Please go to the company in the morning and pick them up then I would like you to bring them to the cabin."

Franco thought about it for a minute.

"Gino stops by the office before going to college. How do I get the books without him noticing?"

"I thought about that already. I'll ask Gino to wait for me at home until I return from Assunta's session. He can leave for school from here instead of the office. That's it boys. You'd better get some sleep."

After they left Paulo stood up and walked to the sliding glass doors. He suddenly felt someone else's presence in the room. He was relieved to see it was Antonio.

"I heard Franco and Michael coming upstairs. I thought you might need some company."

Paulo pointed to the table.

"Thanks, Antonio, have a seat. I try once a month to have a meeting to keep the family abreast on company matters. Michael, Assunta and Gino each own ten percent of the company stock. Anna and I own the remainder enabling us to control the company without interference.

"At the meeting tonight, I told the family of a few changes I made at work. I've appointed a new business manager and a new supervisor. I made the changes because I've found it increasingly difficult to keep up with the demands on my time. Gino attends college during the day and won't get his degree for another year.

"When I announced this at the meeting, Donna snapped out. You might have thought she owned the company. Donna wanted me to tell the two men that I changed my mind. The stock was brought up and she wanted to know why she didn't have any stock in the company.

"To make a long story short, Franco and Gino had a brawl on my conference table."

Paulo pointed out the scratches.

Antonio ran his hands over the scratches.

"There's no major damage except for a few scratches which can easily be covered up."

"I thought about it and decided I'm going to leave them on the table so that every time we have a family meeting the boys will remember what happened tonight.

"Donna, however, is another problem. I fear she may be fooling around with drugs. If my theory is right, I should be able to find out while at the cabin. Maybe you and I can play detective together."

"I've seen the effects of drugs on our youth today. Salvatore and Eleanora's son, David, was using drugs. They were lucky they caught it in the beginning stages. Today, he's clean and sober. He conducts anti-drug seminars throughout the area. Maybe he be can of some assistance."

"If drugs are the problem, then I surely would like him to speak with Donna. No one can tell you more about the consequences of taking drugs than a drug addict himself."

Paulo suddenly felt exhausted.

"It seems I get to bed later and later each night. Let's get some shut-eye. Thanks for hearing me out."

While lying still in bed, Paulo was deep in thought. If Donna used drugs then he didn't want to make the same mistakes he made with Bianca.

The following morning at breakfast everyone ate in total silence. Paulo waited patiently for someone to say something, to no avail. Sensing the hostility, he realized it was time to take control of the situation.

"I see what's going on here this morning and I'm dismayed. All of you came in greeting Mama and myself but none of you greeted each other. Undoubtedly, there are hard feelings among you concerning words said in the meeting last night.

"Each of us, in our own right, may feel bad about the comments that were passed, however, I feel it's better these comments were said openly then said behind someone's back. You're all adults, and as adults, have a right to speak freely at any meeting in our home. I'll allow criticism or disagreement if you feel it is necessary to express your feelings but there's one thing I'll not allow whatever occurs at our meetings shall not cause you to stop communicating with each other.

"As adults, you have a right to your own opinion and should be awarded the opportunity to express your feelings. When this occurs, I hope you'll pay attention to what's being said and try to understand the other person's point of view. As adults, you must learn to accept another's view of a situation without leading to violence.

"Last night's meeting ended on a sour note. That has never happened in the past and I never again want to see it in the future. Mama and I are going to leave the dining room for a few minutes. When we come back, I'd better hear my children talking the same as always. That's all I have to say."

Paulo helped Anna up and left by way of the kitchen door.

Feeling uncertainty about what would occur once they left the dining room, Paulo didn't want to stray too far so he led Anna over to one of the benches at the entrance to the garden.

Anna could see the uneasiness in his eyes.

"Darling, please try not to worry."

Paulo shook his head.

"Last evening left a bitter taste in my mouth. I never saw the boys go at it that way before."

"I know how you feel. I didn't like the sight of my two sons beating each other unmercifully. At the same time, I can't change the fact that it happened. All I can hope and pray is that it never happens again."

"Darling, they may be children to us, but in reality they're adults. They must realize themselves that family takes priority over business. In times of need, it's family that pulls us through."

About fifteen minutes passed before they agreed to return and when they did, they walked into a room full of conversation. It felt good to see everything back to normal, even if it was only for show. They went back to their seats to salvage what was left of their breakfast.

Soon breakfast was over and Paulo made his customary announcements. "Boys, I want to see all of you before you leave this morning. When you're through, meet me in the library. Assunta, I'll drop you off at the hospital as soon as I'm through with the boys. You and I can speak on the way there."

Paulo was on the phone by the time his sons entered the library so he signaled them to sit down. When he was through, he put the phone down and leaned against the desk with his arms folded. They knew by Paulo's expression that this wasn't a casual meeting.

"Gentlemen, I'm very disappointed in the way you conducted yourselves at the meeting last night"

Paulo turned to face Michael.

"Michael, I realize you were only trying to be a peacemaker when you suggested we adjourn the meeting but I was conducting the meeting. Therefore, I should adjourn the meeting and not you."

Paulo now turned his attention to Gino.

"Gino, everything Donna said last night about me favoring Assunta is utter nonsense. I treat all my children and grandchildren equally.

Something is bothering her and I hope you can get to the bottom of it. I'll do all in my power to help, once you find out what the problem is."

Paulo glared at Franco like a lion on the prowl.

"As for you, young man, if you ever display such brutality in the future, you'll regret your actions, so help me God."

Looking at Gino again, Paulo continued.

"What I'm going to say now is in reference to both you and Franco. Your little display at the meeting last night was more then outrageous. I will not tolerate my sons acting like wild animals. I realize you were upset, but that doesn't give you the right to act the way you did. Violence only begets further violence. I've never showed either of you my true temper. I learned a long time ago that violence isn't the answer. You have to learn how to control your temper. Let me tell you a little story.

"When I was a child, my mother worked nights at a club. Someone told all my friends that my mother was a Call Girl. When I found out I went bonkers. I beat that boy up so bad, I sent him to the hospital with a broken arm. Later on we found out that his arm didn't heal properly. There was a possibility he'd never use that arm again.

"The night before the surgery, my mother sat down with me and explained that it was never appropriate to use violence to solve any problem. Instead, I should talk it out.

"To make a long story short, John had an operation and his arm was healed. It would be many weeks of therapy until he was able to get the rotation back in his arm.

"The following spring, you could find us down at the sandlot after school playing baseball as if nothing happened. I learned a valuable lesson from that episode in my life, to control my temper. Violence isn't a way to settle any disagreement especially among brothers. You see, the boy I beat up so badly, was my brother.

"Now, I'm not asking either of you to try and control your temper, I'm demanding it. If not, you'll see a part of your father, you've never seen before! I hope I make myself clear!

"I have to take Assunta for her session with Dr. Cristanzio now.

"Gino, instead of going into work, I'd like you to stay here and wait for a call I'm expecting from a company that produces one of the components that we use. They've come up with a more flexible piece that'll make it easier for us to operate with. When I return from Assunta's session, you can leave for your classes."

"I'll go over some work while I wait for you to return," Gino replied.

Paulo walked out with Franco and Michael.

"Franco, I'll be home around nine o'clock. You can drop the books off around ten."

Before long, Franco, Michael and Paulo all pulled out of the driveway, each going in different directions.

While driving with Paulo, Assunta sat very quietly looking out the side window. She was rehearsing in her mind what she was going to say to Paulo. When she was confident enough, she broke the silence.

"I know I've done something to upset you," Assunta said.

Paulo laid the cards on the table.

"I've watched you in the past during family meetings. You have a way of snickering when I correct someone. I've tolerated it up until now, but feel it's time to stop this childish behavior. If you don't, perhaps we can discuss it further in private."

"That won't be necessary, however, there is one thing that has been on my mind for some time now."

"You have the floor."

Assunta struggled to find the correct words to use.

"I get the impression that I have to walk a straighter line than Donna. If this is true, do you think it's fair to me?"

Paulo knew Assunta was right in her assumptions and was prepared to give her an answer.

"That's correct. You do have to walk straighter than Donna or anyone else for that matter, even if I'm not present. I don't want you ever, for even one moment, to forget you're Paulo Altro's daughter, and, as such, will behave accordingly."

Paulo pulled into the parking lot and parked the car.

Assunta started toward the hospital when Paulo stopped her.

"Assunta, there are reasons why I am so demanding of you at times. I can't explain any of it to you now but in the future you'll understand."

Assunta walked back to Paulo.

"Papa, you owe me no explanation more than I'm your daughter. Hearing those words come out of your mouth makes my heart warm up. You're right. It's a childish gesture. I love you, Papa, and will do anything you ask of me as long as you don't give up on me."

Paulo held Assunta in his arms.

"I'm not ready to give up on you. We have a good many years ahead of us. Just remember who's in charge and you'll be able to see and do things you never imagined possible."

Paulo kissed her on the forehead.

"Now I know everything Donna said last night about the adoption isn't true. I want you to know that even if it were true, it wouldn't matter to me. The important thing to remember is that you adopted me."

Assunta hugged Paulo tightly.

"I love you, Papa, with all my heart."

Paulo's heart filled with pride.

"I love you too, and I'm grateful to God that Franco chose you to be his wife. If he hadn't, I'd have missed the opportunity of my lifetime."

Then Paulo held Assunta's hand and together they went to Assunta's session. When the session ended Assunta started her community service while Paulo headed for home.

When Paulo arrived at home, Franco hadn't yet returned with the ledgers. He let Gino know he was back so he could get started on his way to class. Paulo sat at his desk in deep thought until Franco startled him.

"I believe this is what you wanted."

"Come in and have a seat!"

Paulo skimmed through the books. He was obviously disturbed but Franco couldn't figure out what he had done.

"Since I already spoke with you and Gino this morning concerning your actions at the meeting last night, I'm just issuing a reminder."

"Papa I really . . ."

"I'm not finished speaking, so please extend the courtesy of hearing me out. From here on in, you're to remember at any meeting, whether family or company, you're an extension of me. Being my son is a big responsibility. I'll not tolerate poor behavior. Okay, no more on the subject."

Franco stood up to leave but before doing so, he turned to Paulo to say one last thing.

"I don't know what came over me last night. In the future, I'll keep an eye on my temper. All I ask is if you notice me starting to go off the deep end, signal me so I'll know to get control of myself."

"Don't worry about that, son. If you think I've been tough on you in the past, wait until you see what happens in the future."

Franco knew Paulo was serious.

"Have a nice day, Papa. I love you."

"Love you too, son."

Paulo sat back and reflected. Over time, many have things changed in the Altro household, and most notably was the change in Franco's outlook on life. He has grown into a mature and responsible adult.

The love he found with Assunta and their son Antonio was just what he needed to turn his life around. Together, Franco and Assunta have come a long way, and together, they will travel many more new and challenging roads. There would be many obstacles along the way with countless twists and turns. Paulo and Anna would remain by their side helping and guiding them to conquer anything the future had in store for them.

# About The Author

My name is Susan Rescigno Catrambone, however, my pen name is a combination of my mother and father's first names, Elizabeth Quintino.

When I was growing up it wasn't necessary to lock any doors, coffee was always on, and families lived within walking distance, with neighbors considered an extension of our family and respected as such.

Summertime represented scooters made from wood milk crates, skates, and Coca Cola bottle caps, along with bike riding, roller-skating, handball, and neighborhood swimming pools. Penny candy, ice cream parlors, movie theaters, waffles, lemonade, pretzels, and steak sandwiches added to the enjoyment of summer.

I will carry these memories of my childhood days in South Philadelphia forever in my heart.

Printed in the United States
19905LVS00001B/170